FROZEN AS FRIENDS

❄

AMY PROKOPIS

Amy Prokopis

Copyright © 2024 Amy Prokopis.

All rights reserved. No part of this publication may be reproduced, distributed, or transmitted in any form or by any means, including photocopying, recording, or other electronic or mechanical methods, without the prior written permission of the publisher, except in the case of brief quotations embodied in critical reviews and certain other noncommercial uses permitted by copyright law. For permission requests, write to the publisher, addressed "Attention: Permissions Coordinator," at the address below.

amyprokopis@gmail.com

This is a work of fiction. Names, characters, places, and incidents either are the product of the author's imagination or are used fictitiously. Any resemblance to actual persons, living or dead, events, or locales is entirely coincidental.

Cover image by Amy Prokopis

Edited by Lucia Ferrara

Published by Amy Prokopis

First printing edition 2024

www.amyprokopis.com

*For all the sisters struggling to find their own paths.
Chase what brings you joy.*

Chapter 1

> We will be there at ten!

I CHECKED the message for the second time since the clock on the wall of the airport coffee shop struck ten. If it had been any other day, any typical day back when everything was normal and comfortable, today would've been a nice Saturday. I rose with the sun the way I liked, packing the last of my toiletries in my suitcase and keeping my eyes on the navy carpet of my empty dorm room as I left, and made as quick of a beeline for the Uber outside as I could.

I didn't realize until I got dressed this morning that my entire wardrobe consisted of UCLA gear. Blue T-shirts. Gold hoodies. Even the beanie I settled for turned out to have a little Joe Bruin head on the front. I was comfortable in my navy-blue long-sleeved shirt, UCLA logo free thankfully, and a pair of sweatpants despite the black pants not matching the blue top or the gray beanie. I shoved the hat into my laptop bag as soon as I saw the bear on the front.

Leave it to Madison to be late. I thought at least a little bit of Jared's responsibility would've worn off on her.

I shouldn't be so mean.

Bitter. I was bitter. I knew it and I hated it, but also, I couldn't help it. Of course, I was bitter. I had a lot to be bitter about.

I forced my eyes from the clock on the wall and back to my laptop screen. I'd looked through all the articles on the screen before, but it was an unconscious habit now to Google "best rehab for ankle ligament and nerve damage" whenever I opened a new browser tab. There was nothing new. Sometimes, there was a slightly different result, but it was never a lead. Usually, it was just me typing in the search bar wrong.

I exited the tab, leaving me with the YouTube video that had been playing in my headphones in the background. It was a soccer game from my last season, one of the final UCLA games before we lost out on a shot at a title. My heart fluttered every time I heard the commentator mention my name.

"That's Margot Sinclair with a great pass to teammate Allison Brewers and she's headed toward the goal, dodging a defender, the goal's wide open, and she shoots! GOAL FOR THE BRUINS!"

I backed up the video a few seconds to watch Allison's footwork again, such a slick combination as she sprinted down the last third of the field and passed the ball easily from her left foot to her right and then back again as she faked-out the defender ... All moves I had mastered a year ago. I was quick on my feet, with a better reaction time than most.

Allison Brewers had already taken over my spot on the team and made a name for herself. Her reaction time wasn't as quick as mine was, but she led the team all the same. I could read her tendencies now that I watched the video back. She was more likely to pivot right than left. Her left foot was her weaker side, despite taking a lot of goal shots using her left foot. I was a better player mentally now than a year ago, which only made my stomach twist tighter as I watched myself sprint toward Allison along with my teammates after the crowd burst into cheers at her goal.

"Anyone sitting here?" a woman asked. She had a bored-looking teenager at her side who didn't look up from his phone.

"No. No, you can sit," I told her and motioned to the empty

seats across from me. I glanced around the café as she climbed onto one of the stools. The shop was busier than it had been a few moments ago. I heard a man grumbling a table away about a delayed flight as he, his wife, and a trio of overly excited children sat in a booth together. A glance out the nearest window told me the weather must have picked up in Denver.

That explained why I didn't feel tired the way I was used to. When the winter weather took over, a tingle would settle through my bones. That's how all winter witches felt. It was invigorating. It made me want to go outside and run through the powdery snow. I almost felt a little excited about heading to Crescent Peak.

I heard a pinging sound through my headphones. I paused the YouTube video, so I knew it wasn't the game. It was a notification of an email and my hands returned to the keyboard as the grouchy man started to tell off his kids for being too loud.

I had several unopened emails. Most of them were confirmations that my dorm at UCLA had been canceled. I was leaving California and the campus behind, but not the university. All my classes for the spring semester would be virtual so I could move back home and work with a few specialists my parents swore could get me back in D1 soccer shape. After all my research, I wasn't so sure.

The newest email was from my soccer coach at UCLA. She always had faith in my recovery and was actually encouraging when I made the decision to go home for the semester. My parents, being the overly involved people they were, had talked with her many times and they decided together that there was hope in Denver for some recovery and support.

I can read between the lines.

The joint and pain specialist I would be working with wasn't nationally recognized.

The mental health therapist was, though.

The email wasn't as long as I expected, and my chest tightened, and my stomach sank as I read it. It started strong with the promise that I could have a spot on the team when I returned healthy and happy. I was too good not to make the team, according to the coach. Even at half my best, she said I might see playing time in a game or so next season. I wouldn't have my scholarship, and though she was encouraging, I knew that was probably off the table for good. I would have to return at least as good as before and that wouldn't happen. I knew it wouldn't. It didn't matter how badly I wanted that. She tried to sound hopeful, but I knew it wasn't for the future I wanted.

I could go back to UCLA and play soccer. With a lot of luck, I might even be able to go back and at least play in some games. I might even be good. Could I go further than that? What was I doing? What was the point of going back at all if it didn't lead to something more after college? That was the plan. I was on track and everything and it wasn't even the sport that brought that train to a dead halt. My Jeep took a nosedive into the ditch down the hill from my family's cabin and that was all it took. One day. A short drive to town. A single patch of ice.

My phone buzzed loudly against the table.

> We are like ten away from the airport, I swear. Sorry, we're late. I made Jared stop for hot chocolate and then we ran into traffic.

I TUCKED my phone into the front pocket of my bag. I disconnected my headphones and shut my laptop. I wanted to be anywhere but around these people. The arguing dad and his loud kids, the teenager slouched in his seat as he scrolled his phone next to his mom who kept peering across the table at me with that concerned mom look that made me want to burst into tears and tell her that it wasn't my fault I messed up my whole future even though it kind of was.

I shoved my laptop into my bag and struggled to pull the zipper closed as I started toward the closest exit. Thankfully, speed-walking and looking panicked wasn't cause for concern in an airport and no one stopped me. I passed through the checkpoints and made it to the taxi waiting area before all the emotions could burst from my chest. I walked out into the cold Denver air, icy like knives, and froze in more ways than one.

I felt like I could release my heavy sobs into the thin air, but I didn't. It wouldn't matter anyway. It was no use and the moment the cold air settled in my bones. I didn't feel like going through the motions.

"Whew!"

An older woman with her arm wrapped around a man's elbow patted me lightly on the back. She offered a kind but concerned smile as she glanced over my sweatshirt.

"Is it your first time in Denver, dear?"

"Oh, no. I'm just a little eager to get home."

"Just let one of the attendants know. They can give you a wave whenever your car gets here," the woman said with a smile. She caught the attention of a man at the baggage station and motioned to me. I waved him away before he could approach and hurried back behind the glass doors of the airport.

I pulled out my phone and opened Instagram to mindlessly scroll. Despite my college friends' posts of their arrivals back at their hometowns or holiday photos, I couldn't help but think about that stupid email.

I looked up when someone tapped on the glass door. It was the man from the baggage station. We made eye contact before he pointed toward the line of cars. Holding up the flow of traffic was Madison's bubblegum-pink Jeep, Madison and Jared both waving at me with smiles on their faces.

Jared McAdams stepped out of the passenger's side as I exited the glass doors. He wrapped an arm around my shoulders and took my suitcase before we could finish exchanging greetings.

"It's good to see you," I said and followed him to the trunk. "How's your family?"

"Good. It's been good to be home," Jared said as he lifted my suitcase into the short trunk. "Mom's great. Mark's ... well, Mark. The mercantile is booming." He shut the door with a snap and turned to face me. "You should check out the shop. It's twice the size as last year, thanks to Madison, and her online shop is thriving."

Jared was pink in the face as he looked at me. I was used to this moment, but it didn't make it any more bearable. People would gush about their successes and then realize I was there in my tragic existence. I was happy for all my friends and my family. Madison had a great relationship and finally made her way down to Earth at college. Marlee, our younger sister, graduated high school as the class valedictorian and was thriving in her first year at Yale. I was happy for them. I was.

Jared smiled at me, the awkwardness passing in just seconds and his kind demeanor returning. He was ever the gentleman, exactly what my sister deserved. I hated that I was on the brink of tears. I shouldn't have been sad. What was there to be sad about? It could be worse.

"Everything's fine. Don't tell my sisters, especially not Madison, okay?" I asked and dabbed at my eyes, hating that now was the moment my emotions caught up with me. Minutes ago, I was prepared to cry; I'd accepted the ugly red face and runny nose, and it never came. I loved Jared and all the happiness he brought my sister, but why did he have to be so nice and easy to talk to? He had better things to deal with than me and my stupid, shallow emotions.

"Sure. Yeah. I get it. I do," he said, hesitating with his hand inches from my shoulder before he lowered it. He glanced toward the Jeep, Madison's head curved downward as though she was looking at her phone. "Don't be like Marlee, okay?'

I nodded, thankfully able to swipe away the singular tear that slipped from the corner of my eye. I knew what he meant. Don't seclude myself the way my younger sister did. There was nothing wrong with it. Marlee liked her alone time but that wasn't what I usually did. I wasn't the type to shut myself away for most of the day, even though I wanted to. The idea of sitting with my family after the last year felt like a relief, but I knew it wouldn't do anything but make people more concerned. If I really wanted to be left alone, I had to keep up the ruse.

I nodded and said, "Definitely not."

Jared smiled, finally patting me on the shoulder before pulling the back door open for me. I climbed in as he made his way to the passenger seat. Madison finally looked up from her phone when I pulled the door shut, immediately turning her phone to show me an Instagram post.

"Winnie Maxwell is engaged!" she said with a gasp as though she'd just found out herself. "She only met this guy in like, March, but they just got engaged a few weeks ago and she's already posting to her socials like she's a suburban wife."

"I thought you guys made up last year," I said, clicking my seat belt into place.

"Oh, we did. We're cool now. I'm happy for her. But it's just crazy to me how quickly things go when you just know. You know?' Madison glanced over her shoulder at me before looking ahead. She pulled back into the flow of traffic before I could reply.

Looks like I was even more behind back at home than I was in California.

Chapter 2

I WAS the last to arrive home. I forced myself to be a part of the conversation as we cruised through Denver, but once the trees encroached on the highway my mind drifted along with the snow. I wasn't sure how long I'd been pulled under by my thoughts when Jared turned the radio on, turning the pop station to one that played classic rock. I was surprised that Madison didn't complain about it once on the way home to Heritage City.

Mom and Dad met us on the porch with welcoming smiles. Dad embraced Jared like a son, both of them immediately launching into a debate about professional football before Dad left him to pull me into one of his classic bear hugs.

"Good to have you home, Superstar," he said in my ear, kissing me on the temple before he pulled away and returned to his macho ways.

"All your stuff from your dorm got here yesterday," Mom said and pulled me to her chest before tugging me into the house. "Marlee and I moved it all into your room upstairs. Everything is unpacked. We tried our best to lay it out the way you would."

"Thank you," I said, looking from Mom to Marlee who stood back a few feet from the crowd of people in the entryway. She gave me a nod of understanding that told me she wouldn't bug me. Growing up, everyone used to make comments about how quiet Marlee was. The truth was that Marlee was the only person in our family who really understood anyone. She knew I needed my space, and she wouldn't invade that. I couldn't thank her enough.

"I'm making chili for dinner. It's got a little while though, so everyone get comfortable. There are a few new games in the den," Dad suggested, giving Jared a playful shove as they laughed about a joke that we all had missed.

"Margot promised to go with me to the bookstore event," Marlee said firmly, shooting me daggers before I could utter a word. I kept quiet while Dad floundered, glancing at our mom who shrugged. Madison just rolled her eyes and offered to play a round of pool in the den with Jared. Marlee's expression softened, that subtle smirk that I used to criticize her for now stretching across her face.

"We will be back for dinner," I said before following her toward the door.

❄

Marlee always was the most observant.

"So, what's new?" I asked as we reached the stop sign at the end of the street.

She barely acknowledged me as she glanced in both directions, the blinker of her Jeep clicking rhythmically.

"Just school. Nothing new," she said as she waited for a Subaru to drive past.

"Mom said you really like Yale. She said you made all A's. That's good for your first semester of college."

"Hmm." Marlee looked so uninterested in the conversation that anyone else would've wondered why they were invited along to begin with. This trip was for the sake of escaping. There was no point in denying it. Marlee was already a step ahead of me like always. My eyes stung at the realization.

"Damn it," I groaned and pulled the visor down so I could look at my mascara as it smudged around my eyes. At least it was the only makeup I ever wore. I couldn't imagine how Madison ever managed to look good with how dramatic she could be.

"I do want to go to the bookstore, the new indie one on Elm. They have a really good coffee shop in the back. There's a little lounge tucked back there that people forget about. It's perfect for working on college essays and having existential crises," Marlee said as she sped up to make it through the light in time.

I took a deep breath and then another, the second one making enough of a difference for me to feel a little in control again.

"You are a lifesaver," I said with a sigh.

"I figured you weren't ready for the whole family to look at you like a lost puppy yet. Let them settle in at home. Dad will break out the beers and that will calm everyone down so when we get back, they won't all tiptoe around you," Marlee said.

"That was your plan? We get them all drunk?" I asked, dabbing away the last of the mascara at the corner of my eye with the sleeve of my shirt.

Marlee smiled as we turned into the parking lot of a shopping center.

"Just enough that they can't tiptoe, but not so much that they're all stumbling. That make sense?"

I felt the smile pull at my lips. Marlee parked in front of a section of the shopping center that was painted a dark green color. The name of the bookstore hung over the door in blocky letters that had icicles clinging to the bottom of each letter. Foster's Bookstore and Coffee Shop.

I followed Marlee to the front door. Instead of a little bell giving a dainty tinkle, a deep voice I recognized as Gandalf from *Lord of the Rings* spoke from a speaker above the doorjamb.

"*Speak, friend, and enter.*"

"I see why you like this place," I said.

Marlee didn't look back at me. She continued right on past the rows of chestnut bookshelves that reached so high that each row had a small stepladder, and she went straight for the small coffee bar at the back. The menu was written on the chalkboard wall behind the counter. A section of the counter had leather barstools; one was occupied by an old man who squinted down at his phone.

"Marlee!" The barista looked up from the iPad behind the counter with a smile. "The usual?"

"Two please," Marlee said, raising her index and middle finger before reaching for her wallet.

The whirr of the coffee bean grinder filled the silence. Once finished, the barista placed both drinks on the counter and Marlee paid with a quick swipe of her debit card. She looked at me just long enough to hand me the hot to-go cup and tell me she would be in the fiction section before leaving me at the counter.

I caught the barista watching me as she wiped the top of the coffee bar.

"Where's the lounge?" I asked.

"The next left," she said and nodded her head toward the narrow hall just past the bar. It was narrow enough that I would brush shoulders with anyone who tried to pass. Thankfully, I reached the end of the hall before a man exited the bathrooms to the right. Marlee was right about the lounge being quiet. It was completely empty. The space wasn't very large, just large enough for a plush sofa, a wide coffee table, and four armchairs that sat in front of the glass windows overlooking the parking lot.

I sank into one of the armchairs, the leather emitting a loud groan that made me even more thankful for the seclusion. I pulled out my phone to check my email. Two of the three were ads for Christmas specials from different clothing stores. The third was my coach's email that I'd marked as unread from earlier at the airport.

I'd answer eventually.

I exited my email and opened a browser for the internet instead, my fingers typing before I could think through the action. As soon as I hit search, I deleted the page only to start typing into the search bar again.

Ankle and knee injuries and sports.

Can you still play professional soccer after a severe injury?

Best college major for athletes?

This was stupid. Why was I doing this to myself? Was it even worth pretending that I'd still be going back to UCLA in the fall?

I was going to miss the entire spring training season. My old club coach I trained with all through high school wasn't coaching anymore. He retired after I graduated from Heritage City Academy and moved a state away. How would I even train?

I needed to find something else to do. I needed to get a life that wasn't all about soccer.

I opened the Instagram app and found my way to a list of suggested friends. Unlike the rest of my feed, these suggestions weren't soccer-related. Most of them were people I had taken classes with at UCLA or people I knew from high school. If I knew their name, I added them as a friend in hopes that their posts would drown out the stream of UCLA soccer and professional players that I usually scrolled through.

I spent more time than I cared to admit scrolling through the Instagram accounts of people I went to Heritage City Academy with. Some of them were witches and I could see the subtle hints of it in their photos, like my friend Anne's metal snowflake art pinned on her family's living room wall despite the photo being for a Fourth of July celebration. I saw lots of family photos and even more of my former classmates at college. There were gameday photos of men and women dressed in school colors and sorority and fraternity photos with each participant throwing up their signs with smiles on their faces.

Once I felt the pit form in my stomach, I put my phone in my lap and looked over the empty room.

This had to stop.

I crossed the small room in a few strides and went back into the quiet bookstore. Marlee had wandered her way to the front of the store, three books wrapped tightly at her chest as she looked over a section of autobiographies. She looked up when she noticed me, an annoyed look on her face.

"What's wrong?"

"What do you mean?"

Marlee scoffed as though it was the stupidest question. "You look like you're ready to challenge someone to a duel."

"Not a duel, but I could definitely beat Dad in a game of pool right now," I said and took the books from her arms and turned toward the counter.

"I wasn't done. I'm looking for something," she called out as we walked.

"Order it on Amazon," I said as the clerk behind the counter noticed us. She stopped adjusting her Christmas tree made of paperbacks on the counter to move to the register.

"You can't say those kinds of things in a bookstore!"

I ignored Marlee's protest and sat the books on the counter, already pulling out my debit card as the clerk began ringing me up.

"I want to go home, listen to Jared and Dad talk about football, make fun of Madison when she complains about my sweatpants, and challenge Mom to a game of pool."

"Finally!" Marlee let out a sigh of relief as I slipped my debit card into the chip reader. "I thought you were going to be insufferable all of Christmas Break."

"It's Christmas time!" I slipped my debit card back into my wallet and accepted the paper bag of books from the clerk. "There's no crying at Christmas time."

"Let's go home," Marlee said and took the bag from me. "We all know you can beat Mom at pool. Twenty bucks says you can't be Dad."

"Fifty bucks says I can beat Dad *and* Jared."

"If you lose, you owe me fifty *and* you drive on the way to Crescent Peak tomorrow."

The bell above the door called out to us as we made our way back into the winter air.

"*Speak, friend, and enter.*"

"You're on," I said and glanced back at Marlee's smug expression as we approached her orange Jeep.

"I hope your gas tank is full," Marlee said and opened the driver's door. "Sounds like I'm going to be reading in the backseat."

I took a deep breath and sat back in the leather seat while she turned on the engine.
No crying at Christmas time.

Chapter 3

MARLEE and I were the last to leave the house in Heritage City for the snowy mountains of Crescent Peak. Just the thought of the family cabin with the big fireplace, giant windows looking down the mountain, and the memory of twinkling lights on Christmas trees made me breathe a little easier as I backed out of the garage.

My eyes went from the reflection of the house in the rearview mirror to Marlee curled up in the backseat with a fluffy blanket across her lap and a thick hardback propped on her knees.

"Witchy paradise, here we come," I said under my breath.

Marlee didn't utter a word. She was probably too deeply engrossed in her book to hear me anyway.

The trees grew thicker as we drove farther up the mountain and away from the city lights. It was getting dark enough that the lights on my electric-blue Jeep turned on automatically to guide us through the shadows the evergreens cast over the windy road. I let my mind wander to my favorite memories of Crescent Peak.

The Jeep passed the McAdams Mercantile halfway up the mountain to Crescent Peak. It was a family evergreen tree farm with a little mercantile that sold trinkets. Actually, now, it was more than just a Christmastime giftshop thanks to my sister. Madison expanded the mercantile and it now had a growing section of adorable seasonal clothing, all branded with Madison's name on the tags in elegant cursive. The McAdams had embraced her when she started dating Jared and she was a part of the family now.

I remembered snowball fights on the lawn of the cabin, learning how to use my powers to manipulate the snow alongside my mom, and the many hours spent running soccer drills. Sometimes, I think the snow was the reason for my fancy footwork. I had to get good at the basics in the powder, strengthening my muscles as I dragged my feet through the snow.

Winter witches didn't feel cold, not really. We felt it, but not like most people. It wasn't uncomfortable for us and didn't make us shiver in response. It was invigorating, a kind of relaxed tingle that would settle over your body after completely letting go. It felt the same way I felt letting Madison do my hair when we were teenagers. I'd sit in her vanity chair and drift into my thoughts as she combed my brown hair and curled it to perfection. That was what winter was to us. Winter never felt *cold* to us, not the way I did as we drove past the spot.

My entire body tightened as we passed the guardrail. The road coming down from the cabin was just as steep as it was then, but the guardrail had been replaced. The steel looked thicker now and almost the entire surface was covered in a reflective neon-yellow band. I hovered my foot over the break and gripped the steering wheel in response, focusing on the approaching car and its headlights.

I knew it was just a single car, a black Hummer, but I kept seeing red and blue flashing lights behind it. I was starting to feel dizzy and a little sick to my stomach as the Hummer approached and finally passed and took with it all the images from the accident that flooded my mind.

"Margot," Marlee said in a concerned tone. "We just passed the turn."

"I know," I said a little too firmly. "I just wanted to drive through town."

I recovered quickly, letting out a breath I didn't know I'd been holding as I turned onto the town square. All the buildings were decked out with white lights along the roofs. Tourists walked the sidewalks and into the shops. A man stood on the far corner with a little girl. They waited for a blue car to turn onto the square before crossing the street.

I drove around the entire thing, seeing every shop with their decorated windows and Christmas sale signs. We passed the always busy café and Marlee made some comment about the bookstore across the street that fell on deaf ears. I was more worried about reaching the end of the street, the main road again. I'd have to go back to that intersection and probably replay all the memories. I could feel my chest tighten in anticipation.

I turned left and started driving out of Crescent Peak and farther up the mountain road.

"I want to see the lodge," I said, the lie flowing easily from my lips.

"I bet the mountains are beautiful up there," Marlee said. I heard her close her book with a thump and adjust in her seat.

I knew this way added twenty minutes to the trip. I knew this was stupid, but at least it was scenic with the trees and the glittering snow. It was probably more dangerous than that intersection, but it didn't feel that way to me. My body didn't react as I told myself how this road was traveled less than the main road behind us and how it was more common to come across a deer on the road here than in Crescent Peak. Still, I felt myself relax in my seat the farther up the road we went, and I could fill my lungs completely with air as we approached the entrance to the lodge.

The main parking lot of the building wasn't even half full, but I could tell most of the rental cabins beyond were occupied. The roads here were bone dry thanks to the witches. A group of elders made sure the path was safe to travel so that all winter witches could make it up the mountain for the Winter Solstice Gala. It meant that the trip down toward the cabin would be clear, with no risk of sliding into the ditch, no risk of crashing, and no bad memories.

"That was a good idea," Marlee said as we turned into the long drive to the cabin. "It kept us away from the drama of getting the house all set up, too. I bet Mom, Dad, and Madison already have all the groceries and luggage put away."

"Let's hope so," I said with a sigh, pulling in next to Madison's pink Jeep in the driveway.

❄

I CLOSED the door to my cabin bedroom behind me and locked it. I was glad to be alone, but the reason didn't ease the tension in my shoulders. If anything, they felt rock solid. I could always just tell my parents I did the video call and take a nap instead. I knew as soon as the thought crossed my mind that it wouldn't work. Everyone would be more worried than before. I groaned and went to my luggage and hauled out my laptop, plugging it into the wall in preparation for the battery drain that was Zoom.

My first meeting with the therapist.

She had a name. I just couldn't remember it.

I sat down at the desk and opened my laptop, getting logged in when motion on the street caught my attention. Jared's truck came to a stop, and I saw Madison run across the unblemished snow in the front yard to greet him. Jared rolled down his window and leaned out far enough to kiss her. They talked for a while before Madison leaned for another kiss then Jared used the neighbor's driveway to turn around and head back down the mountain.

I'd been staring out the window long enough that a reminder on my phone went off for the upcoming therapy session. I pulled up Zoom with just a minute to spare when I realized I'd been logged out. I tried all the passwords I could remember before searching my email for the password from the last time I changed it. By the time I joined the call, I was three minutes late.

"I'm sorry. I had a tech issue," I said as soon as my image appeared on the screen. I checked the name under the host's image: Dr. Hadiza Morgan. She was beautiful and made me feel even more pathetic as she sat in her perfectly designed office dressed in a deep-purple blouse accented with a matching diamond earring and necklace set. She had long braids that were tied in a high ponytail that accentuated her slim jawline.

"No worries. This is just a get-to-know-you session," she said with a smile so sweet that it made me feel guilty for the lack of interest I had in this whole thing.

"Well, I can promise that being late is not something to *know* about me because that never happens. I can feel my quads twitch at the thought of being late."

Dr. Morgan did not laugh at my joke. Instead, she gave me a curious look. Classic therapist.

"Why's that?"

"We'd run literal miles for being late."

"Miles? Are we talking like a mile per minute late or ..."

"I guess I should've started with that I play soccer at UCLA. I did play soccer," I said, feeling my insides collapse as I said the words aloud. That was like sports 101, never speak the negative into existence. You didn't go into the huddle and talk about how this was going to be a "learning experience" and how you would "come out stronger" before the game even started. You pulled out all the stops the moment you put the jersey on. Don't give up. What was wrong with me?

"That's about all the information your mom told me on the phone. She said you were a starting player before your accident. She said you'd moved your classes online so you could come home and work with a specialist," Dr. Morgan said.

"Yeah. Just for the semester. I'm going back to UCLA. Coach expects me to be back, and the plan is to rehab as much as I can and return to the team in the fall. I was a strong player and I'm just a sophomore. A junior by the start of the season."

"It's been almost a full year since your injury. Is it just a matter of building up your strength?"

I remembered my last training session with the team. A cone drill that should've been easy, a part of our normal warm-up routine, had me nearly tripping over my feet. Coach was nice and told me I'd get better after a few practices, but I didn't. I got worse. I should've been gaining muscle back and getting stronger, but instead, I felt sorer with each practice and made more mistakes because of it.

"That and other things," I said. "There's some nerve damage. The worst of it is in my right ankle. The concern is that I might not feel if I injure myself and I might make things worse."

"Well, maybe some time focusing specifically on those muscles and getting some medical treatment for the nerves will be exactly what you need. Sometimes, we just have to listen to our bodies and allow ourselves the time we need to fix the real problem," she said without missing a beat.

"I guess I should've asked more about you, Dr. Morgan. My mom would tell me I'm being rude," I said, hoping it would put a stop to the line of conversation.

"Call me Hadiza," she said and flashed another white smile my way. "This is your session, Margot. We can talk about whatever you want, but I guess this is a good time to let you know that everything you say is confidential unless I have concerns that you may harm yourself or anyone else. Have you ever felt that way?"

"No," I said. I didn't mean to sound defensive, but I did. God, what if she thought I was trying to hide something? I wasn't hurting myself. The idea had never crossed my mind.

Hadiza didn't seem phased at all by my reaction. She glanced down at her desk for a moment before reaching for what turned out to be a glass of water off-camera.

"What made you decide to try therapy?" she asked before raising the glass to her lips.

The knee-jerk reaction was to tell her my mom told me to go to therapy. I agreed mostly because she'd asked me on a day when the idea of talking to her on the phone seemed unbearable. I told her I'd go just to put an end to the conversation and quickly found a reason to hang up. I think that was the first day I felt like leaving my dorm room just to get away from the audience of my roommate. I put on my running shoes and left. The rhythmic sound of my breathing and my feet hitting the pavement had been comforting. The memory of that run relaxed me a little now.

I looked out the window and felt my muscles grow heavy at the sight of the road and the growing dusting of snow across it.

"I don't know," I said in an exhale.

Hadiza let the silence stretch for a while before she spoke.

"It's difficult when you work hard for something and aren't able to accomplish your goal due to something out of your control."

"I'm trying to fix everything, but things just keep getting in the way."

"What kind of things are in the way?"

I scoffed. I couldn't help myself.

"I don't see a specialist until after the holidays. The doctor told me not to do anything high-impact until I could be assessed again. I'm only cleared to do low-impact exercises. Nothing I'm allowed to do goes along with my goals."

"Some things are a marathon and not a sprint," Hadiza said with a shrug, her tone light as though we were catching up over afternoon tea and not talking about the derailment of the rest of my life. "It took you a long time to get good enough to play college soccer."

"Yeah, and I don't have another four years to get good and in shape again. I don't even have a year. I need to keep my skills and strength up in the meantime while I fix my ankle issues."

"I'm not saying that you can't heal your injury and play again," Hadiza said. She adjusted in her seat before speaking, looking straight into the camera. "Maybe we can use our time together to reshape your goals and heal your feelings about life not meeting your expectations."

"What does it even mean to heal my feelings? I got in a car wreck that messed up my legs and not only do the muscles not react like they should, but I don't even feel when they're injured anymore. I was known for my precision on the field. I spent all my free time training to do this. My family spent a lot of their free time and money so I could do this. I'm mad! Of course, I'm mad. Why would I be anything else? I did everything I was supposed to and more and I earned my spot."

"You're right. It makes sense," Hadiza said with a nod. "Most people would be angry the way you are. Maybe we just spend a little time talking about that."

"I don't know what else there's to say."

"I know we haven't talked very long, but I get the feeling that you aren't the kind of person who likes to stay stationary when faced with adversity," she said.

I looked back at her. I must not have been paying very much attention moments before, because I could see now that she had a notebook open to her right. Most of the page was off-camera, but I could tell that she'd filled the whole page with notes.

"What do you mean?" I asked.

"You've heard of fight or flight, right?"

"Yeah. Why?"

"Well, really there are more responses. When faced with some kind of threat or problem, people don't always react the same. Knowing how we respond to these situations can help us address how to resolve them in healthy ways. Some people run away from their problems. Some people buck up and fight back, for instance."

"I don't run from my problems," I said with a groan. "If I had things my way, I'd still be back working with the team at UCLA, not here doing a semester online."

Hadiza didn't speak for a moment. She looked past the screen like she was studying something on the wall of her office behind where I would be sitting if we were in person. It made my stomach clench. I could already tell that whatever held her interest was going to hurt.

"You don't run away from your problems, but I think you try to mitigate them," she said. "You're a fixer. You have a great work ethic. Of course you do or you wouldn't have ended up as a starter for a college team at a young age."

"That's what I'm saying. I told you I don't run away. I should be doing *something* in the meantime. I know the specialist is on vacation like the rest of us, but my doctor could've given me something to do during the whole month I have between now and then."

Hadiza smiled a little as she shook her head.

"You want to fix things, but not everything can be mitigated," she said. "You know that there's no fast track to success. There are a couple of ways you can approach this. You can go around the problem and train and hope you don't get injured again and cope with the injuries you already have. You can walk away, which I don't think is on the table. That option isn't even in the same room. Or you can go through the problem. I think you know it's better in the long run to go through, not around. If that's your choice, then we can talk about how to slow down, let things be when they aren't in our control, and learn how to find joy in the parts of your life outside of soccer."

My first response was to accuse her of telling me to take the easy road. I wasn't a wimp. As I held my tongue, I realized from the knowing look on her face that she wasn't doing that at all. She was playing hardball the same way I was. I just wasn't convinced she fully understood. She isn't a professional athlete or even a medical doctor. Had she ever played sports on a competitive level?

This would never work.

"We have a little more time left, but I think we have covered a lot for now," Hadiza said with that wide, white smile again. "We'll meet again at the same time next week."

"Yeah. Next week," I said and leaned back in my chair.

We said awkward goodbyes and I felt my shoulders relax when I exited the tab and shut my laptop. The snow was gathering in a pile along the roof outside my window, glittering under the sunset. The snow was rarely untouched in the front yard the way it was now. Normally, by now, the snow in the front yard would be marred with deep footprints and wide trenches from building snowmen. We used to have contests to see who would build the best one in the front yard and then go to the backyard to use our powers to have snowball fights. There's still a stack of cinder blocks in the backyard that I use to run soccer drills even though the firepit was built years ago.

I stood up from the desk and was halfway to my closet to grab my cleats when a knock came at my door.

"Come in," I said and changed direction for my bed. I sat on the corner just as Marlee opened the door.

"Mom wanted me to let you know we're leaving in twenty minutes."

"Leaving for what?"

"Dinner with the McAdams," she said, eyeing my suitcase lying halfway unpacked on the floor. "We're going to their house and picking a Christmas tree afterward."

"Oh. Well, do I need to change? Is this one of those dinners where Dad's going to try showing off?" I asked, standing up and moving to the side so I could assess myself in the mirror.

"Maybe just put on a sweater or something," Marlee said and left me for the hallway.

I was more dressed up today than the last few weeks and that was just because I didn't want to listen to Madison complain about my hoodies. I exchanged my jeans and Nike sweatshirt for a pair of black leggings and an oversized red sweater. It was casual enough that I could wear my comfortable snow boots, which made it good enough for me.

By the time I stopped brooding at myself in the mirror, Madison was yelling for me to hurry up.

Chapter 4

We couldn't all fit in Mom's SUV, so Madison rode with Mom and Dad in the SUV, and Marlee and I took my Jeep. I followed the SUV down the road, keeping my eyes on the taillights and not on the memories of the pavement and steel guardrail.

"What do you think?" Marlee asked just as my body relaxed and we made our way down the mountain.

"About what?"

It went quiet for a moment, long enough for me to realize she must have been talking the entire time since we left the cabin. My eyes stung as the small bit of relief was overshadowed by a wave of frustration. The hill wasn't even that steep. The roads were dry. How a block of pavement could nearly send me over the edge each time ...

"Do you think blogging is dead?" Marlee asked. "When's the last time you read a good blog that wasn't one of those food sites everyone skims through to get the recipes?"

"I don't know. I guess maybe the bloggers moved to being vloggers on YouTube?" I found myself zoning out as we wound through the trees, resigning to nods and hums of agreement about whatever Marlee went on about the rest of the way to the farm. Instead of turning into the parking lot of the mercantile, we passed it for a gravel road that led toward a little house with a tree in the front window with twinkling multi-colored lights. I parked next to Mom's SUV and before we could all get out of our seats, the front door of the house opened and Jared came out with his mom following behind.

"I don't know about that new coach," Dad said as he extended his right hand toward Jared whose smile only grew wider.

"Give the guy a season at least before you make assumptions," Jared said and shook Dad's hand before he was pulled into a side hug. Jared glanced over his shoulder at Madison, mouthing his apology as our dad steered him into the house to continue their talk about the Denver Broncos.

"I'm sorry, Joanne," Mom said as she stopped next to Jared's mom on the porch. "He forgets his manners whenever someone mentions football."

Joanne McAdams didn't bat an eye at Mom's insult, which was loud enough for Dad to hear. She held open the door and offered to take Mom's coat. Madison slipped past them, giving Joanne's shoulder a gentle squeeze in greeting along the way.

"These are my daughters, Margot and Marlee," Mom said as Joanne hung her coat on the wall of hooks next to the door. Marlee and I moved inside, and I shut the door behind us, immediately getting a whiff of ham and something cinnamon.

"Madison told me about you," Joanne said as we shrugged out of our coats. "Well, make yourselves at home. Mark will be back from the barn in a bit, and we can eat. Mark's my brother. We grew up in this house and I inherited it after our parents died. It's not that big for a dinner party, but it's home."

"Cozy," Marlee said. Her eyes were focused on the photos on the living room wall, half of them photos of Jared at various ages and the other photos of Joanne's adventures around the world. Madison told us Jared's mom spent her younger years traveling from one place to another, but I didn't know that included everything from the wilderness to big cities.

"A lot of stories on that wall," Joanne said as she slowly made her way toward the kitchen.

"Where were you when you held that monkey?" Marlee asked,

pointing to a photo next to Jared's graduation photo. I wasn't sure when she'd left, but I could hear Mom in the kitchen now lecturing Dad about manners.

"That's in Thailand and that little guy climbed into my lap while I was out for drinks with a friend. They're everywhere in Thailand," Joanne said before disappearing into the kitchen. Marlee looked back at the wall of photos in awe. I tugged on her sleeve and we followed Joanne.

It was tight enough in the kitchen that Jared had to lift the platter of ham over Madison's head to move it from the counter to the dining table. Rather than move through the crowd, Joanne told Madison to bring a bowl of mashed potatoes to the table before she told us all to find seats.

"Mark can join us whenever he wraps up," she said as we all settled around the table.

"He's here. I just saw him walk by the window," Jared said just as the front door opened with a creak.

"Hope you didn't wait just for me!" Mark called out.

"Leave your boots at the door!" Joanne yelled back.

"Jeez," Mark said before coming around the corner. "Let me get in the door first at least."

"You were up and down the rows. I don't want mud stamped into the carpet."

"You could always get another rug," Mark said with a laugh, ruffling Jared's hair as he squeezed past for the empty chair next to his sister. Jared elbowed him playfully in the gut before he could take a seat.

"I was ten and I thought the paint would cover up the stain," Jared said, smiling despite the pink tinge to his cheeks.

"This boy is the reason for all the house rules," Mark explained, taking a roll from the breadbasket and signaling for the rest of us to fill our plates. I noticed the annoyed look Mom shot Dad as he reached across her for the gravy boat.

"Again, I was ten," Jared laughed.

"Not when you let a rat loose in the house," Mark snorted.

My mom's hand stilled inches from the casserole dish.

"Gross," Madison moaned, shooting Mark a disgusted look and swatting Jared's hand when he laughed.

"I thought it would be funny to scare Mom with it. I didn't know they could jump like that," Jared said and looked back at his mom apologetically. "I found it a few minutes after I dropped it. My plan didn't even work. Mom wasn't scared at all! She didn't even flinch when it launched itself across the hall."

"That's because I grew up with him and then raised you," Joanne said and pointed from Mark to Jared, barely containing her smile.

"Should've heard the way Jared screamed," Mark chuckled, passing the ham to Jared.

"Speaking of rats …" Dad started, pointing at Jared with his fork.

"I swear, Peter. You got to the give the guy a whole season before you can decide if he can improve a team," Jared laughed, opening the floor for yet more football talk.

"I'm glad he has someone to talk about the Broncos with, because he knows it won't be me," Joanne told the rest of us while they engaged in their debate. "I don't think I've watched a whole football game since he played in high school."

"I'm just glad he has someone to go to the games with who will actually know what's happening," Madison said.

She hadn't spoken that loud, but somehow, Jared heard. He looked at her with a challenging expression.

"I'm taking you to a game and I swear you'll like it. It's a lot more fun in the stands than watching from the couch," he said.

She rolled her eyes. "Whatever."

"I'm serious," he said and bumped his shoulder against hers. "I'll get you in an orange T-shirt before you know it. Maybe we can get matching jerseys."

"Keep dreaming," Madison smiled.

The cozy kitchen was filled with the scraping of forks on plates and the hums of satisfaction. Madison accidentally kicked me once, blushing bright pink as she apologized and cast Jared a knowing look as he tried to contain his laughter before going back to whatever game of footsie they had going on under the table.

"How are classes, Jared?" Dad asked, helping himself to another round of ham.

Jared shrugged. "Good. It's slowing down a lot as we get closer to graduation."

"And the plan is to graduate and come back here to run the family business?" Mom asked, taking that tone that I knew so well. It was almost challenging, like warning him against giving the wrong answer, whatever that was.

"Expanding it," he said and glanced at Madison. "We have a lot of plans, mostly Madison's ideas. She's going to take over primary operations with the mercantile. I have already secured a few connections with some artists and business owners around Colorado that I think would be great to bring into the mercantile side of things. The farm will stay mostly the same, but I have ideas to expand that into more of an event space for things like sleigh rides through the trees and maybe even weddings."

"He wants to put a zipline through the field," Madison said teasingly.

Jared blushed. "I've always thought a zipline over all the rows with the lights at night would be really cool."

"Keep thinking about the logistics of that one," Mark said and pointed at him with the end of his fork before spearing a slice of ham.

"Marlee, aren't you at Yale?" Joanne asked, scooting her empty plate aside.

Before Marlee could answer, Mom jumped in.

"She just finished her first semester. She's planning to study law. She's making straight A's and is part of the honors college," she said.

Marlee shrugged as everyone around the table congratulated her.

"It's not as exciting as it sounds."

"Maybe not the school part, but Yale has a beautiful campus," said Joanne. "I really liked the East Coast when I was still traveling. I liked the cities. There's just nothing like New York City. I'd love to get back there again." She turned her attention to me with a smile. I could feel my chest tighten as she asked the dreaded question. "How's school been on the West Coast?"

"Margot is back home with us for the next semester," Mom said. "Still with UCLA, but she's doing classes online."

My stomach sank at the drop in her tone. You could feel the room deflate. Joanne kept the smile on her face, but the twitch at the corners of her mouth and the way she looked down and reached for her water confirmed what everyone else was thinking.

"You know, I could really use someone like you at the company, Jared," Dad said after the silence settled in the room.

Mom slapped his bicep. "He just told you what his plan was."

"I know and I'm just saying that I could really use a guy like him," Dad told her before looking up at Jared with his business smile plastered across his face. "We'll have an opening not long after you both graduate. It would keep you back in Denver. You wouldn't even have to move."

"Dad," Madison groaned.

Dad held up his hands in resignation as Jared laughed and thanked him for the opportunity. The conversation shifted to dessert. I passed on the apple pie. It wasn't part of my soccer diet and besides, my stomach was too knotted to think about food, and the longer I sat the more it churned. I worried I might even be sick. I was relieved when Jared suggested we all go to the mercantile and sit on the patio behind the barn.

The fresh air was comforting, but the chill only eased the tension in my shoulders a fraction. My powers surged toward my fingertips; a little burst of energy, like a warm cup of coffee that made taking a seat on the outdoor couch a little easier. It had started to snow while we had dinner, large flakes falling softly and leaving a thin dusting across the deck. Mark moved around the deck, a new addition since last Christmas season, turning on the three heaters while Joanne lit the firepit in front of the couch.

"We're going to take a lap around the row. I want to show Madison my idea for a new sleigh route," Jared said, taking Madison's hand and tugging her toward the nearest row before she had a chance to agree.

"Whew!" Mark said and rubbed his hands together. "Leave it to Jared to pick the coldest day this week."

Joanne shot him a look of warning, turning back to add one more log to the firepit before she stood up.

"You got the lights?" she asked him.

"I got the lights," he confirmed and turned for the barn. He slid both large doors aside to reveal the inside of the mercantile.

It was dark inside, but I could see that some kind of backdrop was set up in the middle of the shop. It looked almost like the setup for a photographer. I noticed four dark shapes on the floor, split so two sat on one side of the backdrop and two on the other. I had just realized they were vases of flowers when the lights turned on and blinded me for a second.

I was right about the backdrop. Someone had set up a large, black backdrop in the middle of the shop and framed it by draping a long strand of pink roses across the top and down the sides. The vases on the floor were filled with the same pink roses and hanging in the center of the backdrop was a neon sign with the words *Jared & Madison* glowing in beautiful cursive.

I looked at the deck, which was now illuminated by the bulb lights that stretched overhead. I followed the lights across the rows of evergreen trees, down a row where Jared and Madison were standing. My sister was looking up at the lights above them when Jared touched her shoulder and pointed at the lights behind them. I couldn't make out exactly what was hanging from the wire, but I had an idea that it was a piece of mistletoe.

With Madison's back turned Jared pulled something from his pocket and sank onto one knee. When Madison turned back around, her hands immediately covered her face. A moment later, we could hear her squeals of excitement and Jared rose to scoop her into his arms. They kissed for a long time, long enough that the answer was obvious, and our families started to cheer and clap from the deck.

I cried alongside my mom, the smile making my cheeks hurt.

Mom wrapped an arm around my shoulders and squeezed me, crying happy tears too. Only, the tightness in my chest and the unsettling way my stomach twisted to the point of cramps made my breath catch in my chest. I was happy. I was excited.

Then why did I feel dizzy then and why did my lungs not want to accept the deep breaths I was trying to take?

Jared and Madison pulled away, keeping their hands linked. Madison let out another squeal and held up her left hand to show off the engagement ring we were too far away to even see. She started to run toward the deck, stopping after a few feet to turn back and pull Jared along behind her by his hand.

"Show us the ring and let's celebrate!" Mark announced as he returned from the barn with a bottle of champagne.

Madison gladly held out her hand. I took a step forward to join my mom and Marlee despite the growing pain in my stomach. The ring was beautiful; diamonds along the band and more clustered together in the center to form a snowflake.

My heart flew into a race at the sound of a pop. I stepped back from the group as Mark began filling glasses with champagne and Joanne helped pass them around to each of us. Her smile dimmed a little when she reached me, and she didn't offer the glass right away.

"Um, would it be all right if I go lie down in the house for a minute?" I asked before she could speak.

"Sure. You feel okay?"

"I think I just need some water, maybe something sugary. I just feel ..."

"Right," she said with a nod. "Help yourself to anything in the kitchen. Make yourself at home."

I was glad that my family was too occupied with the toast to notice me, and I left the deck. I could hear my breathing as I crossed the yard for the house. It had gone from shallow breaths to a full-on panting. My eyes stung and my vision blurred as I reached the front door. The sob was building in my chest, and I stayed in the house just long enough to grab my purse before I hurried to my Jeep where I fell apart in the front seat.

Chapter 5

I COULDN'T STAY, not there. I felt better the farther up the mountain I drove; even better as I passed the fork in the road where I should've turned to go to the cabin. Instead, I kept driving, and the more trees I saw the more my body relaxed until my sobs had quieted and fewer tears rolled down my face.

I'd forgotten to grab my coat, but I was glad for the cool air that filled the Jeep. Once I was aware of the silence, I turned on the radio and listened to the pop songs as I drove. I couldn't remember the name of the next town, but I knew it was larger than Crescent Peak. I wasn't sure I was going to stop there anyway. I didn't really know how long I would drive.

What was I even doing?

The Jeep skidded for just a second on the road, a moment too brief to have done any damage, and yet that single second was enough to throw me into a panic. My scream died out and as the Jeep continued along the road as though nothing happened. I cried again. A laugh came across the radio, only adding insult to injury.

"Let's get to more serious topics," the DJ began. "Temperatures are set to drop drastically in the next two hours as heavy snow moves through the mountains. Visibility will be reduced as these large flakes move through the area, so stay home if you can. Drive slower than normal if you have to travel, and make sure you keep informed of your driving conditions. Lots of rural roads may be too snowy or slick to pass through this evening and overnight until we go into a very sunshiny Saturday," he said before the next pop song began.

I read the sign for the next town as I passed. *North Ridge.*

The first building in the city limits was huge, a sprawling campus I thought was a school until I saw the silver words plastered across the side labeling it as North Ridge's city athletic complex. Under the words was a description of its campus.

Ice rink, Olympic-size swimming pool, power-lifting gym, indoor track, and soccer field.

Soccer field.

I turned into the parking lot. It was mostly empty, with a few snow-covered cars in the front likely those of employees. I was right about it being a quiet spot. There was no one at the front desk and aside from the people I could hear to the left where the gym was, it was quiet. The sign on the front of the desk said the ice rink was straight ahead, the gym and track were down the left wing, and the pool and soccer field were down the right wing.

I didn't wait for the receptionist and thankfully, the hall leading to the soccer field was unlocked. There was no one around to stop me and when the hallway opened at the end to the giant space beyond, I finally felt relaxed. The turf was sprayed with the logo of the complex in the center, and the entire space was set up to host matches.

Along both sides of the field were metal stands. The far side was smaller than the one I was on, just a few rows that sat in front of the windows that showcased the pool in the next giant room. I stepped onto the turf and walked toward the nearest goal, imagining that I was back at UCLA and on my way to make a game-winning shot. I dropped my purse as I went and started to jog, even feigning a kick when I made it to the goal. It felt a little silly, but it did help me relax. When I turned from the goal, I saw a soccer ball wedged under the bottom row of seats in the stands.

I ran over and eased the ball from under the metal with my foot. I started by dribbling up and down the field, feeling more and more excited as my heart rate increased. I incorporated more footwork with each lap until I was nearly back to my UCLA drills. I easily slipped into my team's warmup routine and after reaching the end of the field again I stopped to slip out of my red sweater so I could better move in my leggings and sports bra.

I thought back to my last practice with the team, the drill that finally got me called to the sidelines to talk with Coach. It was the first panic attack I'd had. I knew what she'd say, and the panic attack had already started before I even reached her on the sidelines. It was bad enough that we moved into the locker room, and I nearly fell apart right there as she told me that I should see the doctor again and how the trainers thought I needed more than the physical therapy they could provide during the season.

I took a deep breath and started the footwork drill, imagining the cones along the field as I went. I pushed and pushed myself as my ankles and shins started to burn, muscles aching until they didn't ... and I tripped. I got up and started again, finding that my feet responded less and less to what I needed them to do, what I knew they could do, and I fell earlier and earlier into the drill. I tried again and again until I was breathing heavily, and it was too hard to focus past the tears and the pain in my ankles.

I let out a groan as I kicked the ball as hard as I could, watching with my hands on my knees and heart racing as the ball shot into the goal several yards away and settled on the turf. I went to the stands against the windows, going to the very end and taking a seat. The metal was cold, and it felt nice against my skin as I lay down, a contrast to the hot tears that ran down my cheeks. I closed my eyes and tried focusing on my breathing.

It's fine.
It's fine.
It will get better.

❋

I WOKE with a jolt when I heard a loud tapping sound. I nearly fell off the seat. We were separated by inches and thick glass. The guy waving at me from the poolside of the building looked familiar, but I didn't have time to sort through my memories. He held up his phone, placing the screen against the glass so I could read the message he'd typed out.

Are you okay?

I looked up at him, surprised by the shock on his face before the glow from the LED screen behind him caught my attention. The time across the top read five-fifteen in the morning.

The morning!

I did fall off my seat this time. I ignored the pain at the back of my head from where I'd bashed it against the metal stands and I scrambled to my feet, looking over the soccer field. Where did I leave my purse? Had anyone else been in here overnight while I was here? I ran to the far side of the field, panic beginning to grip my chest as I looked over the turf.

"Are you okay?" he asked.

"I need my purse. I can't find my—"

I took a deep breath when the man ran a few feet to my left and leaned down to pick up my bag from the turf. As he straightened up, a new kind of shock came over me.

First, he was nearly naked and dripping wet.

Second, I did know him. At least, I used to.

Dax Krune walked toward me with my purse held in one hand. He wore nothing but a pair of swim trunks that fit tightly against his thighs and were low on his hips. Water slid over his broad shoulders and down the creases of his abs, his arms, and onto the leather of my purse. He attempted to wipe it away with his other hand before he offered it to me.

"Are you all right, Margot?" he asked, more concerned about me than the fact that he was barefoot and half-naked on a soccer field.

"Why are you here?" I asked after I'd recovered.

He gave a small laugh, offering my purse to me again. This time, I took it.

"Swimming," he said. "Why are *you* here?"

"Just soccer," I said and draped my purse on my right shoulder, realizing now that I was in my sports bra. Holy hell. Where was my shirt?

"In snow boots?" Dax laughed again.

I turned from him and raised my hands to the top of my head as I scanned for my shirt. I was starting to get a headache. Not only that, but it was five in the freaking morning. I stayed out overnight in a whole different city, in a gym, and my family was probably flipping out.

"Oh God," I groaned as I thought about the party I'd left. My sister's freaking engagement. What was wrong with me? How stupid was I?

"Hang on a sec," Dax said and came around me so were face-to-face again. "For real, what are you doing here?"

Tears stung my eyes. No. Absolutely not. I was not going to cry and whine about my problems in front of Dax freaking Krune.

"I need to find my shirt," I said with a sigh and walked past him again. If it wasn't on this side of the field, surely it was on the other. Dax caught up with me as I walked.

"I haven't seen you in years," he said.

"I saw you last year at the Winter Solstice Gala," I pointed out. The Winter Solstice Gala was the event of the year for the winter witch community. We gathered at the lodge in Crescent Peak for the ball and danced and celebrated the day when our magic was the most powerful. The Krune family had always attended since we were all little kids. Dax and his brother both went to Heritage City Academy where my sisters and I went.

"Yeah, but we haven't talked since high school," Dax said.

I opened my mouth to disagree when I saw my red sweater on the field near the stands. I must have run right past it when I panicked about my purse. I picked it up and slipped it over my head, a little annoyed when I saw that Dax was still standing next to me in his tight shorts.

"We used to be friends, you know," he said teasingly.

Not totally wrong. We were in the same circle in high school. We had a lot of the same friends, attended the same social gatherings, and we were both athletes. That's really about all we had in common then. We were the only athletes at our private school that got scholarships and we both got big scholarships to Division One colleges, both of us coincidentally accepting scholarships to California schools. I got a full ride to play soccer at UCLA. Dax got a full ride to swim at UC Berkeley.

"Pro athletes don't exactly practice in their street clothes," Dax said. I didn't know what to say. Part of me worried that everything would just come tumbling out if I opened my mouth. "Come on."

Dax led the way down the field, and I followed him from the turf to the stained concrete and through the door to the swimming pool. It was complete with ten lanes and a giant LED screen that could display times during a competition. A smaller pool was on the far side of the room, probably for warmups or maybe recreation. It was warm in the room, humid even. We passed the end of the pool and started toward that smaller one, Dax leading me straight to the door of the men's locker room.

"I'm the only one here, I promise," he said and held the door open for me.

"That doesn't exactly make a girl feel more comfortable following a guy into the men's room," I said and went inside anyway.

I understood as soon as I rounded the corner for the main room why we came here. The first area I walked into was a large changing area with lockers against the right wall and mirrors and sinks on the left. The door opened directly to those sinks and gave me a perfect view of my mascara-smeared face and red-rimmed eyes.

Holy hell.

My face flushed with embarrassment, and I quickly went to

the first sink to try scrubbing off the makeup. I tried my best and even after scrubbing my skin until it was sore, there were dark smears at my lash lines. Dax left a towel for me on the counter along with a black toiletry bag where I found a face scrub that I gladly took. When I finished washing my face, I noticed he added a pair of sweatpants and a hoodie to the counter.

I dried my face on the towel and turned to look at him. He sat on a bench with a towel draped around his shoulders.

"My family is probably freaking out," I said with a groan.

"I'm the only person who's ever here this early. Most people don't even use the pool this time of the year," Dax said and stood up. He tossed the towel onto the bench behind him. "No one should come in here, but there is a lock on the door. Feel free to use anything in that bag. There's shampoo and stuff. I'm a bit bigger than you, but the sweats should fit you."

"What?" I asked.

"Call your family and let them know you're okay. I don't want to offend you, but you did just run around a soccer field and it's noticeable," Dax said with a snort as he started toward the door. "Besides, you'll feel better after a shower. Like I said, no one should come in here, but there is a lock on this door if it makes you more comfortable. I got to start my workout. Come find me at lane four when you're done."

He left the locker room and after considering all my options, I locked the door behind him and picked up my purse from the counter. Just like I figured, I had a bunch of text messages and a few voicemails. No one told Madison I was missing. It was clear that at first, everyone thought I went to the cabin. Marlee left a voicemail telling me that Madison was staying with Jared at the farm and to let her know where I was. Dad's voicemail was not as calm. He demanded that I come home or at least call and he told me how thoughtless it was that I chose my sister's engagement to disappear.

I didn't want to, but I knew Dad was the person I needed to call.

"Superstar," he said with a sigh.

"I'm fine. I'm at the gym in North Ridge."

"North Ridge? Where the hell have you been all night? We thought maybe you went back home to Heritage City, but we never saw you on the cameras and the alarm system said the door hadn't been opened since we all left. What were you thinking?"

"I'm sorry. I know I should've called."

"At least send a text, Margot," he said before talking to Mom in the background. "I know things aren't going the way you planned. You have plenty of reason to be pissed off, but please don't shut us out. I haven't pried. I know you need your space, and you'll talk when you're ready, but we need to make sure that you're safe."

"I am safe," I told him, suddenly feeling like a seventeen-year-old version of myself.

"All right," he said with another deep sigh. "I want you to turn on location sharing on your phone. Make sure your mom and I both have access. If we can't see your location in five minutes, we're coming to get you. Come home before dinner."

"Okay."

"Okay," he said, ignoring my mom's questions in the background. "We love you."

"I love you, too," I said, feeling the tears burn my eyes again.

He hung up first and just like he asked, I made sure to share my location with him and Mom. He texted me to let me know that he saw my location and that he loved me, repeating his warning to be home before dinner. I tucked my phone back in my purse and gathered everything I would need from Dax's bag for the shower.

Despite the locked door, I undressed behind the plastic shower curtain to be safe and hung my clothes on the hook just outside. As the water warmed my skin and eased the tightness of my muscles, I let the tears fall again and was annoyed enough with myself that the crying stopped minutes after it started. I had to figure it out. I needed to get myself figured out. There was no use in crying about it all when I could be doing something.

No crying at Christmas.

Dax's shampoo smelled woodsy. He kept his blond hair short, so it made sense that the guy didn't have any conditioner. I hesitated as I rubbed the *Cedar & Cypress* scent over my arm, my stomach twisting from the awkwardness before I scrubbed the body wash across my chest and down toward my naval. I wasn't sure how much I'd need and decided to be liberal, which meant that bubbles clung to my skin, dripped over my hips, and slid down my legs before I could do anything to avoid it.

This shouldn't be that awkward. I was completely alone. The door was locked. It was just soap. I was just soap that smelled exactly like he did. Maybe it was just because I didn't have brothers and I'd never had a boyfriend. I had barely kissed a guy, unless you counted the wet mashing of lips that was me and Aiden Harrington at the eighth-grade spring dance.

That did it.

I no longer had that strange butterfly feeling in my stomach.

I finished rinsing off and hurried from the shower stall to the dressing room with the thin towel wrapped around me. It dawned on me that I had no clean underwear. I could feel the heat from my face as I quickly pulled on the sweatpants and sweatshirt. What would my family think if I walked into the house in some guy's clothes?

I looked up at the mirror and felt a little better. Dax had given me his Berkeley swimming sweats, so they looked almost exactly like my soccer sweats, other than the obvious size difference and the university name across the chest. I could make it work. What I couldn't do was ignore the smell of cedar that clung to my skin. I got a whiff of clean linen when I got dressed; the same laundry detergent I used, I was sure.

There was no way I could face Dax. I knew I wouldn't be able to look him in the face and I really should get home anyway.

I grabbed my clothes from the hook outside the shower and tossed them toward the counter where my purse was. I thought I might have to try all the lockers but found his backpack on the floor instead. I paused before I opened the front pocket and found several things. His phone. Wallet. Keys. A notebook with the Berkeley swimming logo across the front. There was a pen clipped to the spiral notebook, so I pulled it out and opened it up to the first blank page.

Sorry. I can't stay. I'll get your stuff back to you. Thank you!

I WROTE down my phone number and left the notebook out on the bench so he wouldn't miss my note. Then, I gathered my things in my arms, unlocked the door, and practically jogged around the perimeter of the room toward the exit. I didn't look at the pool until I reached the glass door, catching a glimpse of him speeding down the middle lane before I left the pool and hoped that no one would question me on my way out of the building.

Chapter 6

I COULD HEAR my parents arguing in the den when I got back to the cabin, so they were distracted enough for me to make it up to my room and change out of Dax's clothes and into a pair of leggings and a T-shirt.

"Do Mom and Dad know you're back yet?"

I jumped at Marlee's words and knocked my dirty clothes and purse off the corner of my bed. When I turned around, she was leaning in the doorway with her arms crossed.

"No," I told her and let out a sigh. "They were a little busy."

"Yeah. They've been like that all morning," Marlee said and rolled her eyes.

I bent down to gather my things, surprised at how far I'd tossed it all. I found a sock so far under my bed that I decided it was a lost cause and I couldn't find the other at all. I gave up picking it all up and just kicked it toward the closet instead.

"So, you slept in the gym?" Marlee asked.

"Um, yeah. Kind of," I said and set my purse on my dresser, removing my phone and noticing that it had died at some point during the trip home. "I just needed to get some energy out. After that, I sat down and ended up falling asleep in a corner. The area I was in was dead, so I guess no one noticed."

Marlee let out a single laugh as I went to the side table to plug my phone in, making sure that it was charging before I turned my attention to her. She had her glasses on, which told me she'd been doing some serious reading. She'd probably spent the entire morning in her room avoiding our parents' argument downstairs.

"Are they arguing about who gets to work when during the holidays?" I asked. That was always the big point of tension at the cabin. Who got to work in the office? Who got the mornings and who got the afternoons? Who ruined dinner by taking a work call?

"Surprisingly, no," Marlee said and moved farther into the room. My heart skipped when she pushed Dax's sweats aside to make space for herself on my bed. I reached over and grabbed the clothes, tossing them toward the closet. "Mom bought the wrong syrup for pancakes and Dad got mad, but apparently it's his fault because we always eat waffles at the cabin and Dad forgot that."

"Well, maybe Mom can just use the syrup and Dad can make waffles instead."

"That would be too easy."

"Well, when you expect one thing, I guess"

"It's petty and you and I both know it," Marlee said with a groan. "Let's just call it what it is."

"Okay. Well," I started, not really sure where I was going with the words. I let out a groan in frustration that I knew Marlee wouldn't ask me to explain. That's why I did it. I knew she wouldn't press. I let the room go quiet for a moment before the words came to me, the explanation I wanted to give to our parents, my sisters, and even Hadiza.

"I just want people to stop looking at me like I'm going to fall apart if they bring everything up, you know?" I said, grabbing my pillow and setting it in my lap. "I want everyone to give me the space to do the stupid therapy and train like the doctor says I can and not act like I'm going to do something crazy."

"You're not going to do anything crazy, right?'

"No!" I tightened my grip on the pillow, the polka dot pattern looking more like a bunch of ovals stretched across the fabric.

"Okay," Marlee said with a casual shrug.

"Okay?" I asked.

She shrugged again and stood up from the bed.

"Yeah. You haven't done anything to make me think you're going to go postal or anything. I mean, you left the party yesterday and slept in a gym, but I kind of wish I'd left the party earlier, too."

"Really?"

"Oh yeah," she said with a snort. "Most people got pretty tipsy. Madison slapped Jared's ass. It was a little weird."

"Yeah, I guess there's that, but you don't think me sleeping in the corner of a gym is—"

"It's a twenty-four-hour gym. You're, well, you. You take soccer so seriously that staying in the gym overnight doesn't seem that weird." Marlee adjusted her glasses on her nose as she backed toward the door. She waited for just a moment before she left for her room across the hall, shutting the door just as I heard Mom tell Dad to run to the store to pick up more groceries and to get her some Advil for the headache that he was giving her.

I closed my door after that.

❋

MADISON CAME by in her pink Jeep to rescue Marlee and me from the house that afternoon. She was still living on cloud nine from her engagement, and I was convinced she'd reside there for the next several months. Marlee must've been right about a lot of the partygoers getting drunk because Madison never mentioned a word about me leaving the farm. The more she talked about the night and Jared as we drove to the coffee shop the clearer it became that she didn't know I'd been missing most of the night.

"God, why is there not a single place in Crescent Peak to go get a beer?" Marlee asked.

Her comment put an abrupt end to Madison's discussion of wedding planning, which was pretty much already planned out aside from booking and ordering everything, as she put the car in park at the curb and turned to glance at our younger sister in the back seat.

"It's like two in the afternoon and you aren't old enough to drink yet," she said.

"Sure, but still, There's a lot of things to do in Crescent Peak if you're outdoorsy or like to shop or like fancy coffee, but the town pretty much shuts down at nine every night," Marlee said as she gathered her things from the floorboard.

"I thought nightlife was about putting on your pajamas and reading Jane Auburn to you," Madison said as she opened her door and stepped out. I could hear them arguing despite stepping onto the sidewalk on the other side of the car.

"It's Jane Austen. How do you *still* not know that?" Marlee asked.

"Whatever it is, you're still not old enough to drink."

They came around the front of the Jeep to join me on the sidewalk, Madison leading the way in a neon pink sweater with the cursive words *snow bunny* arched around the collar. It was a piece of her own design that she sold in the McAdams Mercantile. Even in a sweatshirt she managed to look like a fashion icon and a billboard at the same time.

"Like you didn't go to parties at Kent all the time. I've seen your fake ID," Marlee said as she walked toward the coffee shop.

"Yeah, fine. Don't we all? Well, maybe not all of us," Madison said when her eyes fell on me. "Still, even if there was some kind of nightlife in Crescent Peak, I doubt you'd be spending your Christmas Break up late every night."

Why did I always have to be the goodie-two-shoes, even with everything I had going on? How was it possible that I could have a whole mental breakdown, uproot my entire life plan, and still be seen as the responsible one in the family?

"Only in Crescent Peak does the coffee shop get busier as the day goes," Madison said as we walked into the packed room. Almost every table was full, and several people stood around the room absorbed in their conversations.

"Hence the need for some kind of nightlife activity," Marlee said before Madison led the way toward the register.

We placed our orders: a hot chocolate with chocolate shavings for Madison, a black coffee for Marlee, and a caramel latte for me. We waited in silence for our drinks at the counter, Madison smiling at her phone and Marlee reading what looked like an article or maybe an eBook on hers. Once we all had our orders, we started the hunt for a table and after at least fifteen minutes, we found a small table we were able to pull three chairs around.

"So, what's Yale like? What is this nightlife that you're using a fake ID to experience?" Madison asked, setting her phone to the side and taking a sip of her hot chocolate.

Marlee looked so annoyed for a second that I didn't know if she'd answer, but she cupped her drink in both hands and leaned forward in preparation.

"There's this brewery near the dorms that does a trivia night."

"Beer? You're going out to drink beer?" Madison asked.

"I'm not shotgunning shitty beer at frat parties," Marlee snorted. "I have the fake ID in case I need it, but if you know your stuff and walk in like you belong there, no one bugs you in the first place. One of my friends is older, so we go to trivia night, and it gets competitive. We like to go on the nights they talk about liberal arts and politics."

"I guess I thought you'd be into something like wine tasting or, I don't know." Madison shrugged glanced down at her phone again. I pulled mine from my purse just to avoid the tense conversation, surprised that I had a text. It was from an unknown number, but once I opened it up, I knew exactly who it was from.

> You can give me my clothes tomorrow morning when I pick you up. I got a workout at six at the gym. I actually have something of yours to give back too.

SOMETHING OF MINE? What did Dax have? My missing sock? Probably.

"You both will definitely be in the wedding," Madison said. "I'm thinking about wearing a champagne gown and I kind of want to make it myself. Is that crazy?"

"You, controlling every aspect of your wedding all the way down to the construction of your dress? Not crazy at all," Marlee said, her tone thick with sarcasm.

Rather than tell them both to be nice like normal, I reread the text from Dax. Going tomorrow would be an excuse to get on that practice field again, an excuse that I could argue was also a morning out with a friend. Maybe everyone would stop sending me those worried looks when I walked into the room.

I texted him the address of the cabin while Madison talked about her vision for the wedding. Marlee sipped on her coffee as she talked, scowling down at her phone and offering supportive hums of approval whenever cued.

"The next dress you wear will be at the gala," I pointed out and tucked my phone back in my pocket.

"Yes, and ..." Madison leaned her elbows on the table and started scrolling through her phone until she found what she was looking for with an excited gasp. "I needed a project, and I've always thought it would be fun to open up my online shop for custom orders. I thought that the gala would be the perfect opportunity to create a portfolio for the website, so I made you both dresses."

"How did you know what sizes to make?" I asked as Madison slid her phone across the table to me. Marlee groaned, hiding her face behind her hands.

"Don't hate me," Madison said, unable to contain her smile as she waited for my approval.

My first response was to refuse to wear it. Holy hell! Did it have to reveal that much skin? The gala was in the middle of winter in Colorado! But Madison made it herself. Not only that, but she made it so well.

The dress hung on one of her dress forms in the work shed at the McAdam's farm. It was snow white, the same color everyone would be wearing per tradition, and made entirely of a sheer fabric she'd draped and pleated and gathered in all the right areas to keep it from being too sexy. It was a spaghetti strap dress with sheer fabric that gathered at the bust, almost like a bra top, draped just so to create a scoop neckline. The midsection was boned, pulling the sheer fabric into an hourglass shape at the waist where it relaxed at the hips. Fabric gathered at the right hip, creating a slit just below that allowed the rest of the fabric to drape across to the left side and to the floor.

"I know it may not look like it, but it's structured the way you like. You aren't going to fall out the top of the dress or flash anyone," Madison said and reached over to scroll to the next photo of the dress from a different angle. Somehow, there was more exposure from the back than the front. Other than the folds of fabric that wrapped across the butt the way they did in the front, the rest of the dress was mostly see-through.

"What am I supposed to wear under this?" I asked.

"That's the best part," Madison said and pulled her phone from my hands.

Please don't say nothing.

"What? That every man at the gala will want to buy her a drink?" Marlee asked, realizing she was out of coffee as she raised the cup to her lips.

Madison ignored her and turned her phone to show me a pair of white, high-waisted silk shorts. Were they shorts or underwear? Whatever they were, they looked like they would go to my naval and keep my entire butt covered.

"The dress should actually be really comfortable. The bottoms are full coverage, like a swimsuit. The slit in the dress will show off those soccer legs. No offense, but you aren't very large up top, so you can get away with going braless, which is basically every girl's dream anyway," Madison said. Before I could give my final opinion, she scrolled through the photos again before turning the phone to an entirely new dress.

"Oh no," Marlee groaned.

This dress had a similar top to mine, only the sheer fabric was lined. It had ribbons for straps that were tied in bows at the shoulders. The skirt was flowy, the sheer tulle decorated with lace snowflakes. Marlee didn't say anything for a moment as she looked at the photo.

"It's okay," she said with a shrug, which was basically like acing a math test and scoring the game-winning goal on the same day.

"I can't wait until you both try them on! I swear, you will be totally in love," Madison said with a gasp before she set her phone aside and took another drink of her hot chocolate.

"I think I'm going to go across the street to the bookstore," Marlee said and stood up, not waiting for approval before she went to the counter to order another cup on her way out the door.

"Before you defend her, I know that it's not her personality and that she shows her love in other ways that I don't understand. I get that," Madison said, holding up her index finger in that accusatory way she always did before jumping up on her soapbox. "But I wish that for once she would gush with me about the exciting stuff, like how I'm freaking engaged!"

It was always the same story and I launched into the same lecture I always did, defusing the tension and circling the conversation back around to wedding details and watching as my sister's face lit up again at the talk of different shades of pinks and venues.

Chapter 7

AFTER THE SMEARED makeup and bench-sleeping debacle, I couldn't help but be a little self-conscious about going to the gym with Dax. I barely wore any makeup at all and never at the gym, so that didn't change. But I did put on my favorite gym clothes, the only matching leggings and long-sleeved top set that I owned. It was also not UCLA-branded, which made me feel both sad and empowered.

If that's your choice, then we can talk about how to slow down, let things be when they aren't in our control, and learn how to find joy in the parts of your life outside of soccer.

I'd imagine that Hadiza would call this a first step, even if it was pathetically baby-sized.

I packed my toiletry bag and a clean change of clothes in my gym bag, opting for a pair of jeans despite wanting to stuff a pair of sweatpants into the bag. Was that another step? Maybe it was just me being self-conscious again about Dax seeing me all sweaty and red-eyed. Honestly, it was probably Madison in the back of my head telling me to dress up a little around guys.

It was just Dax Krune. He was the awkward guy in high school who didn't exactly fit in with the athletes even though he was the best one in the entire school.

I tightened my ponytail and made sure I'd packed my soccer gear for a second time before my phone buzzed on the dresser. A glance outside told me he was here. A blue truck large enough to block the entire driveway was parked in the road. I wasted no time heading downstairs, catching my dad's gaze as he stood at the coffee maker.

"Up before the sun like old times, Superstar?" he asked.

"Headed to the gym," I said and pulled open the pantry door. I took a couple of protein bars from a shelf before shutting it. Dad leaned against the counter as the coffee maker hissed behind him.

"Take it easy, okay? Keep to the list."

Right. The list. The list of approved activities, given my injuries.

"Yeah. I don't want to risk anything," I said, ignoring the itch in the back of my brain that told me running a single mile wouldn't kill me. It would probably keep me in better shape. It didn't have to be a fast mile ...

I let the front door swing shut behind me and I hurried down the driveway to the truck. I could feel the warmth envelope me before I'd even climbed into the passenger seat. It smelled like pine, like those little cardboard-tree air fresheners you buy at gas stations to hang from your rearview mirror, and sure enough ... Dax had a stack of old trees sitting in a tray under the dash.

"Morning," he said, flashing a kind smile at me before putting the truck in drive and pulling away from the curb.

"Why did you invite me along?" I asked. I'd been thinking about it since I got the text, and I couldn't avoid the elephant in the room anymore. If it was because he heard about my accident and how I lost my spot on the team, because everyone had heard, then I wasn't sure this would work. I might even decide to find my own way back home when I finish my workout.

Dax shrugged and adjusted the heater.

"Seemed like you needed to get away the other day. I hate sitting around, you know? I can't. I really can't if something is bothering me, so it helps to get out and move a bit. I figured it might be nice to include you."

"Move a bit?"

"Yeah," he said with another shrug. "It's what I do to keep focused, move. I was diagnosed in grade school with ADHD because I was driving my mom and my teacher nuts. I just couldn't sit still, and my grades weren't super great. They weren't bad or anything, but the grades I got on homework were way low and I would walk in and ace a test before half the class was done. I needed stuff to do, so my mom basically tossed me in the pool to keep me busy one day and had to drag me out after. I've been swimming every day since, competing, you know the rest."

"So, you are so good and dedicated to swimming because you can't focus?" I asked, feeling the smile pull at my lips.

Dax chuckled.

"Kind of," he said and laughed again. "It's weird. That's how ADHD works. It just so happens that swimming is a kind of hyper-fixation for me. It gets all that energy out, too, so it helps me focus the rest of the day. That's how I made school work for me. I went to morning practices with my private coach and then went to school. It made sitting through classes a lot easier and then by the end of the day … Boom! Time to go to swim practice for school."

I jumped a little when he slapped the dash, which only made him smile wider.

"It's a little weird, but it also makes sense in a way," I said and looked ahead. We had already passed the fork in the road that usually sent me into a panic. I'd completely forgotten about it when Dax started talking about himself.

"How did you get started in soccer?" he asked.

That was a question I got a lot and always answered the same way: I've always played since I can remember. Rather than spouting my usual response, I stopped. The way he'd asked it was different than I was used to. It just seemed more genuine for some reason, like he really wanted to hear the whole story and not just the gist of it.

"Um, well," I started and adjusted in my seat. "I was six and it was spring. My dad was working all the time and Mom was stressed out because her company was merging with another company and she was getting ready to take over the whole department, including hundreds of new employees. She was in a lot of meetings in person and on phone calls and she needed something for the three of us to do so we wouldn't interrupt her. Marlee went to daycare, but Madison and I thought we were too old for that. Madison took up cheerleading at a gym in Denver and I went to a Denver soccer club.

"We were both able to carpool with teammates to most events, so it left Mom free to do her thing while Dad did his. By the end of the season, I was taking extra lessons, and my team won the league in Denver. Dad was so excited that he moved games and practices into his schedule, and he was the one driving me around from there. Mom knew a couple of people who had connections at a few colleges, and she started coming to games to record me and make highlight reels for YouTube. I guess that's kind of the story."

"You go to all the camps at colleges, too?"

"Uh-huh," I hummed in agreement, laughing when I saw the knowing look he gave me.

"When did you go through your burnout period?" Dax asked as the windshield wipers swooshed across the glass to clear the new snowflakes away.

"Burnout?"

"Yeah, you know?" Dax shrugged. "I was a sophomore. It was summer and I competed in Fort Collins. You already know that winter witches and warlocks don't feel a hundred percent in the summer anyway. It's like what the winter months feel like to most people and I had it. I was tired, not feeling like myself ... I just needed a break and wasn't listening to my body. It was an outdoor meet, and it was warm. I hadn't had enough water that day and things just didn't feel right. I ended up passing out before I could swim in the finals. I woke up and felt better an hour later, but I decided to call it quits and walk away. I took a month off from swimming entirely, didn't even hit the gym. I went to a friend's house for a pool party, and it made me miss it, so I called my coach, and we were back at practice the next week. It was like I'd never taken any time off."

"Huh. Weird," I said, thinking through my own history with

soccer and all the practices and private lessons. "I've never taken time off. Well, I mean ... That's why I'm so frustrated right now because that's just not something I do. I want to play all the time. It's what I want to do for as long as I can. I want to do it for a living. It's driving me absolutely insane that I'm not with a team right now. That's why I was in the gym late when you found me. I couldn't stand it anymore and I had to play."

"I heard about the accident," Dax said carefully. "I'm sorry. I bet you'll feel like yourself again soon."

"Maybe," I scoffed, pushing my toes against my soccer bag on the floorboard.

"You'll be okay."

I disagreed. My brain was already doing that thing where it ran through all the worst-case scenarios in double time. My heart thudded heavily in my chest, but Dax looked so positive with his megawatt smile and the relaxed way he sat with his hands on the wheel.

We took the same path through the gym, Dax waving at the girl seated behind the main desk with her headphones on and a half-awake expression on her face. She barely acknowledged us as we slipped by. Dax and I parted ways when we reached the soccer field. I laced up my cleats and started my warm-up routine before ever thinking of looking for a ball. After searching around the field, I tried the locker room and found a metal bin full of soccer balls with a printed warning that anyone who didn't return all equipment would be fined.

I took the ball back to the field and ran the same warm-up drills I normally did. It was a rush to race down the field, passing the ball from one foot to the other. I practiced control with my left foot and then my right, ignoring the slight ache in my ankles when I reached the end of the field for the second time. I felt my stomach drop when I thought about that drill. I hadn't been able to complete it since the last season at UCLA.

Maybe, if I just went slower?

I started at a light jog, passing the ball from right to left as I approached the various marks that I knew so well. I hadn't bothered setting up any cones. I knew this was too slow to be productive. This wasn't fast enough to be competitive at all; a middle schooler could steal the ball from me right now. I ignored the negative thoughts and continued until I finished the drill. Just as I felt a little flutter of success in my chest, I remembered that I'd left out two of the marks.

Should've put the stupid cones out after all. No wonder it was easier.

I took a water break, set up the cones, and started again. I took the drill slowly again, making it through the entire thing once before I gave in and picked up the speed. This time, the pace wasn't the problem. I'd barely hit the first mark and my right ankle turned under me instead of holding my weight when I pivoted.

My heart was in my throat as I stood completely still. It didn't hurt. I looked down at my foot and rolled it from one side to the other, feeling the stiffness set in the more I moved it until I knew that practicing on it was no use. It started to ache as I made my way toward the locker room to return the soccer ball.

This locker room only had three shower stalls and the space must not be used super often, because it wasn't nearly as nice as the space by the pool. I grabbed my duffle back and slipped into my boots before making my way through the connecting door to the pool. The sound of sloshing water met my ears before I saw Dax emerge from the pool in a butterfly stroke. Two more and he rolled into a flip turn and started the other direction for several beats, fully submerged before he burst from the surface again.

I watched him as I made my way around the pool, deciding to meet him at the start instead of hitting the showers in the locker room. I didn't know a lot about swimming, but I knew he was fast just from watching as he pulled himself through the last half of the lane and came to an abrupt halt at the wall. He raised his head as he clung to the side, panting heavily for a second before he lifted himself and reached over the side. He tapped his phone screen twice before he receded into the water again and breathed deeply.

When he noticed me rounding the corner of the pool, his lips turned up in a smile and you never would've known he'd just swam for his life back there. He pulled his blue swim cap from his head and his blond hair stuck up in several directions. A quick swipe of one hand and he plastered it flat again. He was just out of the pool enough for me to see how he was obviously a swimmer.

His shoulders were rounded, broad, and muscular from the same event he just completed in the water. The rest of him was slender, though I'd imagine you'd gain quite the six-pack just from the muscles it took to come out strong after a flip-turn. I was so focused on the anatomy of it all that I didn't realize how long I'd been standing in front of him until he snickered.

"So, practice was good?" he asked. His smile dimmed a little and I knew I'd given myself away. Why couldn't I keep a poker face the way Marlee could? "What's wrong? You look a little like you want to hit me."

"My stupid ankle is all jacked up," I said, fighting the thickness growing in my throat.

Dax lifted himself from the pool and sat on the ledge in front of me, pivoting so I could see that I was right about that six-pack theory. He looked concerned and dropped his gaze to my right ankle.

"Which one?" he asked, letting out a relieved sigh as I shifted from one foot to the other. "You think a sprain or ..."

"I don't know. I twisted it a little, but it didn't hurt. It could be anything. The doctors said my nerves aren't registering pain right," I said with a groan.

"Roll your leggings up and put your feet in the pool. It's not the same as icing it, but it's cool," Dax said, sliding his phone behind him and reaching around the starting block to pat the stretch of concrete in front of the lane.

I slipped my shoes off and rolled my leggings up from my ankles. They looked normal. The right looked like the left. No bruising, but now that I lowered myself to place them in the water, I could feel how sore they were. Dax was right about the pool. It wasn't cold, but it was cool enough to provide a little relief. I leaned back on my hands and bumped his phone, turning to see that he was using the timer. Two minutes flat with a few seconds to spare.

"I'm decent at most events, but 200 butterfly is my best. It's my best shot at qualifying for the Olympics this year," Dax said.

"What time do you need to make the cut?" I asked.

"One minute and fifty-five seconds," he said with a shrug.

I glanced back down at the timer just to make sure I had read it right.

"You're only five seconds off," I said in awe.

"Well, maybe not," Dax said and lifted his swim cap from the ledge. "The problem with practicing alone and not having the system set up is that I have to hit the timer myself to start and stop. That takes a bit off my actual race time, so I think I'm under that already."

He said it like it was the most everyday thing to have an Olympic team qualifying time.

"That's amazing!"

He smiled, cheeks flushing pink as he stretched the swim cap back over his head.

"Now that I have you," he said and stood up, "let's see just how fast I really am."

"Do I start timing at a specific point or?" I asked, taking his phone from the concrete.

"An old-fashioned *on your mark, get set, go* will do," Dax said as he stepped onto the block. He waved his arms aggressively across his chest the way I'd seen swimmers do on TV. He gave me a few more pointers, mostly explaining how the 200-meter butterfly worked and when I needed to stop time. Once he'd finished his stretches, he turned his eyes down to the still water. He took a deep breath and did the strangest motion I knew was a Dax thing and not a swimmer thing.

He placed both of his hands on the top of his head, then his shoulders, then his knees as he crouched, and then his toes before he took a position with one foot in front and both hands on the edge of the block.

"On your mark," I said.

Dax let out a loud breath.

"Get set."

The muscles along his back braced, shoulders tensing. His back leg was tight, calf round, and prepared for the forward launch. He looked so powerful that I made him wait a little longer for the call.

"Go!"

My words had barely slipped past my lips when he lunged forward with a gasp. He disappeared under the water's surface and the entire room echoed with silence before it filled with a splash of his first stroke. It was a rush watching him race to the opposite end. My heart beat faster when he turned, and I didn't know I was holding my breath when he came out of the kick turn until he emerged again in the final sprint back toward me. He didn't slow as he approached me, practically slamming into the wall.

"I see why people like this sport," I blurted.

Dax looked up at me with his chest heaving, smiling despite the exhaustion.

"So?" he asked, nodding toward his phone.

Oh.

I looked down at the dark screen. When I turned it, the lock screen lit up with a photo of him on a mountain with a German Shepard at his side. Dax laughed as he lifted himself from the water. I handed him his phone and pressed my hands to my face.

"I'm so sorry," I groaned.

"Don't be," Dax said and laughed again. "I got this gem now."

I lowered my hands as he turned the phone so I could see a photo I'd taken of my face, the angle far enough below my chin that it gave a clear view up my nose.

"And this one," Dax said and swiped to another photo of me from the same angle but with my mouth hanging open. "And this."

The next photo made my face hurt with embarrassment. The

angle was better, but my mouth was still open in awe and my eyes were so wide that it looked like I'd been caught moments before something bad happened.

"If this thing wasn't between us, I'd push you in," I told him and patted my hand on the starting block between us as he laughed. Dax set his phone aside and looked back at me, his amusement fading to a look of curiosity that made my stomach twist.

"Did you pack a swimsuit?"

"Not in my gym bag, no," I told him and looked for my duffle which was still sitting against the wall behind us. "I'm training for the season. All I have is my soccer gear."

"Could you bring a suit tomorrow?" he asked and plucked the swim cap from his head. Just like before, his blond hair stood straight up until he ran a hand through the wet mess.

"I don't know that I have time to swim after practice."

"No practice," Dax said and shook his head. "It's time you took that break we were talking about."

Break? Like, from soccer? My heart raced just thinking about it. If I took more time off than I had to it would only put me further behind. At least, if this didn't work, I could say I really tried. I was not a quitter, and I wasn't going to do anything but my best. My whole future could be determined by the work I put it on the field tomorrow. I felt a little dizzy just thinking about it.

"Hear me out," Dax said, placing his hand on my arm.

A jolt went through my body at his touch, like he'd hit some kind of reset button that pulled me out of my thoughts and halted the panic rising in my chest. I looked back at his sincere blue eyes and took a deep breath.

"Swimming is one of the best workouts and it's also low impact. It will be good for maintaining your endurance and you can also safely work those muscles in your legs that were weakened by the accident. You can run a few drills on the field after if you want. Call it a warmup."

"I don't know," I said, feeling that pit forming in my stomach.

"You'd be doing me a favor too, you know?" Dax said with a

smirk. "We start in the pool, and I show you some exercises to help rehab your legs. Then, you keep time for me and let me know what you see. What do you say?"

I still wasn't sure, but the puppy dog look on his face was the kind you didn't say no to. I liked the idea of having him close during a workout. His encouragement and seeing his success were helpful. It was the most stable I'd felt in a long time.

"Okay," I said.

"Okay," he said excitedly before standing up. He extended a hand and helped me to my feet. He promised that it would be worth my time to do some exercises in the pool before we parted ways at the locker rooms. This time, I had my own shampoo and body wash.

Chapter 8

"Ugh! This looks even better than I thought it would," Madison said as she took a step back to look me over. "This suites you so much."

I had to hand it to her. She was right about my gala dress being surprisingly comfortable. I understood what she had envisioned by the shorts once I had them on under all the mesh and draping. I felt like I was on a red carpet as I admired myself in the full-length mirror propped up against the wall of the mercantile. Even Marlee stared in shock at me when I turned back to look at them.

I never dressed like this, not even at my high school prom. My gala dresses were all similar, full-coverage, and never this revealing. It was a big change and despite the butterflies that did loop-de-loops in my stomach at the idea of wearing this dress in public, I liked the new look.

"Okay," Madison said and clapped her hands together. "Your turn, Marlee."

Our youngest sister groaned as she stood up but didn't resist. She went to the little changing booth at the back and pulled the red buffalo plaid curtain closed behind her.

"So, you actually like it?" Madison asked, sending me a suspicious look.

"Yeah. It's ... different, but I do. I think different is good right now," I said. My stomach sank as her smile faded.

"You know, you'd make a really good coach. I bet Heritage City Academy would let you help the soccer team in the spring," she said.

"I need that time to train."

"Yeah, but you need to ease back into it and maybe looking at the sport from a different angle will help. I don't know," Madison said with a shrug, not doing a good job of masking her frustration.

"Exactly. You don't know," I said and kicked off the heels she made me wear to make sure the skirt wouldn't drag on the floor.

"Margot, come on," she moaned and kicked the heels out of the walkway.

I started for the other dressing room.

"I'm ready to twirl and stuff, if anyone cares!" Marlee called out, sarcasm so thick that it was obvious that the last thing she wanted to do was twirl.

I stayed in the dressing room as the rings on Marlee's curtain scratched on the curtain rod. Madison did her usual squealing of excitement while I peeled the mesh from my body and slipped into the warmth of my sweats. I lingered behind the curtain after I'd dressed. I took stock of everything I had with me.

Phone. Wallet. Keys.

Phone.

I opened my phone and went to the usual social apps. For once, I didn't want to see a thing about soccer. I felt heartbroken and angry all at once as I scrolled past the photos of players on the field, only to see more UCLA photos or an ad for new soccer gear. I needed to get out of here before I exploded on Madison again, or worse, Marlee.

My fingers were typing the message before I could decide if texting him was a bad idea or not.

Are you busy right now?

It didn't take long for Dax to text back and in a matter of minutes, I pushed the curtain aside and walked past my sisters before they noticed where I was headed. I pulled open the passenger-side door of his truck.

"Where to?" he asked.

"Away from here."

He let out a laugh.

"I have some ideas."

❇

Dax didn't ask any questions as we drove. We fell into the familiar route toward North Ridge. He filled me in on his family drama. His brother, Daren, had been in Madison's class and hadn't changed since high school. His antics were what made him popular in high school, but he was now in college and had nothing going for him except for his social life in his fraternity.

"My parents told him that he had to pay back the tuition and books for the classes he failed last semester. He's already an entire semester behind on his degree plan," Dax said with a laugh of satisfaction. "It's funny."

"What's funny?" I asked as we passed the sign welcoming us to North Ridge.

"They never really acted surprised when he did stuff like that in high school. I remember getting a lecture because I failed a math test in high school. The same week, Daren snuck out and drove my dad's car into a stop sign while he was trying to send a text message. They gave us both the same lecture about responsibility and how *your actions set the tone for your future*. It was word-for-word the same. The expectations have just always been different until now."

Wow. Everyone knew that Daren Krune was the wild one in the family and that Dax was on his way to great things. I never thought it was because his parents treated them differently.

"Does it bother you that things aren't fair between you two?" I asked.

Dax shook his head and then shrugged. "It used to, maybe when we were kids. I don't have a lot in common with my brother and we didn't really interact that much during school. We were both just so busy and I was so serious about swimming. I knew what the path to success looked like for me and I wasn't focused on what anyone else thought about that. Don't think that my parents are horrible or anything. I think things with me were just easier and maybe when the oldest child has always taken so much of your time and energy, parenting the second one just ..."

I felt a little like a piece of me had just fallen away.

"It feels like you tell everyone else what to expect from you," I said.

Dax nodded and gave a low hum. "And people will treat you exactly the way you allow them to. No one ever asked if I needed a break because I focused so much on what was ahead and I was always high achieving in the pool. When I decided to take time off, my mom and dad just accepted that. They didn't challenge me. They didn't ask if I was sure. They just said I needed to do what I wanted to do because I was a junior and I needed to start making decisions for myself that I could live with. We had a lot of conversations about it."

Here we go with the whole break thing again. My stomach tightened in anticipation of my upcoming workout. At least we agreed I could run drills on the field after swimming.

"What made you decide?" I asked with a scoff. "A few months later you went on to win the state championship, get a scholarship to swim at Berkeley, and now you're on track to win a spot on the Olympic team."

"I missed swimming the entire time and I just felt wrong not going to practices. I would wake up and just lie in bed doing nothing and feel bad about myself. I decided to start again when I realized that after senior year there would be a whole world of opportunities for me outside of swimming. I used to ask myself when I did warmups if I still wanted to compete. I got comfortable enough with myself and my goals that if I felt like chasing a different opportunity, I would let myself. If I had to give up swimming to do that, then I guess I would adjust my goals. When I get ready for practice now, I ask myself what I'm chasing that day. All this time since and I've never found anything else worth chasing, at least not yet."

"That sounds like ..."

"Not like something a lot of top athletes would say?" Dax said and cast me a smirk before looking back at the road.

"A lot of people would say that you're casting doubt."

"I'd say that I'm just making sure I don't have any," Dax said with a laugh, giving me a smug look that eased the tension in my shoulders. I looked away from him, feeling my lips pull into a smile. "Opportunity is out there. What would you like to do?"

That put a damper on any humor I felt from the moment.

"I don't know," I said and sat back in my seat, setting my eyes on the road ahead. I almost mentioned the gym as I saw it ahead, but something stopped me. I didn't want to think about soccer. I didn't want to face the sore muscles and poor performance that had become my everyday occurrences at practice. I mean, part of me wanted to. I should want to. Still, I wanted to forget all about it and pretend that I was still the old version of myself that easily slipped between defenders on my way to the goal, took a shot that was so easy that I could do it in my sleep, and turned around to celebrate with my teammates as they surged around me on the field with wide smiles on their faces ...

"I've never been to a bar," Dax said, pausing a moment before casting me a waiting look.

"Yeah. Me neither," I said. I had to think for a minute to make sure, but yeah ... I'd never been to a bar. I'd been to a few parties with my roommate, but we were never close, and I usually stayed just long enough to check out the place and then I'd leave so I could wake up for a morning workout.

"There's got to be one somewhere close," he said as he turned off the highway. My heart skipped in my chest.

"What? Isn't it too early for that? We have a workout in the morning," I said as we cruised down a street lined with shopping centers.

Dax let out a laugh. "And we are both in our twenties. A beer or two once in a while isn't going to mess up our training. It's on me."

I wanted to protest, but I didn't know what else we would do. I didn't know why I was even here. I just wanted to get away from my sisters' prying eyes. I wanted to leave. I didn't mean to leave Crescent City, not really. Before I could think of anything to say, he pulled into a parking spot just as the streetlamps came on along the sidewalk.

"Just one," he said as he turned off the ignition and got out of the truck.

I froze for a moment, long enough that he slapped his hand on the hood of the truck twice and motioned for me to follow him. I groaned, shoved my phone into my pocket, and hopped down from the seat. I was of age, but my stomach still twisted when I saw the sign bolted to the metal door. Dax went in first, holding the door open so I could follow him into the dimly lit space.

The bar was small with two pool tables at the back where a pair of men were mid-game. A pair of dartboards hung on the wall to the right of the pool tables. The rest of the room was filled with tables and wooden chairs surrounding the oblong bar in the center where a young man stood emptying a dishwasher. He looked up as we approached the bar; Dax took a seat on one of the wooden stools.

"Want to start a tab?" the man asked as I climbed onto a stool next to Dax.

"Sure. On me," Dax said and pulled his wallet from his back pocket before I could utter a word. He handed his card to the man who took it and looked at me.

"I've never had beer," I told him and gave an awkward shrug.

Dax laughed, ignoring the embarrassed glare I sent his way.

"Do you want to try one?" the bartender asked without missing a beat.

I glanced at Dax who was still smiling. My cheeks heated.

"I don't really like anything too sweet, but I don't like anything super bitter or anything. I can't drink coffee straight unless it's a weak roast, you know?" I said, stopping myself before I could embarrass myself any further. Thankfully, Dax didn't laugh.

The bartender took a glass from the cabinet below him. "So, maybe something like a pale ale or an amber?"

"Sure," I said with a shrug and looked at Dax, so I didn't have to look at the expert in the room anymore.

"And for you, bro?" the bartender asked, returning Dax's card.

"I'll take a beer. Surprise me," he said and pocketed his wallet.

The bartender took a second glass from underneath the bar and turned his back to us. I caught Dax's eye and saw that he was holding back his laughter the same way I was. I felt like I'd walked into the place underage and gotten away with it. It was so ridiculous, but it felt good to do something a little rebellious. Dax gave a laugh and something about his blue eyes made me laugh in such a way that I hardly recognized the sound.

"Tell me what you think, and I can try to make a better recommendation if you don't like it," the bartender told me as he sat a dark glass in front of me and another before Dax. It almost looked like a cold brew, a thin line of foam at the top.

"Cheers," Dax said and lifted his glass. I clinked mine against his and raised it to my lips before I could think too much about it. All I registered at first was the light foam at the top and then the taste coated my tongue. It was bitter, but also not. It was almost like bread, but something about it being a liquid did not appeal to me.

Dax laughed as I sat the glass down and stuck out my tongue. I wiped the back of my sleeve across my mouth with a grimace as he laughed and took another sip of his beer.

"I hope this doesn't ruin all beer for you," the bartender said with a smile and pulled a new glass from beneath the bar. "You don't like anything overly sweet. Do you like Coke?"

"Yes, but I haven't had it in years because of"

"She'll take a rum and Coke," Dax told him and slid my beer in front of himself. He took a sniff and then a small sip. He shrugged and sat the glass down again. "Try this," he said and slid his beer to me.

I hesitated but accepted his glass and followed his lead. It smelled pretty much like mine had, which almost made me push it back his way. I took a small sip and immediately sat it back in front of him with a grimace. I was glad when the bartender sat a small glass in front of me. I drank, recognizing the taste of Coca-Cola immediately along with something that warmed my throat.

"Is that better?" Dax asked with a smirk.

"Much," I told him and offered him the glass. He took a sip and nodded.

"That's good, but I think I'll stick with the beer."

"So, you've never had alcohol before?" I asked and took another sip of the rum and coke. It was better than I thought it would be. Somehow, I thought it would be stronger, and have more of an effect than it did.

Dax shook his head. "Nope. I've tasted stuff at parties and such, but I've never had a whole drink to myself. It's not so much to do with swimming as it is that I just haven't liked anything I've tried."

"Do you not have a diet for Olympic training?" I asked.

Dax snorted and took another drink. "Yeah, but I'm not going to skip the cake at my birthday, you know?"

Not really. I hadn't had a birthday cake since I was in high school. Now that I thought about it, there had been mini cupcakes at one of our team dinners, but I did skip them. Maybe it was just me. Had I always been so high-strung?

"Let's do a shot." The words were out of my mouth before I could stop them. I didn't take them back. I ignored the voice inside telling me it was a bad idea and focused instead on Dax's sideways grin.

"I'm the one driving," he laughed.

"Come on! Just one. I can't do it alone," I said and waved the bartender over as he handed a pair of drinks to a couple on the opposite side of the bar from us.

Dax shook his head, his smile widening.

"We'll take a couple of tequila shots," he told the man.

"Lime and salt?"

"Please," Dax answered and watched me with a challenging look as the bartender set two small glasses on the table and picked up a bottle. He poured a small amount into the glass, almost to the rim, and then set two lime wedges on a small ceramic plate. He sat a little bowl of salt on the plate between the wedges and then moved the two shot glasses and the plate toward us.

"What do I do?" I asked Dax after the bartender left.

"Lick, shoot, suck," he said.

Something about the words made my stomach twist and my face heat. I had to look away from him, especially when his smile widened, and his own cheeks flushed.

"Lick your hand here," he said and pointed to the spot between his thumb and pointer finger. I watched as he ran his tongue along the spot, my heart fluttering. He took a pinch of salt from the bowl and sprinkled it on the spot and then pulled one of the shot glasses toward himself. I quickly did the same, unsure just how much salt I needed to adhere to my skin before I lifted the shot glass.

"Lick the salt first and then take the shot," Dax said before I could raise the glass any higher. I paused and then lowered it to the table again.

"Okay. Do we count or what?"

He snorted. "On three."

"One," I started.

"Two."

"Three," I said and licked the salt off my hand. I tossed the entire glass of tequila into my mouth and swallowed before I could second-guess the decision, the liquid burning down my throat. When I looked back at Dax he had a lime wedge in his mouth.

"Lime, Sinclair!" he laughed and picked up the wedge from

the plate. He held it to my lips, and I bit down, my mouth puckered at the sour taste, and I nearly spat the entire thing on the floor before I caught the lime in my palm. I recovered for a moment as he laughed before lifting the lime to my lips again and sucking the juice that was left.

"It really wasn't that bad," I said, unable to find it in me to tell him off for laughing. It was a little funny. I was sure I'd made the ugliest face, and I didn't even care. I'd never been to a bar, had a beer, or a shot, and I was enjoying myself more than I thought I would. I understood why my roommate stayed out late Friday nights and didn't complain that much about the headache it would give her into the next morning.

"So, what's next?" I asked and sat the lime down in the empty glass.

"You're not even halfway into that rum and Coke. Take it slow." Dax laughed and looked around us. The room had filled with a few more people since we'd entered. I'd been too engaged in the new drinks to notice them. "How about a game of darts?"

"Fine, but I'm competitive," I told him and hopped down from the stool with my drink in hand.

"If you're so competitive then let's make it interesting," he said as he followed me to the corner of the room. I turned to face him as I reached the dartboard.

"Have you played before?" I asked.

"A few times," he said and reached behind me for a red Solo cup filled with darts on a shelf below the board. "You?"

"Of course," I said, doing my best to feign confidence. I'd never played before, but I understood the concept. You wanted a bullseye. It was based on points. You wanted to hit zero first. This dartboard was part of a machine and had a scoreboard. How hard could it be?

"If I win, you take a whole week off from soccer and do my workouts in the pool," he said and backed away from me to take his place at the mark on the floor.

My heart leaped into my throat, and I took a long drink to settle my nerves.

"Fine. Okay," I said and joined him, downing the last of my drink and setting it on the nearest table. "If I win," I started, glancing at the scoreboard as it illuminated with our starting scores. What did I want? I couldn't think of anything I could take away from him and I couldn't think of anything I wanted. I'd already agreed to work out with him in the mornings and to help keep track of the times when he swam. I was a little surprised that I was looking forward to it.

"If you win," Dax said, pulling me from my thoughts. "I will go with you to the Winter Solstice Gala, so the elders won't bother you about not having a date this year and so your mom won't try setting you up with one of the obnoxious frat boys."

I let out a loud laugh. It wasn't the best prize, but I would be thankful for it when I had to endure the entire evening at the gala. If I had to be there, and I did *have* to be there, according to my family, then at least it wouldn't be horrible like usual.

"It's a bet," I said, accepting a dart when he handed one to me.

"Ladies first," he said and backed away from the gray duct tape on the floor that marked the starting line.

"Can you grab me another drink? You'll be back in time for your turn," I said as I took my place, a little worried now that my first throw might not be as good as I'd hoped.

Dax snorted and crossed his arms. "No way. You might cheat."

"I don't cheat!" My stomach twisted when I saw the playful smirk on his face. I turned to the dartboard as mine flamed, hiding the color of my cheeks that I was sure matched the bullseye of the board. Before he could finish laughing to reply, I sent my dart flying at the board where it sank into a green section in the middle ring.

"Eight. Okay," Dax said, his tone not telling me much.

"How about that drink?" I asked and turned to face him. He smirked again, lowering his half-empty glass from his lips and setting it on the table.

"Another or something different?" he asked.

"Surprise me," I said. Dax gave me a salute before heading back to the bar, leaving me with the cup of darts.

I'd already had one drink. I was already here, back home for good and not just for the holidays. The thing is, I *was* here in Colorado. I wasn't going back to UCLA, and even though I'd be taking online classes, I'd be missing practices for therapy sessions and weightlifting for doctor's appointments. I'd been telling myself it was all temporary, but what if it wasn't? What if I was just left chasing something I couldn't get back?

"My turn," Dax said, pulling my attention from the board. Something flashed across his face for a brief second, making my stomach twist so tight that I almost didn't trade him the dart cup for the new rum and Coke out of fear that I might throw up. Whatever I saw vanished as quickly as it came, and he was smiling back at me again. "Eyes forward, Sinclair. You wouldn't want to miss anything worthwhile."

"Do your worst, Krune," I said as he took his place at the starting line.

Dax kept ahead of me the entire game, never once faltering. I did okay for having never played before, but it was also obvious that I'd never played before, and Dax called me on my bluff just before taking the final shot of the game.

"Let's even things out," Dax said as he raised the dart, aiming. "If I finish the game with this throw, you take a week off from soccer *and* I'll be your date to the gala."

"Whatever. You'd need exactly—"

I was cut off as the dartboard flashed its lights and played a short tune. He cleared the board, winning the game by a margin I hoped we'd never speak of again. Dax turned to me with his arms held high and laughed.

"That was a bit of a long shot," he said. "I wasn't sure I'd make it."

"Well, you did," I said, not sure what else to say. I burst out laughing as he did until it hit me what that would mean. No soccer. I'd be in the pool with him doing whatever kinds of drills you did in the water.

"Do you have a swimsuit?" Dax asked and took a drink from his glass. I followed him to the table and took a seat opposite him. I had to think for a moment. I packed all my clothes and shipped them home when I moved out of my dorm room. I had a swimsuit, more than one, but I wasn't sure what I'd tossed into my duffle bag to take the cabin. I hadn't paid much attention when I packed.

"Somewhere. Yeah," I told him.

"We can make a stop tomorrow morning and just get a later start."

"No. We work out at six. I know I packed it," I told him. My heart had skipped a beat at the idea of getting to a workout late. Once in a while was one thing, but after skipping the soccer drills entirely for swimming ... I didn't think my anxiety would allow me that much flexibility and I didn't dare test the thought.

"Okay. I swear, what we will do will be strength training like you've never had. You'll definitely be sore after," he told me and took a drink. "I don't know if you noticed, but that's why I hopped in that little pool in the corner after. It's a cold plunge pool. There's a hot pool, too."

"Why not just go to the pool outside?" I asked. The side doors opened to a gated outdoor area where there was another lap pool, complete with blue flags hanging over the top and a set of metal stands on one side for spectators.

Dax shrugged. "I guess, I could do that. I think the idea is that the indoor plunge pools will stay the same temperature year-round. I think they keep the outdoor pool temperature controlled. It's probably not all that cold even this time of year."

"No way they heat that whole thing," I said and took a long drink.

Dax sent me a knowing look. "North Ridge has a whole mountain of cabins that rich people own. You think Lawson Rathbone would let the pool at the rec center look less than Olympic?"

Who? I knew there was a lot of money in North Ridge, and famous people, too, but I had no idea who that was.

"Who's that?"

Dax looked a little shocked before he caught himself, took a deep breath to reign in his excitement, and sat forward with his hands around the base of his beer.

"Lawson Rathbone is a swimmer, or was a swimmer. He went pro, missed making the Olympic team twice, and then retired from swimming for a job at Speedo. He worked his way up and now he gets to work with the pro swimmers and Olympians that partner with Speedo. He's a cool guy. We met when I was in middle school. He thought I had potential. I used to swim at the rec center after he'd finished his workouts. He said that Speedo would be behind me when I made the Olympic team, or if I would post regularly to social media."

"Wow," I said. "Sounds ... tight?"

I was sure it was all over my face. The image of Dax Krune standing on the starting platform in a red, white, and blue Speedo that barely covered his muscular body ...

Dax burst into laughter and after a moment, I joined in. A few people in the room glanced our way, most of them waiting for tables to open up.

"That reminds me," he said after he recovered. He finished the last of his drink and took my empty glass, setting it inside his and scooting both to the middle of the table. "I have something of yours. Come on."

I didn't protest as he led the way to the door, even though part of me wanted to sit at that little table and laugh a little while longer.

Chapter 9

I SAID that tacos sounded good as we passed a Taco Bell and Dax made a U-turn to pull into the drive-through. He ordered a little bit of everything and the poor teenager working the window eyed us curiously when she handed over the two bags of food and a pair of large drinks. I was a little disappointed when I found out the drink he handed me was water and not Coke. I ate a taco as he merged onto the highway, not going far before pulling into the parking lot of the rec center. The lot was mostly empty, with only a line of cars near the front that likely belonged to employees. He pulled into a spot in the far corner of the lot that backed up to the trees.

"This is the most fun I have had in ..." I didn't know how long, and the realization made me sad.

"It only gets better," Dax said and pressed a button on the ceiling between us. The tan fabric began to slide backward, revealing a large window that stretched to the back seats. The night sky beyond was littered with stars. A hum pulled my attention away to watch Dax recline the driver's seat and fold his hands behind his head. I did the same, letting my seat lay back as I focused on the stars and tried to forget about everything I faced in the morning.

"This is the most fun I've had in a while," I said again, my voice so soft that I wondered if the words were meant more to reassure myself after the night of drinking. This was not like me at all, but it felt so good, so good that I could feel myself seconds away from tears.

"Don't take this the wrong way," Dax said as he reached into the back seat. "I wasn't being creepy or anything, but it looked like it might be team gear, and I thought you might want it back." He held up a piece of blue fabric and it took me a split second to realize that he was holding a sports bra. It was my UCLA sports bra. I pulled it from his grasp before I could control my shock. It was just a sports bra. It wasn't like it was a pair of underwear, well, a pair of underwear that I didn't show up to practice in for everyone to see on a hot day.

"I should've told you sooner," he said and sat up in his seat.

"No. It's just a sports bra. It's not like—"

I took a deep breath, the tears stinging my eyes. I blinked frantically, managing to chase them away as I reminded myself that I'd left that stupid bra in the men's locker room, the locker room I'd left wearing a boy's clothes. God, what was I doing? What happened to me?

"It had your jersey number on it, so I figured it was part of your team gear," Dax said gently. "I have a couple of pairs of jammers from the swim team and I think coach would be pissed if I lost them."

My coach felt the same way. We all showed up to practice in uniform, always the same matching gear. On hot days, we'd stripped down to our shorts and sports bras, running drills under the California sun. My stomach twisted at the memory. Part of me wished he'd just thrown away the bra; I would never have known he'd had it at all. It would be easier to think I'd lost it than have to face taking it back when I wasn't sure I could take back my spot on the team.

I rolled down the window and pulled myself halfway out of the truck as Dax called for me to sit down. I pulled the elastic of the sports bra taut like it was a slingshot and released, watching as the blue fabric shot through the air and landed high in the nearest evergreen. I slipped back into the silent truck and rolled up the window, setting my eyes ahead on the streetlights that illuminated the sidewalk to the rec center.

"I'll pay the fine or whatever," I said as the window rose with a hum, finally settling back in place.

After a quiet moment, Dax snorted, and I turned to look at his shocked expression. He let out a laugh and lay back in his seat again.

"Atta girl," he said, unable to hold back his laugh. Soon enough, I'd joined the laughter again. I laughed so hard that I thought I'd lose a lung and then my entire chest hurt, tightening, my lungs burning in a way I wasn't used to. I tried controlling my breathing, holding my breath until my heart stopped pounding away, but it never did. I sucked in a deep breath and as I did, it was like I'd surfaced from the depths, everything sounding loud. Surely, I didn't sound like that. There was no way I sounded like a fish out of water, but that's what I heard.

A sensation on the back of my left hand caught my attention and switched my mind from my suffocating thoughts to the realization that Dax was holding my hand. I saw how white my knuckles were and loosened my grip immediately. Dax ran his thumb back and forth across the back of my hand, thankfully, still lying against his seat and staring up at the sky with the other arm folded behind his head. I felt the tension in my chest ease and then it felt like my entire body had collapsed and all I wanted to do was curl up in the seat. When I pulled my hand free, Dax sat up.

"Take this," he said and offered a Heritage City Swimming sweatshirt he found in the backseat to me. "Nothing UCLA about it."

"I think I want to go home now," I said and balled up the sweatshirt.

Dax nodded and put the truck in drive.

I rolled onto my side, snuggling my cheek into the fabric of his sweatshirt. I wanted to sleep, but I could feel every bump and turn as we drove, my stomach churning more and more the longer we went. I couldn't tell if it was the alcohol or my nerves and just as I was deciding that I hadn't had enough to drink to be more than a little tipsy, the passenger door opened, and Dax stood there with his arms open.

"How do you feel?" he asked, pausing a moment before waving a hand as though he could push the words aside. "Don't answer that. We're at your house. I can walk you in if you want."

"It's fine," I said and sat up, undoing the seat belt and sliding to the ground where I nearly slipped in the snow. Dax held me to his chest, keeping me upright. He took a step back once I gained my footing and closed the passenger door, following me around the front of the truck and to the driveway. Despite telling him I was fine, he followed me all the way to the door where I struggled with the key in the lock and felt like I might burst into tears until the damn thing finally turned and the door opened.

"Thank you," I said and hugged the sweatshirt around my chest, inhaling the clean scent. "I'll see you in the morning. I'll wear a swimsuit."

I pulled the front door shut before he could respond, and I hurried up the stairs as quietly as I could. The house was silent. There was the glow of a lamp from beneath Marlee's door and I could tell from the sound of his snoring that Dad was sleeping in Madison's room instead of with Mom. I shut my door behind me and realized as the pressure released just how tense my shoulders had been. I went to the window and watched as Dax climbed into the driver's seat of his truck. He sat there for a long time, and it wasn't until my phone buzzed in my pocket that I realized why.

> Tonight was a lot of fun. I promise not to be too hard on you during tomorrow's workout, but I think you're up for the challenge.

THE WINKING FACE emoji he sent with the message made it easier to take a deep breath and as his truck pulled away from the front of the cabin, I wished I had said more on the doorstep. I turned to my closet, planning to search for a swimsuit for tomorrow morning, but found myself lying across the foot of my bed instead, staring at that text message.

❄

I FOUND a swimsuit when I got ready the next morning, but not the one I had hoped for.

"Ready to go?" Dax asked when I tossed my gym bag into the backseat of his truck. I shut the door and opened the passenger-side door. He was dressed in yet another Berkeley sweatsuit, this one navy. Did he bring any other clothes home with him? Did I really have the room to talk when my wardrobe was all team gear and a few nice sweaters?

"Yeah. I'm good," I said and climbed in, pulling the door shut.

"Shit! I should've grabbed an extra swim cap for you," Dax said as we turned onto the main road. I was sure he'd said something before, but I was so focused on the end of the road and trying to forget the bad memories to hear anything. I eased my grip on the door handle as we continued down the road and passed downtown Crescent Peak.

"It's fine. I doubt I'll be swimming laps like you anyway," I said. I didn't know what was worse, the fact that I'd soon enough be standing at the edge of the pool in my swimsuit or that I could have been standing at the edge in my swimsuit with a tight swim cap on.

"What do you mean you won't be doing laps? You'll be doing laps, Sinclair," Dax corrected, adjusting the radio so a soft indie song with an acoustic guitar filled the truck.

"Fine, but it's not like I'm going to set any records, so it's fine," I told him. The truck went quiet, and we drove until the trees were thick over the shoulder of the road and there was nothing but wooden mile markers along the way.

"You okay? You seem tense," Dax said as the first sign of buildings bobbed above the next hill.

"I'm just ... It's the stupid bet," I told him and adjusted in my seat, going through the mental list of items I'd packed in the duffle bag to avoid the flush from spreading across my face.

"Ah!" he said with a gasp. "Scared."

"I am not scared!" I practically turned sideways in the seat, noticing the teasing smile on his face. If he hadn't been driving, I would've slapped his arm as he laughed.

"All right, Sinclair," he said as we pulled into the rec center parking lot. I didn't talk as he found a parking spot near the front and hopped out, grabbing both our bags from the backseat before I'd even climbed out of the truck. "Come on, Soccer Star!"

He didn't wait before heading toward the entrance, leaving me to scurry after him like a lost puppy. God, was I a lost puppy? I might as well have been, as anxious and directionless as I felt.

"Margot!" Dax called back as we turned the hall for the annex. He flashed a playful smile before pushing past the first set of doors, waiting for me just inside. "Did you wear your suit under all that or do you need to change?"

I had worn my suit under my sweats, but I wanted to stall as much as possible before disrobing.

"I'll change in the locker room," I told him as we passed from the field to the humid air of the indoor pool.

"Use the men's. The women's room—"

"It's always locked. I remember," I told him and passed the women's door for the men's locker room. I peeked inside before entering, a habit I didn't think I would ever get rid of even though it was always just the two of us at the pool. I dropped my duffle bag on the floor and sank onto the wooden bench before the lockers.

Maybe he wouldn't react if I just walked out like it's the most normal thing.

Maybe he would just be nice and not say anything or even look.

God, I was screwed.

I kicked my bag aside and stood up. I turned so I wouldn't have to look at myself in the mirror as I shoved my sweatpants to the floor and stepped out. I pulled the sweatshirt over my head and tossed it onto the bench, forcing my feet forward.

Dax was floating on his back in the closest lane when I came out of the locker room. I held the towel I'd grabbed at the last second on my way out in a tight ball at my stomach as I walked toward the first platform. He straightened up as I approached, pushing a hand through his blond hair so that it was slicked back.

"What?" I asked.

"What do you mean?" he asked.

"You're staring."

"I'm not staring. You just stopped. I'm waiting for you to get in."

"It feels a lot like you're staring."

"I practically swim for a living. I see people in swimsuits all the time."

"You're staring at—"

I let out a huff, a mix of embarrassment and frustration painting my cheeks. I wasn't even sure why I was frustrated. He didn't act like he'd been checking me out or anything. He truly was waiting. Treading water might as well have been the swimming equivalent of tapping your foot impatiently.

After a moment, a small smirk spread on his face. "Okay. Well, sure, you're not exactly aerodynamic in that suit."

"Yeah. Well, don't expect me to do the breaststroke today," I said and looked down at my bikini top. It didn't even have any underwire, and it was a wide cut to make the most of my cleavage, the only feature I had that wasn't completely flat.

Dax let out a laugh that quickly turned to a gasp when I turned to put my towel on the metal bench next to his. Ugh! The bikini bottoms I wore were the same shade of blue to match the top and while they did sit a little high-waisted on my hip, the back was cut so cheeky that I was sure my entire ass would slip out after a quick lap down the lane.

"It's all I had, okay?" I said and turned around, glad to see that he seemed more amused by the ridiculousness of the situation than distracted by my few assets. "What do we do first?"

I sat at the pool's edge and Dax swam a little closer, no longer laughing.

"Get warmed up. Do a slow and steady swim down and back, not too fast. Try to make all your strokes long," he said before ducking under the water to move into the next lane.

The water was cool, just cool enough that I could feel my winter powers tingle and it set my mind at ease. My body followed shortly after, and I remembered a moment later as I felt my skin prickle at the calming chill that this bikini top had very little padding.

Well, shit.

I pushed away from the side of the pool before Dax could notice any more about my chest, trying my best to follow his instructions to take long strokes. I was sure I wasn't doing it right because when I took long strokes, I could feel myself sinking.

"Move your arms and legs quicker!" Dax called from the opposite side of the pool as I rested with my hands holding the edge of the pool.

"I thought the point was to move slow and steady!"

"Yeah, but you need your entire body to work together. Think about using strong and even force between your legs and arms."

"Whatever," I grumbled, surprised that my voice still rang clearly in the open air.

"Come on, Sinclair!" Dax called back, his tone almost teasing. He clapped his hands until I threw myself back into the lane, pulling my arms and legs through the water at the same time as much as I could. I knew how to swim. Why was this so hard? What the hell did he expect me to do?

I pushed the flyaway hairs away from my face as I straightened up at the end of the lane. Dax shrugged as he leaned on the lane divider separating us.

"You'll get better," he said. When I snorted, he continued with his coaching. "It's your form. We'll correct that tomorrow. Let's move on to the backstroke. You're going to go down and back just like before."

"Assume I don't know what I'm doing," I told him, trying and failing to mask my frustration.

He smirked and moved back off the lane divider. "Think about reaching far past your head. You want your hand to contact the water behind you, pinky first. Then, when you pull, you want to drag your arm through the water beside you at an angle. You should be angled so you can feel the water move past your hip. Ideally, your hips should kind of rotate with your shoulders. Keep your back straight to stay streamlined. You don't want to go totally tits up."

He said it all, including the boob joke at the end, so casually that I debated if it was even worth telling him off. I could tell from the smirk on his face and that onery gleam in his eye that he was waiting for the comeback. I let it slide instead and took a deep breath before lying as flat in the water as I could. I looked straight up at the ceiling and focused on dragging, no, pulling my arms through the water. This was already better than the freestyle and I sort of understood what he meant now when he talked about keeping a smooth and steady pace.

I reset when I felt myself reaching the end of the pool, this time pushing off the wall harder and moving quicker than before. I could feel my muscles ache as I pushed the pace. It felt like I was moving a lot faster than I actually was and I only knew that from how slowly the ceiling tiles moved above me. The blue flags hanging across the middle of the pool slowly passed overhead and my muscles screamed for me to slow down. I maintained the pace, focusing on each stroke, determined to keep the exact form he'd shown me.

Suddenly, there was a strange, garbling noise and then I saw stars. The top of my head ached, and I sank under the water. I surfaced and sucked in a deep breath and with it, a mouthful of pool water that immediately turned into a coughing fit.

"Are you all right?" Dax asked, hands grasping my biceps to keep us both treading water.

"Fine," I said once I'd managed to control the coughing. Dax took his arms off me and pushed his hair away from his face.

"You swam into the wall," he said as I massaged the top of my skull.

"I know," I said and pulled myself up, so I was sitting on the ledge.

"You know what they call swimmers who swim straight into the wall?"

"What?"

"Names," he said, the corners of his lips pulling into a smile.

It took a moment for the full weight of the joke to hit me; the horrible, cheesy joke that really wasn't funny at all but still managed to make my cheeks hurt as I tried to keep from smiling. It was a lost cause when he started laughing. That boyish sound was infectious. I kicked the water at him, sending a wave over his face that made his hair fall across his brow again.

"Want me to time you now?" I asked.

"Hold on! You're not done yet, Sinclair," Dax said and sent a splash over my calves. "I'm having too much fun with you."

He motioned for me to join him in the water and despite my head telling me I should get out, dry off, and go straight for the soccer field ... a bet is a bet. So, I slid back into the pool for my next lesson.

Chapter 10

By the time we moved from my workout to Dax's, my muscles ached way more than I would ever admit. I hadn't expected to feel this way and sitting on the pool's platform with my phone in my hand to time his sprints was a welcomed break. After getting a taste of the easy drills, watching him train was impressive. He cut through the water like a blade through butter, so seamlessly that it seemed impossible for it to be real. His slow times weren't far off from Olympic trial admittance and his faster sprints had me so excited that he had to remind me to read them back to him.

He always responded with the same words.

"That's great! Let's see what else I can do."

I followed him into the men's locker room when we were done. He talked about his plans for tomorrow's workout, for both him and me, as he gathered his shampoo and body wash and a fresh set of clothes.

"I swear, I won't flash you or anything," he said before closing the shower curtain of the first stall. It wasn't until I saw his clean clothes appear over the shower curtain that I realized what he meant. The squeak of a faucet sounded and then water pounded against the tile floor around his bare feet. A second later, and his swimsuit was tossed over the top where it draped over the metal bar and hit the shower curtain with a slap.

Once he resumed the conversation, which included his plan to set up his phone behind me to record his sprints so he could check out his form afterward, I relaxed again. I came prepared to shower too, so I took the opposite stall just like he had and we continued to talk as we showered.

"I guess, the first stop should be to get you a new suit," Dax said, the rings of his shower curtain scraping against the bar as he exited. I turned off the water in my shower and squeezed the water from my long hair.

"It's the middle of winter in the mountains. Where am I supposed to get a swimsuit?"

"You forget that I have a contact with Speedo right here in North Ridge."

I pulled my sweatpants from the shower curtain, pulling my underwear from the pocket. Once I had them set at my hips, I reached for my shirt and lifted it to grab for the black sports bra that I'd hidden beneath it. As I pulled, the bra caught on the shower curtain ring and in my scramble to free it, my shirt slipped over the top and onto the other side.

"Shoot!" I gasped, whirling around to face the shower wall when I accidentally flung my bra over the top as well.

"No worries. I got it," Dax said. I heard his feet shuffle over the tile floor and then I turned when I heard something settle over the top of the shower curtain again. My shirt appeared first, draped over the top like before. "That's the second time you've done that. Do all girls sling-shot their bras when they take them off?"

I could feel my face flame. If his comment hadn't been so funny, I might have yelled for him to leave the room.

"Thanks, and no, they don't," I said when the bra made its reappearance. I pulled it from the curtain and quickly pulled it over my head, reaching for my shirt before I had fully adjusted the bra so that it sat comfortably.

"So, want to try for a new swimsuit this afternoon?" Dax offered. "I think I can set something up by then. We could grab lunch in the meantime."

I pushed the shower curtain aside and moved to the wooden bench where he sat. I pulled a clean pair of socks from my duffle bag after tossing my toiletry bag inside. I opened my mouth to accept, ready to ask about the food in North Ridge, when I remembered my only obligation for the week.

"I can't. I have a video call thing this afternoon." I finished tying my shoes and then leaned over for my bag. Dax lifted his onto his shoulder and moved to the locker room door, holding it open for me as we left.

My stomach twisted at the thought of my therapy appointment. Hadiza was nice. I liked her. I did, but I didn't want to talk about soccer or the what-ifs. This entire bet with Dax made my heart race as I thought about my goals to get conditioned and healed enough to play in the fall.

"Maybe another time," Dax said and we left the pool for the soccer field, where I should've been all along. The longing was fleeting as we moved into the hall and started for the main entrance, but it felt like I'd left every ounce of the excitement I'd felt this morning behind and was left with just the guilt to carry to the truck outside.

❄

I WAS EARLY for my therapy appointment with Hadiza. The words *waiting for host* remained on the screen as I sat at my desk and watched the snow fall softly outside. I watched as my dad left the front of the house, my mom following after him until she stopped at the front of the driveway wearing just her work clothes. She folded her arms across her chest as my dad climbed into the dark SUV and backed into the street. Mom stood there for a moment as he drove up the mountain, likely to the big clubhouse where the Winter Solstice Gala would be held in just a few days.

"How are things, Margot? What's new since last week?"

I turned back to the computer screen where Dr. Hadiza Morgan sat in her tidy office with her braids wound into a thick bun on top of her head, complete with a red scarf tied around it that matched her blouse.

"Well, I drank beer for the first time," I said with a shrug.

It started as just a tremble and then it built through my chest until it felt like my lungs were collapsing. My bottom lip quivered, and I bit down on it to keep from losing my grip.

"Take a deep breath through your nose. Hold it a moment. Good. Now, blow it all out your mouth like it's your birthday and you're blowing out the candles on your cake," she said, her voice so calm and matter-of-fact that it made relaxing again easier. There was no Madison spewing all these girlish fantasies and bombarding me with questions. There was no Marlee with her sarcastic quips and depressing reminders of Mom and Dad and their fighting or that I was stuck at home with them for the next semester at least while I tried to repair broken dreams and lost opportunities.

"So, you had your first beer. The way you say that makes it sound like that's not something you would have done in the past," Hadiza said, pulling me out of my thoughts and back to our conversation.

"I went to a few parties at college, but I never got too involved," I said and let out a deep sigh. "I've always been the responsible one. I always had it all together. I never jump into anything without a game plan."

"Do you feel like you're without a plan now?"

"The plan isn't working."

"What is the plan?"

I let out another breath, feeling restless in the desk chair.

"I moved home for the spring semester. I'm doing classes online with UCLA. I'm seeing you to clear my head and after Christmas, I'll see a specialist who will hopefully look at my ankle and get a plan together to get me back in shape so I can be back on the team in the fall."

Hadiza thought for a moment, staring through the computer screen in a way that made me run through the plan again in my head.

"So, the timeline on that plan doesn't start until after Christmas. Is that why you had your first beer? Are you taking some time before then to enjoy the holidays?"

I opened my mouth, ready to shoot down the idea immediately, but something stopped me. In a way, I kind of was taking the time. I had no choice. The doctor's office told us several times that there was no availability until after the holidays. I had a list of approved workouts I could do in the meantime, but they were general. As I thought through them now and how sore I was from the morning with Dax, they were all designed for muscles that I was already exercising in the pool. Then there was the bet ...

"I switched to swimming workouts," I said and pulled my legs into the chair so I was sitting crisscross.

"That sounds like a good compromise. Swimming is low impact, but good for the muscles," Hadiza said with a smile. The room went quiet again for a moment, my mind going back to that feeling as we left the pool, walked through the soccer field. "But it's not soccer."

"Yeah. That's pretty much it," I said, glad that she didn't ask me to express the guilt I'd tried so hard to shove down each morning on the way to North Ridge.

"You like to have things planned out. You like goals and you're stubborn about them. Would you agree?" she asked, moving a notepad onto her desk.

"Yeah. I'm not afraid to go after what I want," I said.

Hadiza nodded and began writing on the pad of paper. Her pen scratched across the page for a moment before she looked up and set it aside.

"Okay. Then let's get into some real talk so we can focus on setting the path to what you want for yourself," she said and held up the notepad. She'd drawn a big circle, a medium circle inside that one, and an even smaller one inside of that. Each one was labeled. The outer circle was *out of my control*. The middle one was *some control*. The center circle was *in my control*. "This is your locus of control. When we experience anxiety, we often feel out of control. A tool I think might work really well for you, since you like to be goal-focused, is grounding. You can ground yourself in reality by reminding yourself of what is completely in your control, what you have a little influence over, and the things that are out of your control. For instance, you can't control that you can't see your doctor until after Christmas, so that would go here."

Hadiza laid the notepad down and scrawled the word *doctor* in the ring that symbolized things out of my control. My stomach sank at how finite it was. She turned the page back so I could see it. I stared at the truth that made it hard to sleep at night, and which was both motivating and difficult to get up and go to the gym.

"Your turn," she said and pointed to the middle circle with her pen. "What is something you *can* influence or something you have a little bit of control over?"

I thought for a long moment. My chest started to tighten again. It felt like there was nothing. I didn't feel like I was in control of anything. I didn't want to be back home because it meant I wasn't at practices with the team anymore. I didn't want to be at UCLA because it meant I sat on the sidelines and watched the team practice while I felt sorry for myself.

"I guess, I kind of have control that I'm here to see a specialist and that I can do school online."

"Sure," Hadiza said and began writing on the pad again. "You also said a minute ago that you changed your workout to swimming, making it lower impact. You might not be able to do soccer drills right now, but you can have some control in modifying those workouts and you're already doing that."

I hadn't thought about Dax's bet as a modification of soccer, but I suppose it sort of was. I hadn't exactly meant to, but I was following the doctor's list of approved workouts perfectly by swimming. I couldn't deny that my entire body ached from the effort, so it wasn't like I was taking things easy.

"Last," Hadiza announced and turned the pad so I could see the final empty circle. "What do you have control over?"

It felt stupid. It shouldn't be this hard. Everything couldn't be out of my control, but it really felt like it. I started with what was already on the list, trying to think realistically past the fog of anxiety.

"You can control how you choose to see your circumstances," Hadiza suggested, starting to write again a moment later. "You can control what you believe about yourself."

"I can control what I do right now while I wait for that doctor's appointment," I said, not feeling as disappointed by the truth as I thought I might, hearing it come out of my own mouth.

"You're right," Hadiza said and turned the list so I could see the entire diagram. "You can add as much as you want to this, because there will always be things out of our control, things we can influence, and things that we have control of. I'll make a copy and email it to you."

"Okay. That works," I said and checked the time on my phone.

We talked for another ten minutes. Hadiza walked me through a breathing technique I could use if I felt another panic attack come on. I was a little shocked when she called it that. Panic attack. I'd had moments like that before, like during games when I wasn't playing particularly well or when we played in a close game. Our session ended, and I sat at the desk watching the front lawn fill with snow. After a while, my phone dinged, and I opened an email from Hadiza. The attachment was a photo of my locus of control diagram. I exited the app at first. Then, I opened the email again and saved the image to my camera roll.

Chapter 11

DAX COACHED me through the same workouts the next morning and I could already tell that I was much better than the first day. He told me my form was better, but I could also feel as much as I took even strokes through the water. I learned as we moved from my workout to his that he was also lifting weights at his parents' cabin in the evenings. I knew he had to be doing more than just timing sprints in the pool to be an Olympic contender. After a little prodding, I convinced him to let me tag along one night, promising not to overdo it or do anything that wasn't on my doctor-approved exercise list.

He told me about his family's Christmas plans while we showered, him in the first stall to the left and me in the first stall to the right. It was just the second day and even though we were both in very vulnerable positions behind thin shower curtains, it didn't feel that way. I was just glad to be working out and Dax wasn't bad company. We had more in common than I realized, and I couldn't believe we hadn't been closer during high school.

"What did you talk me into?" I said as we drove through downtown North Ridge. I hadn't brought any styling tools aside from my hair dryer, so my long hair was pulled into a bun at the top of my head, and I had no makeup on. Dax said the night before that he wanted to show me something after our workout and I hadn't put much thought into it until I sat next to him in the truck. He was wearing jeans instead of sweatpants. At least I had my nicest pair of leggings on, but I still was far from dressed up for

"Don't worry. It's a casual thing," he said with a laugh as he turned onto a mountain road.

"This isn't like ... Did I miss some signal or am I just reading into things?"

"What? Oh!" Dax started laughing again. "You think I asked you on a date?"

"No! I mean, kind of? I didn't until just now. Don't think that I *wanted* it to be a date," I said.

"Ouch!" Dax laughed, clutching his chest. "Okay, so I'm not your type or what?"

"It's not that you're not attractive or not date-worthy or—"

I stopped defending myself as his laughter filled the truck, putting an end to my brief questioning about our surprise outing. Not a date. Got it. Thank God.

"I promise that this surprise is worth the wait," Dax said as we wound up the mountain. He turned onto a gravel road, which soon led to a paved road that led to a large gate. Dax rolled down his window and pressed the call button, only waiting a moment before a man's voice came through.

"Hey, Dax! It's good to see you again! Well, it will be here in a moment," he said. There was a buzzing sound and the gate before us slowly swung inward. "Just park anywhere and come in through the front doors. I know you're coming from the pool, so I made an early lunch."

"Will do. See you in a bit, Lawson," Dax said before rolling up the window.

"This is your Speedo friend," I said as the truck passed the gates and started down the long concrete path toward a large cabin at the end. It was three stories with a circle drive that had a statue of an elk in the center. As we grew closer, I noticed a second building. It was a free-standing garage large enough for several big vehicles. The garage matched the same log cabin style as the main house, which had a pair of oversized wooden double doors beneath a chandelier of antlers. Dax parked the truck next to the house and climbed out, pulling our duffle bags from the back of the truck while I took it all in.

"This is nice," I told him when he joined me.

He scoffed and led the way to the door. "Your family's cabin is at least this nice."

Well, maybe he was right. This cabin was just so … woodsy. My parents wanted our cabin to scream luxury and mountains without the outdoorsy parts. This looked like a high-end cabin for a true outdoorsman and my assumption was proved correct just moments later when we moved into the foyer.

There was a lot of taxidermy, all well done and still stylish among the lavish furniture and mahogany floors as we passed the main entryway. It was clear that Lawson Rathbone was an avid hunter, as the closest bust of a ram's head had a gold plate beneath the mount with details of the date of the hunt and listed Lawson as the marksman. The rooms we passed, a small sitting room and a den, all had different animal rugs.

A man padded barefoot from one of the side rooms. He wore a pair of joggers and a long-sleeved shirt with Speedo written just over his left breast. He smiled, the small creases that appeared at the corners of his eyes the only feature that gave away his age. Dax extended his hand to him and was pulled into a hug instead.

"Good to see you again, man," Lawson said before pulling away.

"Same to you. Thanks for inviting us over," Dax said and motioned to himself and me. "Well, letting us come by."

"No worries. You're not intruding at all. You know, we could see a lot more of each other if you'd take me up on my offer," Lawson said and held his hands out as though weighing the options.

Dax shook his head with a smile. "Another time."

"Ah! Okay. Fine. After you make the Olympic team then," he said and turned to look at me next, already reaching for a handshake. "Did you finally take a break from the pool to hit the dating scene?"

"We're old friends," I told Lawson as I shook his hand. "We sort of grew up together."

Lawson cast a look at Dax who told me he didn't fully believe us.

"I'm Lawson Rathbone. I met Dax when he was ..." Lawson turned to look at Dax as though staring at him would bring the memories back. "I don't know. You were probably like sixteen? Either way, not the man you are today."

"Thanks. You've expanded a lot since we met, too," Dax said and motioned at the house around us. Lawson snorted and waved away the compliment.

"I had this place when I met you. I've added the garage outside since then and the outdoor area is where the house really shines now. How about a tour?"

Lawson was already motioning for us to follow up the stairs. He took us all the way to the top. Three large bedrooms and a bathroom complete with a jet tub sat off the large entertainment space where a full bar was in the corner along with a pool table and a large TV and sectional that looked comfortable enough to fall asleep in. The second floor had three more bedrooms, one of which was his. Lawson's luggage sat open on the bed as he showed us the space. The entire back wall was a glass sliding door that led to a shared balcony between the room next door.

"You weren't kidding about that outdoor area," Dax said as he moved onto the balcony ahead of me. I approached the railing and looked over the yard. The grass was still green, probably turf, and a small pool sat in the center with a waterfall made of rocks along one side.

"The pool is heated, but it's mostly just warm. It's the perfect temperature in the afternoon. It's too cold in the evenings, so that's why I added the hot tub. It's under the awning below us," Lawson said and led us back inside with a shiver. I took it that he was not a winter witch like we were. It wouldn't matter if the pool was heated to us.

"This place is beautiful," I said as crossed the bedroom again.

Lawson let out a gasp and turned around. "Since we're up

here," he said, brushing past Dax and heading for the closet, "I got what you called about."

He returned with a large cardboard box that he plopped on the floor in front of me. When he opened the top, I understood why we had made the surprise stop. Inside the box were dozens of women's swimsuits, all packaged in clear wrapping.

"Thanks, Lawson. You should've seen the workout we tried in the suit she had on," Dax said, flashing me a smile when I elbowed him.

"Do you take Venmo?" I asked and reached for one of the suits on top to get a better look at the design.

Lawson shook his head. "You take whatever you like. No worries. These are mostly suits we send out to influencers and for other advertising."

"Okay. Well, thanks," I said and started actually looking at the swimwear. I didn't look long before picking a simple black one-piece with an open-back design. Lawson offered his bathroom to try it on, but I declined and tucked the package under my arm while he put the rest of the suits away. I'd refused to take a second suit and Dax swore he had enough swimsuits when Lawson tried getting him to dig through the box of men's swimwear he also had tucked in his closet.

"All right then," Lawson said and shut his closet door. "Lunch is ready downstairs in the kitchen. We can talk over a bite."

We ate a venison stew over rice, a two-pot meal that tasted like it had taken hours to make. Dax and I both had seconds while Lawson told us what he knew about the Olympic trials and which athletes were expected to be top-contenders in each event. He made sure to mention that Dax's name was listed among them and that he'd gained national attention ahead of the trials. That's when he tried again to get him to partner with Speedo and Dax did his best to change the subject.

"You just get here?" Dax asked before putting another spoonful of stew in his mouth.

Lawson shook his head as he chewed and reached for his

phone. He scrolled for a moment before turning the phone so we could see a picture of him with his arms around a dark-haired woman so pretty that she could've been a model.

"I have a girl now. Fiancée," he told us and turned the phone again and started scrolling. "She's a sportscaster. We came here for a few weeks. She just left a couple of days ago to head to Denver to work a basketball game. She's going to fly back to California from there."

"Congrats on the engagement," I told him.

"Yeah, congrats, man," Dax said and took my half-empty bowl when I pushed it aside. I felt the smile tug at the corners of my lips as he set it on top of his and began eating the last of my meal. He lowered the spoon to pull his phone from his pocket, his brow furrowing. He looked up at Lawson. "What's with the numbers?"

"The first one is for the gate and the second goes to the front door," Lawson said and took the last bite of his stew before standing up. "Before you dismiss the idea, hear me out."

"Lawson," Dax said, the smile on his face contrasting his chiding.

"You're here every day to train. There's still food in the fridge and pantry that I'd have to throw out before I leave tomorrow anyway. Someone might as well get some use out of the place. Do a cold plunge in the pool after a workout, soak your sore muscles in the hot tub, or cook the steak in the fridge. Stay overnight if you want. Enjoy it," Lawson said as he rinsed out the bowl. Dax froze for a moment before chuckling and shrugging.

"Okay then," he said and pocketed his phone. "Thanks."

"Like I said, someone should enjoy it when I'm not here."

"I don't mean to eat and run, but Dax," I said and showed him the time on my phone. "I did promise my sisters I'd meet them for coffee this afternoon."

"Right. Well, thanks for lunch, Lawson. I appreciate everything, you know that?" Dax said and rose with our bowls in his hands.

"You don't have to thank me. Friends do nice things for each other," Lawson said and took the bowls from him.

"Is there anything we can help with before we leave?" I asked, itching to do the dishes left in the sink. Lawson repeated the phrase "Friends do nice things for each other" as he led us to the foyer where we said our final goodbyes.

I tucked my new swimsuit into my duffle bag before Dax loaded it into the backseat of his truck. A strange feeling built in my chest as we passed the buildings of downtown North Ridge and made our way onto the highway. It was a strange, heavy feeling that made me want to take a nap. Part of me wanted to stay in North Ridge and avoid everything waiting in Crescent Peak.

Chapter 12

Dax dropped me off at the coffee shop in Crescent Peak, pulling to a stop in the street next to Madison's pink Jeep and Marlee's orange one. They were both sitting in the back of the mostly empty café where the nice lounge chairs were, Madison with her hot chocolate and Marlee with her dark roast.

"You're late," Marlee noted, a pinch of surprise to her tone.

"I know. The workout ran late," I told them as I dropped my gym bag on the floor next to one of the leather chairs before plopping down.

"I hope you're not overdoing it," Madison said as she began pulling a notebook and a laptop from her handbag.

"I'm not. I've been swimming actually," I told them, wishing I hadn't said anything when they both flashed looks of shock my way. "It's low impact and it's approved by the doctor."

"That's not the part that surprises me," Marlee said and let out a laugh. "Swimming?"

"I hit the soccer field too," I added, the lie twisting my stomach with guilt for so many reasons. Maybe I should be at least running laps on the field after or doing some basic ball-handling drills.

"Onto the reason I wanted to meet with you guys," Madison started and opened her laptop. "I made a few wedding decisions that I wanted to tell you about and I need some opinions on the theme."

The next hour was consumed with wedding planning, all of which had Marlee groaning. Thankfully, Madison was too excited to engage her, and the entire session was argument-free. Madison had already booked the main hall at the country club. She wanted the ceremony to be outdoors so we could enchant the venue so it would snow the perfect amount, perfectly do-able considering the amount of winter witch power that would be among the guestlist. The theme was pink, of course, with a black-tie flair. The country club would take care of most of the details, so we spent most of the time scrutinizing the tiniest details from shades of pink so close it made me go cross-eyed to table settings. You would think the wedding was in a month and not a full year away.

"Oh! Text from Mom," Marlee said with more excitement than she normally would. She groaned yet again and shoved her phone into her pocket and began gathering her things. "Mom said we are having a Sinclair family dinner, and we need to all come home."

"You think they're trying to play nice?" Madison asked as she stood up with her purse over her shoulder.

"Can I ride with you, Marlee? I had Dax drop me off," I told her, knowing that a ride with Madison would just mean more wedding talk.

"Sure," she said as the three of us left the coffee shop. We followed Madison's pink Jeep down the road and up the mountain. The driveway was full as soon as we pulled in behind Mom and Dad's SUVs. I stared as the sight as I climbed out of the front seat. I couldn't remember if they'd both driven their cars or not. We usually left as many behind as we could. We spent more time together at the cabin than at home, so we didn't need as many cars.

"Here we go," Marlee said with a sigh as we followed Madison through the front door. The house smelled of garlic and steak. When we got to the kitchen, Dad was moving the steaks onto plates for each of us. Mom drained water from a large pot of green beans. They both smiled back at us before continuing their work.

"Take a plate and go to the table," Dad said, holding a plate for Madison to take.

"Wait! Don't forget to get some green beans and there are baked potatoes in the oven. Just pull one out," Mom said as she finished seasoning the green beans. Madison started the buffet line, filling her plate as we all fell in line silently. The kitchen was a symphony of forks and knives on plates for a long while before anyone spoke.

"So, what's the deal? Why the sudden call for a family meal?" Marlee asked, spearing a hunk of potato and popping it into her mouth.

"Your mom wanted to tell you something," Dad said as he sliced into his steak. Mom let out a sigh, jaw tensing for a moment before she looked at each of us in turn.

"We are getting a divorce."

The room was silent. Dad sat his fork and knife down and watched carefully for our reactions.

"Who ... Who wanted ... How will the wedding work? What about the house and everything?" Madison asked and then gasped. "What about the cabin and the country club?"

"You're wedding is a whole year away, Madison. This changes everything right now," Marlee said. Madison shot her a glare across my plate and Marlee rolled her eyes right back.

"I know that, which is why I asked. I mean, are you both going to move?"

"We've never had any joint accounts because of all our businesses, so separating will be easy enough," Dad said with a gentle smile. "We will still be at your wedding. Graduations. We both decided we are better apart."

"What does that mean for now?" I asked, just starting to wrap my head around what a divorce would even entail.

"Your dad travels for work more than I do, so it makes the most sense that I get the house. He will move out over time when we get back home. We are going to sell the cabin," Mom said.

"Well, we want to do a few remodels first. Next Christmas we will finish them up, so we will have one more holiday here before it's sold," Dad added.

Madison looked like everything had fallen apart around her. Marlee looked a little relieved and I couldn't blame her. Mom and Dad always fought when they were together. I didn't always notice, but they didn't interact like other couples and our family dynamics were strange. There weren't ever really any family dinners except for holidays and those still functioned around work calls. When they were together, in the same room and off their phones and computers, the room felt strange the way a silent waiting room is before you go to the doctor for something unpleasant. Still, this only complicated things more than they already were.

"I'm staying in the guest room," Dad said, filling the silence for just a moment before it returned heavier than before. Neither of them seemed emotional about it. It was as though we were around a boardroom table discussing annual numbers.

"The gala is at the end of the week," Madison said quietly.

"We'll be at the gala as a family," Mom said like it was a no-brainer. "We aren't keeping all this a secret though, either. Your dad and I are going into this amicably. It will get around sooner than you think."

No one moved for a long moment until Dad picked up his knife and fork and began cutting into his steak again.

"You've been at the gym a lot with Dax Krune," he said and looked up at me with a smile.

"I'm timing his swims and he's coaching me through pool workouts," I said.

Dad nodded. "Swimming is easier on your joints. Smart. He's also going to the Olympics. I'm sure that will help. A few more weeks and you'll be back to soccer training."

"He's hoping to make the Olympic team," I corrected, though no one seemed to be paying attention to the meaning of the words we exchanged. Dinner continued with the same silence and awkward conversation peppered throughout. No one stayed up late and despite the closed doors down the upstairs hallway, the glow beneath the doors lasted for hours.

❄

My thighs ached as my boots crunched through the snow at the McAdams Mercantile. Madison convinced me to wear a pair of jeans and snow boots, saying something about wanting photos next to the evergreen trees. Marlee paired her jeans and boots with a thick leather jacket over a Yale T-shirt. I wore a maroon sweatshirt with a cute design of a reindeer. Madison waved at us when we arrived, but quickly found herself swept up in the bustling mercantile, and then Jared pulled her away to help with a custom wreath order a woman was placing at the register.

"What are you so focused on?" I asked Marlee as we reached the last row of trees. She'd been studying her phone screen as her fingers typed away. I caught a glimpse of the bright screen filled from top to bottom with text. "You writing a novel over there?"

"It's a project I've been working on," she said, and the screen went black. "School stuff."

Marlee shoved her phone into her pocket, and we started walking back the way we came, waiting for a family with their four kids as they dragged a red sleigh with a downed tree lying across it. The parents thanked us while their young boys bound along behind them excitedly.

"What kind of remodel do Mom and Dad want to do to the cabin? Have they said anything?" I asked.

"Why would they tell me their divorce plans?" Marlee said with a snort as she raised her coffee cup to her lips.

"I only meant—"

"I know what you meant. I'm home all the time. I might have overheard something, but I haven't. Well, not much. I heard him yesterday talking about meeting with one of his country club friends again that has something to do with construction. I think he owns a patent or something on some kind of closet system. Whatever the deal is, it seemed like the friend had a connection," she said and swirled the to-go cup in her hands, trying to take a peek through the small opening in the top to see what was left. "Sometimes, I wish I wasn't the informant all the time or the cover story or the easy child."

"Crescent Peak has things to do. You could go out and do things besides just visiting the bookstore."

Marlee groaned. "I don't have anything left here I like except for that bookstore. My friends in high school weren't winter witches and we haven't talked since high school. If I wanted to go out, I'd have to join the gossip among all the witches and warlocks, and I don't want the drama."

I couldn't fault her for that. I didn't know how Madison stood it during high school. Even now, she didn't have a lot of drama going on, but her personality was dramatic and everything that happened to her seemed to be out of a fairytale.

"Margot," Marlee said, stepping in front of me so I had no choice but to stop walking. She looked so annoyed that I worried I'd said something until she glanced toward the nearest row of trees and then rolled her eyes. "That guy keeps staring at you."

"Who?" I asked and looked to the right. Three guys were standing next to each other holding to-go cups and sporting sweatshirts with fraternity letters. I recognized one immediately as Dax's brother. I didn't know the other two, a dark-haired man and one with brown curls. "Darin Krune?"

"No! The one with short, dark hair," Marlee said and chanced another look.

"How do you know he's not checking *you* out?"

"Because if looks could kill they would all drop dead," she said under her breath.

"They're coming this way," I said and pulled her to my side as she groaned.

Darin led the charge, the two boys sauntering behind.

"How's Christmas Break been?" Daren asked, looking from me to Marlee, not fazed in the slightest by Marlee's pointed stare.

"It's been good," I said, knowing that it had been far from good. It had only gotten worse since we came to Crescent Peak.

"These are my friends from college. They're warlocks too, based in Denver," Darin said. The dark-haired guy must've taken that as his introduction because he stepped forward and extended a hand to me.

"I'm Noah Porter. I'm studying meteorology," he said and shook my hand. He was the textbook warlock from the air of magic that exuded from him to the fact that he was studying the weather. There was a reason so many meteorologists were witches and warlocks. It was an easy gig. "This is Quentin Hayes. We'll be here through Christmas Break and we've been learning our way around town. Darin told me a little about you. I was wondering if you'd like to be my date to the Winter Solstice Gala, maybe show me more of Crescent Peak?"

Oh boy.

My stomach churned and soon it had gone quiet, too quiet. As I came out of my surprise, I wondered how long that silence had stretched. Man, I was awkward. I only had to say one word.

"Um, well, I'm actually going with someone. I'm going with Dax, actually. Dax Krune," I said and motioned toward Darin who seemed just as taken-aback as the rest of the group, Marlee included.

"My brother asked you to go with him?" Darin asked.

"Yes. Well, it might have been me who asked? I don't remember. Either way, we're going together, but just as friends. I did tell him I would go through."

"Sure. No worries. Maybe I can steal a dance the night of?" Noah asked, flashing a smile and a pair of deep brown eyes dreamy enough to drown in.

"Yeah. Maybe. I'll see you there then," I said and skirted around the trio, Marlee catching up a moment later.

"You're going to the gala with Dax Krune?" she asked.

"As friends," I added. "We've always been friends. We have a lot in common and he's been helping me with strength training. I've been keeping his times for his workouts. I don't want to take a date anyway, because I was hoping that I could leave early. He felt the same way, so it made sense."

"Yeah. Makes sense," she said in a way that made me question if it did make sense or if she just didn't believe me. "If Madison makes us wait any longer, I'm going to freeze her solid the next time we do see her."

I felt my body relax at the change in subject, not even sure why I'd been so nervous. I wasn't interested in Lucas Porter even though he was one of the more handsome guys I'd seen around Crescent Peak. Things were already complicated enough, and it was hard to focus on my goals now without the added distraction of a gala date.

Marlee had her phone out and was tapping out a message across the screen. I felt my phone buzz against my hip and I pulled it out to see her message in our Sinclair sister group text.

> I'll turn you into a popsicle if you stand us up.
> Boys are being annoying here.

I FELT the smile pull at my lips at her message. Marlee had the highest expectations for boys. Madison still swore that she was gay or at least bisexual. Marlee never bothered to deny any of the assumptions Madison threw at her, just rolling her eyes and going back to whatever solitary activity she was doing. I was closer with Marlee, and I was sure that whoever she ended up with would be brilliant, the type of guy who ran a multimillion-dollar business and could still go to a sporting event without anyone giving him a second look. Hell, Marlee would probably graduate from Yale and become that person herself. Maybe she didn't care about dating at all.

My phone buzzed in my hand.

> Sorry. Jared and I have a lot of orders to work on in the shop.

"She stood us up to get laid," Marlee said as I read the message.

"What? Why do you immediately think that?" I asked, looking away from my phone to watch my younger sister roll her eyes.

"Because she said this morning that she was actually ahead on orders and the display on the way through the mercantile was still full. She's not lying about Jared being with her, but they aren't making orders."

I turned away from her and we continued walking back toward the big red barn. Part of me wanted to stay here, walking through the rows of trees in the winter air that was so crisp that it made me feel more relaxed than I was used to. I wasn't sure the last time I felt so comfortable and that alone was enough to make my muscles ache. I could feel my chest tighten and my stomach twisted so tight that I worried I'd throw up all the coffee I'd just drank.

"I might do some gift shopping inside," Marlee said and was halfway up the deck stairs before she turned to face me.

"I'm going to walk for a bit," I managed to say, the words nearly choked off from the lump forming in my throat. I didn't wait for her approval before I turned and started for the nearest row. I hoped she just turned around and went inside. I hoped the family of three I just passed didn't look at me as I passed between their group, wishing I was wearing a pair of leggings instead of these stupid jeans that chaffed as I quickly walked through the snow. My boots crunched in the compacted snow and once I made it to the row, I moved into the deep grove left by a tractor tire. I picked up the pace, hoping that the exercise would even out my racing heart. Worse yet, it only felt like it was harder to breathe. Tears were already halfway down my face before I felt the coolness of them.

There was no one for yards at the end of the rows and once I realized how alone I was, I let myself sink to the ground behind the last evergreen. I scooped handfuls of snow and held it to my face, hoping the coolness would help to ease the panic. I tried focusing on my breathing, closing my eyes, and breathing the way Hadiza had coached me. I sat there for a long time, nearly losing it again before I breathed through the sobs and managed to center myself again. I thought about the circles on my chart. My locus of control. I couldn't control the fact that I was home trying to rehab an injury that might end my soccer career. I had some control over the things I could do now like swimming and still going to classes when the semester started again. I could control what I did now. I could control how I wanted to think about anything other than soccer right now. That thought alone should've felt blasphemous, but it was somehow freeing. Giving up for just a moment felt good, but just for a moment.

I opened my eyes and my heart burst into a sprint for a different reason. Dax Krune sat in front of me in the snow with his legs crisscrossed and something like pity in his blue eyes. I brushed the snow in my hands against my jeans and I stood up, face burning.

"I thought you could use the company," Dax said as he stood.

"Who wants company while they ugly cry and lie in the snow?"

"It would be a dick move to let you ugly cry and lie in the snow alone," Dax said with a snort. "Friends don't let friends wallow in sadness."

"Wallow in sadness?" I asked, standing taller than I'd ever felt. The humor in Dax's face was gone now, replaced by such a sincere concern that it only made my stomach twist more with anger. My eyes burned and I focused instead on the anger and all the things I wanted to scream at the world instead so I wouldn't cry again.

"I didn't mean it that way. You're allowed to be sad. You're allowed to be pissed off too."

"Well, I am pissed off. I'm really pissed off, Dax. You aren't helping," I told him.

"Tell me how to help," he said and scooped a handful of snow from the ground.

"Unless you can time travel ..."

Dax didn't say anything and for some reason, that made me hesitate. I turned from the path to face him, noticing that he was following me. He stopped walking and continued to pack the snow between his hands, and he waited for me to speak again.

"What are you doing?" I asked. He didn't take the question the same as I meant it. Rather than explaining why he'd turned into a labrador, he turned his attention to the snow between his hands. He rolled it between his hands again until his powers hardened it into a solid sphere of ice. He held it up for me to see, his expression distorted by the ice so that his nose took up most of his face.

"Catch." Dax tossed the ball to me and I caught it with both hands, the ice so cold that it began to stick to my fingers. I passed it between my hands as I adjusted the temperature so my skin wouldn't freeze to it before I looked up at him again. "You have a crystal ball. What do you see?" Dax pointed to the ball.

"This is so stupid."

"What do you see?" he asked again, his tone more insistent.

I looked down at the ball, trying to see past the crystals of snow suspended in the ice and see what kind of future there was for me.

"I don't know, Dax. I don't see anything in your stupid crystal ball."

"You're the stupid one."

I thought I misheard him until the words settled around me. The air was silent as I stared back at him. He gave me a challenging look and I wanted to lob the icy sphere right at his face.

"What did you say?" I asked.

Dax let out a deep sigh and took a few steps forward. He stood tall and set his hands on his hips, the positioning enhancing his muscular shoulders and biceps.

"You aren't stupid. I didn't mean that, but you are acting stupid," he said with a snort. "You act like your entire life is over.

You are so tightly wound. You always have been. You acted like that night at the bar was the first time you had ever allowed yourself to have a little fun and then you beat yourself up about it on the way home. You can't do that."

"I already have all of Crescent Peak and Heritage City telling me to give myself some grace while I heal. I don't need you doing it too," I said and started to turn again.

"I didn't mean that you can't beat yourself up. I meant that you can't keep denying yourself a little fun in life," he said, pulling my attention back to him again. He looked frustrated, so frustrated that I could see the tension in his body now. "You can't let soccer be the only thing that brings you happiness. It can't be your only goal to go pro."

"Why does it matter?" I said with a sigh. My eyes hurt and I was sure that I would start crying again if I had to continue to defend myself.

"Because we're friends," Dax said and moved close enough that he could put a hand on my shoulder. "And I care about you, Margot, enough to tell you when you're being stupid because any soccer team, career field, friend, or lover would be lucky to have someone who is as stubborn about what she cares about as you are."

That was all it took to send me over the edge again. This time felt different though. It was a little like that feeling I got when I stepped out of the Denver airport and into the cool winter air. It felt wholesome and honest and as I worried that the unbearable weight was just moments from settling in my chest, Dax pulled me to his instead. I sucked in a deep breath, smelling the woodsy cologne on his neck and the clean linen scent of his sweatshirt. When I exhaled, tears still slid down my face, but I didn't feel out of control like I normally would.

"Let's go," Dax told me as he pulled away, sliding his hand into mine and tugging it down the row of trees.

"Where?" I asked as I swiped the remainder of the tears from my face.

"I don't know," Dax said with a simple shrug and an encouraging smile. "To find the finer things in life? To find more joy?"

I didn't ask any more questions and gladly followed him to his truck.

Chapter 13

Dax parked his truck in a gravel driveway of a two-story cabin. An iron snowflake hung over the garage door, a signature sign of a winter witch family, and another iron sign with the words *Krune Family* hung over the address on the porch. The cabin wasn't as modern as my family's, but I could tell that it was nice and well-kept. It was just a few blocks from the country club, true mountain living, and had a balcony on the second floor that wrapped to the back of the cabin.

"Daren won't be home for a few hours, if that. My parents are home though. They like to hole up in the cabin when we're here," Dax said as he led me to the front door of the cabin. He unlocked it and we walked inside.

Just like I thought, the Krune's cabin had the traditional rustic feel rather than the modern look that ours had. It was nice and was exactly what I imagined Dax growing up in. The foyer opened to a large room, a living room with a pair of tan leather couches on the left and a kitchen on the right with so much wood that you'd think at least one of parents' was a master carpenter.

"My parents are both on call a lot of the time, so they really soak up the downtime when we're in Crescent Peak. We have a whole closet that's just board games," Dax said with a laugh. He led me past the living room and to a pair of wooden stairs that were open to the downstairs space. I got a full view of the open-plan kitchen and the many black appliances on the counter. Someone around here liked to bake.

"There's a bathroom just off the kitchen. Daren and I share this one upstairs," Dax said and pushed the first door to the left open to reveal long counter with double sinks. The shower was a glass cubical in the corner opposite the toilet and I recognized the dark packaging of Dax's haircare sitting on the white tile floor just beneath the shower head.

"All the bedrooms have sliding doors that open to the wrap-around balcony. This room is Darin's," Dax said and didn't bother to pause outside his brother's room. It was so pristine inside that you'd think he never came home. The next room was much more lived-in. Dax moved inside and stayed standing next to the bed. The walls were decorated with swimming photos and awards that added more color to the otherwise earth-tone house. His closet door was slightly open, revealing a messy pile of shoes on the floor and a small collection of nice sweaters that I have never seen Dax wear.

"I know. It's messy," he said and held his hands out to his sides.

"I wouldn't say that. It looks like you're comfortable here," I said, and I noticed the drawer of his nightstand was open. Dax Krune liked boxer briefs.

He smiled at the comment and moved to the curtain on the far wall. He slid it aside and sunlight came streaming in. He unlocked the door and slid it aside before stepping onto the balcony and turning to the right.

"Hey! You're home early," a woman's voice greeted.

"Have you heard about this thing called a Borg? I just read online that it's a trend among college students," a man's voice said as Dax motioned for me to follow.

"Yeah. Borg. You fill a gallon jug with alcohol and go to parties," Dax said, taking my hand and pulling me onto the balcony when I took too long. Both of his parents adjusted in their wooden rocking chairs. Dr. Danielle Krune put her bookmark in her book and sat it next to the mug on the table between her and her husband. She had blonde hair that hung just past her shoulders and a pair of blue eyes that matched Dax's.

"Margot Sinclair," Dr. Lucas Krune sat his phone on the side table along with his mug. I saw the recognition flash across his face, more than just recognizing my family name. It was more than acknowledging that our families had grown in Heritage City, their children attending the same schools, and appearing at the same social events. His smile was genuine when he spoke next. "How are you? Your family doing well?"

"Yeah. Well, we're good. My family is good," I said. God, if only that were the truth. I hoped it wasn't obvious, but it felt like a slap in the face to be asked about the state of my family just a day after I found out that it was cleaved in half. Neither Danielle nor Lucas seemed to miss a beat, offering one of the free rocking chairs on the balcony to me.

"I have to admit. I don't know either of your parents that well," Lucas said as Dax pulled a rocking chair next to his mom and motioned for me to sit. I did, surprised at how comfortable it was considering there was no cushion on the wooden seat and back.

"My mom saw you after she injured her knee playing tennis at the club in Heritage City," I said and turned to Danielle. She gave me small smile in reply.

"Yes, well, I didn't want to say anything. HIPAA and all." She laughed and pivoted in her seat to turn toward me. "I'm sorry to hear about your injury. You have a great medical team behind you, though. Dr. Melon does great work."

My stomach dropped. I forgot that my parents had spoken to her about my injury. They did a lot of research and talked to a lot of specialists, and Dr. Danielle Krune was an orthopedic surgeon with a lot of knowledge and training in sports injuries. Now that I thought about it, she was the best in Heritage City, and we went outside our community to seek more opinions. She didn't look offended in the slightest, however. I had to tell myself that it was normal to get a second opinion, that not all doctors were a good fit, and that it made this interaction a whole lot less awkward since she wasn't treating my injury.

"Margot, do you like tea? We just made a fresh pot, so there's still hot water in the kettle. We have lots of different kinds," Lucas said, leaning in his chair so he could see me around his wife.

"Um, well, I'm fine actually," I said, still figuring out how to fully relax in the chair I was in.

"I'm going to make some coffee for myself. You like yours with a bit of caramel and a little milk, right?" Dax asked, saving me from answering his dad. I nodded, clearing the thickness in my throat before answering.

"Yeah. I'll take a cup, if you're making coffee," I said, sure my expression conveyed my gratitude based on his reassuring smile as he went back to the sliding door. It wasn't until he was gone that I wondered how he knew how I liked my coffee anyway. It wasn't like we'd gone out for coffee before. I guess, I had ordered coffee in the drive-through at a place in North Ridge.

"It's, um, really pretty up here," I said, hoping that changing the subject would take the focus off me and allow a little room to decompress. It wasn't just a matter of changing the subject. It really was beautiful on the balcony. The back of the house overlooked a pretty steep decline into a valley. It meant there was no backyard at all, but I could only imagine the things the Krune's had witnessed as they had morning coffee out here. I was sure a deer and even elk sighting was fairly normal for them. Since we were all winter witches and cold temperatures didn't chill our skin the way they did for normal people, sitting outside to enjoy the seasonal nature was a reality and a pleasure not granted to many. This cabin really was paradise for anyone who enjoyed the outdoors.

"It's the best seat in the house," Lucas said and took his phone from the side table.

"Dax said you've been helpful at the pool. He said you track his times and give feedback," Danielle said.

"I don't know that I've been that much help, but I have been trying. His times are more accurate now and I try to pay attention to his form, not that I really know anything about competitive swimming. I just tell him what I see that I think might be a little strange."

"What have you noticed?"

"Well, when he pulls during the freestyle, his right arm is just a little different than his left. It's not a huge thing, but it is different, and even though it's a small thing I would think that it might change something in his muscles over time. He doesn't act like it bothers him or anything, but I wonder if it's adding a second or two to his time. I don't know. I'm not a swimmer or anything, so I don't know how it really works," I said, hoping my rambling wasn't too awkward. A curious look crossed Danielle's face that made me turn toward the railing ahead and focus on the mountains. I started to count the trees nearest us as I took deep breaths, getting to forty by the time Dax returned with two mugs of coffee. He handed one to me and leaned against the railing with his own in his hands. I noticed that he'd changed into gym clothes, a pair of shorts and a long-sleeve shirt were not at all weather-appropriate for anyone but a winter witch.

"How's your shoulder been, Dax?" Danielle asked as he raised his mug to his lips.

"Fine," he said with a shrug. "Why?"

"Margot said you pull your right arm at a slight angle when you swim," she said. I dribbled a little coffee in my lap before I could rest the mug on my knee. Dax glanced at me before returning his focus to his mom.

"It doesn't hurt at all. I've been lifting normally," he said with a shrug. "Well, I guess it's been a little sore, but I didn't think much of it."

"You're swimming form is off. I bet it's adding more resistance to your right arm than your left. I bet you'd swim faster if you focused on keeping both sides even and then you wouldn't be sore on the right side," I said, wondering if I should have said anything at all as I watched the smirk spread on his mom's face.

"We should get a video tomorrow morning, and we can watch it back," Dax said glancing at his mom. "I know what you're thinking. I have been rehabbing it. I do the band exercises when I do weights downstairs."

"Yes, but the reason some people are so prone to reinjury is because they aren't practicing good form, or they get lax about it after an injury. Margot is right. You wouldn't be sore if you focused on keeping even strokes," she said.

Dax nodded slowly. "This is why I keep you around." He smiled my way.

"Remember that first day you gave me lessons and you harped on me about keeping my pull even?" I raised my eyebrows at him as I lifted my mug to my lips, the steam warming my face.

"Fair point," Dax said with a laugh and lifted his mug in a toast to me. "Anything else I should know?"

"You look like a toe in your swim cap."

The cackle the comment got out of his father practically bounced off the mountains. His mom covered her mouth as she laughed, sitting so far on the edge of her rocker now that I worried it would dump her onto the deck. Dax's mouth was agape, amusement in his eyes as he stared back at me.

"A toe? That's all you got, Sinclair?" Dax asked, arms out by his sides.

"After practice, you smell like one too," I said, barely holding in my laughter as I said the words. His dad only laughed harder, red in the face.

"It's the swim cap, babe," Danielle said over her husband's laughing. "You're blond and the one you wear is gold."

"The gold is easier to see in the water," Dax said like it was obvious.

"And it makes you look like a toe," his dad said and decended into laugher again that quickly turned into coughing.

"Geez! I'll wear the blue from now on." Dax leaned against the rail and switched his coffee from his left to his right hand. "At least it covers more than what Margot had on."

I nearly spit out my coffee.

"Um, hot," I explained before anyone could ask. Neither of

his parents seemed to read too far into his comment. "There was nothing wrong with my, um, swim cap."

"Just a little small," Dax said with a shrug. It was so subtle in his expression, just the slightest twitch at the corner of his mouth, but that onery look was there and it warmed my heart more than a steaming mug of coffee ever could.

"Good thing I got a new one," I said before hiding my surely reddening face behind my coffee as I took as long a sip as I could stand. Dax laughed when I lowered the mug.

"Isn't that, like scalding hot still?" he asked with a smile. He knew exactly what he was doing. I tried nudging his foot but missed and kicked his shin instead. He flinched, sending a wave of coffee over the sleeve of his shirt.

"Oh! I'm sorry," I said.

"He deserved it," Lucas said with a wave. "It's about time for your lift anyway, right?"

Dax looked at his watch and then used his clean sleeve to wipe the drips from the bottom of the mug. Typical boy.

"You're right," he said and then looked at me as he inched toward the sliding door to his room. "Give me like five seconds to change and then you can come with me to check out the gym."

Dax slid the door shut and immediately pulled his shirt off, walking into the middle of the room and tucking his fingers into the waistband of his sweatpants without giving the curtain a second look. I pivoted in my chair before he could pull the pants down, catching his mom's eyeroll.

"Dax! Curtain's open!" Lucas yelled. A moment later I heard the door slide open again.

"Well, I guess that officially makes us friends now," Dax said and patted me on the shoulder.

"If that's what makes it official then you're friends with every neighbor and guest at the country club," his dad grumbled and reached for his book on the side table. Danielle nudged him with her foot before lifting her mug from the table.

"Come on," Dax said, giving me little time to climb out of the deep rocking chair. I sloshed coffee onto the deck as I stood. I closed the sliding door behind us, pulling the curtain shut for good measure. I heard Dax chuckle behind me.

"For the record, I wasn't looking," I said and turned around.

He smiled back and crossed his arms. "Why are you so red, Sinclair?"

"Because I'm embarrassed for you," I said, a little surprised at myself by the bold comment. Dax gasped and clutched his chest like I'd just shot him.

"Ouch! You don't have to dog on a guy's manhood," he laughed.

I walked past him, kicking a pair of underwear he'd left on the floor out of the way as I went.

"For the record, I wasn't looking," I said and looked up at him. "But I think you just told me all I need to know. Doesn't sound like I'm missing out."

It took a moment for it to sink in. Dax stared at me in shock until that onery grin spread across his face and he shook his head. His cheeks were turning pink.

"Some friend," he snorted.

"Friends don't wonder what friends look like naked," I said with a shrug.

Dax pointed a finger at me. "You're right. It's weird. Touché."

He was still snickering when he led me back into the hallway.

Chapter 14

It was strange being in a gym and not working out, strange but kind of nice. I sat on the padded bench while Dax did squats with the barbell loaded across his shoulders. He let out a deep huff each time he straightened up, powering through his final set with his eyes set on the closed garage door ahead. He let the bar clatter to the floor once he finished, slowly walking toward the garage door and then back, offering a tired smile when he noticed me watching.

"What does your family do for Christmas?" he asked as he stopped in front of the barbell.

"We do a big meal on Christmas Eve and then we open presents in the morning. That's pretty much it. Winter Solstice is the big winter holiday for us," I said.

Dax leaned over to pull the weights from the bar, carrying them one at the time to the stand in the corner.

"A true winter witch, through and through," he said and sat on the opposite side of the bench from me. I stood up and lifted the now empty barbell and carried it to the rack on the opposite wall. Once it was back in place, I pull the thickest resistance band from where it hung next to a pair of ten-pound plates.

"You need to work on your shoulder," I told him as I looped the band around the lowest rung. I waited as he crossed the room to join me.

"I've been doing more weights," Dax said, "Focusing on that shoulder."

"It's not that. It's your form. It's like you've conditioned it into a particular position, and you're not used to how it should feel. How long has it been since you injured it?" I asked, stepping aside and holding the ends of the band out for him to take. He did with a sigh.

"I've always had some issues with it since I injured it in high school. Do you remember? Daren and I were in that car accident and it tweaked my shoulder right before the state swim meet. I shouldn't have swam, but it was state and I just pretended that it wasn't that bad. I got out the pool and asked to go straight to the trainer who told me I was an idiot," Dax said with a laugh.

"You won," I said.

Dax's smile dimmed when he looked up at me. God, why couldn't I be better at hiding my frustrations? Why was I comparing my accident to Dax's now? They weren't the same. It didn't hospitalize him. It didn't leave him with tendon issues and nerve damage. It wasn't the same and it wasn't like he was acting like it was or trying to throw it in my face that he was able to power through the pain and win the state title just weeks after the accident and I couldn't even complete a stupid warm-up drill.

"All right," Dax said, pulling me out of my thoughts. "What do I do?"

"Hold the bands and move your arms as if you're doing the backstroke," I told him, moving to stand behind him so I could watch his form. Just a few reps in, I noticed the slight difference in his shoulders. It was so subtle, subtle enough that I was a little surprised with myself that I'd noticed it at the pool at all.

"They feel the same," Dax said.

"Because I was right, and you're used to bad form. Your right arm should be angled a little more," I told him and moved forward. I pressed a hand to his back, and he froze with his arm raised, muscles tensed against the resistance bands. I ran my hand over his hard bicep, lifting his elbow just a fraction so its position matched the other. I held his elbow there for a moment.

"Do you feel the difference?" I asked.

"Oh. Yeah. I see what you mean now," he said after a beat. He relaxed when I backed up, lowering his arms and turning to face me with the resistance band between both his hands. "Margot, can I say something, one friend to another?"

I looked up from the outline of his sweaty abs through his T-shirt and wished I hadn't. I could tell from the serious look on his face that I wasn't going to like whatever he had to say.

"Sure," I said.

"I say this because I care about you," he started, twisting the bands between his hands before letting out a sigh and tossing them aside. "Your family is the richest is the whole coven. You go to a great college, make good grades, are so down to Earth considering the number of countries you visited before you could even drive ..." He snorted and used the hem of his shirt to wipe the sweat from his face before he looked straight back at me and continued. "Things aren't going the way you want them to. You have to wait to see a doctor. You are back home. It sucks. I don't want you to think that I'm insensitive or anything, but you have to accept that you have to wait and find something to do in the meantime that doesn't lead to self-destruction."

Locus of control.

I was sure it was what Hadiza had been itching to tell me since I started therapy and was just waiting for me to come to the same conclusion on my own. Was I self-destructing though? I was following the doctor's orders and not doing any workouts that were high impact. I wasn't even lifting weights. I was doing everything I'd been told I could do while I wait to see the specialist. How was I being self-destructive? Why did everyone act like I shouldn't be pissed about it?

"I'm not self-destructing," I said as calmly as I could.

Dax nodded for a moment.

"You're different when we hang out. It's like you let your guard down and just enjoy the moment for once, forget all about being sad. I just want you to know that you can be like that all the time, if you want."

Again, why did everyone act like it was a choice to be sad?

"Thanks," I told him. "Can I tell you something, one friend to another?"

"Sure."

"You stink. You stink bad. So, if we are done in the gym, I think I'll just head home for the night," I said, glad when he smiled back at me. He pulled his shirt off and tossed it at me as I started for the door. I tried to dodge it, but it wrapped around my pants and I had to do an awkward jiggle to dislodge it. Dax laughed and pressed the button for the garage door and I waited for it to roll up enough so I could slip out.

"If I stink so bad, you sure you want to be stuck in the truck the whole drive down the mountain with me?" Dax asked as he followed me to his truck, swiping his shirt from the garage floor and pulling it back on once he reached the front of the truck.

"Good point. I could just walk. The cold doesn't affect winter witches, so it's not like I'd be cold and then I could avoid smelling like an onion when I get home," I teased.

Dax let out a mocking laugh and patted the hood of his truck.

"Get in, Sinclair," he called out as he climbed into the driver's seat.

❄

CHRISTMAS EVE FELT weird from the moment I got out of bed and went downstairs to help my mom get started on the waffle bar. We talked about school and training with Dax as we put toppings in bowls and made the batter, but she seemed tense, and I couldn't blame her. It wasn't until Marlee and Dad joined us that I realized the weird feeling I had was sadness, sadness, and maybe a little anger that even now on Christmas Eve and after their so-called amicable divorce announcement they still managed to slip away to check their emails and make notes.

I'd caught Marlee's expressions enough times across the table to know that she felt the same way. The trend continued, not even lunch with Jared and Madison easing the tension. Madison talked on and on about wedding plans and what changes they were making in the mercantile for the spring. Jared was a good buffer between Dad and Mom, but even their talk of the Superbowl didn't totally distract from the tension in the room which only got worse when they left.

"I think we should eat the leftover ribs from lunch and toss together a salad," Mom said after unloading the dishwasher. She held a pan between her hands as she spoke, looking down at it like it would be a shame to dirty it again with yet another meal.

"It's Christmas Eve," Dad said.

"I'm tired. I don't want to cook."

"We always do a big meal for Christmas Eve."

"Yeah. I don't really want to cook. You can take the lead, if you want," she said and sat the pan on the stove. A beat of silence passed through the kitchen as my mom and dad exchanged positions, Mom sinking into a bar stool and opening her laptop while Dad pulled out a package of ground beef from the fridge and plopped it on the counter.

"Did someone disconnect the printer? My computer says it's offline," Mom said, turning in her seat to look at Marlee and I on the couch. Marlee looked up from her book just long enough to shake her head.

"I don't go in the office," I told her.

"I took the printer to the country club cabin," Dad said as he plopped the beef into the pan. He turned around and pulled a cutting board from beneath the counter, not pausing until he caught the look on my mom's face. "What?"

"Why did you take the printer? Why would you take a whole printer to a space you're only going to be in for another week?" she asked.

Dad shrugged and turned to the fridge again. "I use it more than you do for work, and I had work to do."

"I also use it for work, and it was already set up her. That office was set up specifically for you. I've never had a workspace here and now you get to take the printer and have two?"

"No. I took the printer so that my office can be in the country club cabin where I am staying. I have an office there and now you finally have an office here."

"If it's my office then why are all your things still in there? I can't use the desk because you have files there that you say I can't move."

"And you can't move them. I'll take them with me when I get a briefcase or something I can lock them in. I can't just have files in the new cabin with the cleaning ladies in and out all day," Dad said and turned from the fridge, setting a plastic bag of bell peppers on the cutting board hard enough that one rolled out and onto the floor.

"Margot," Dad said as he picked up the bell pepper from the floor and began to wash it in the sink. "Can you take over dinner? I'm making a chili."

"Where are you going?" Mom asked him as he put the pepper back on the cutting board.

"There's a lock on our suitcases. I'm going to take the carry-on and lock the files in there," he said and moved to the end of the counter. "That way you can have the office."

"But I was using the carry-on," Mom said, her laptop screen going black behind her.

"Then I don't know what you want me to do," Dad said, his frustration finally creeping into his tone. "Margot, can you come stir the meat? You should add a little more seasoning too."

Marlee's book was sitting in her lap now and the way she looked at me reminded me of that time she was missing three front teeth and insisted on wearing her hair in two braids every day. Madison would pull her hair when she helped braid it before school if she was annoyed enough, sometimes to the point of tears. Marlee would never cry though. She'd just shrink and go quiet and stare off at the buildings that whizzed by on our way to school or disappear in some corner with a book where I would inevitably find her and talk to her until she would force me out and go back to whatever she was doing, much less tense and looking far less stressed than before I stepped in.

"Can you stir the meat, Super Star?" Dad asked again, his

tone so much sweeter than before, almost reassuring, that something deep inside me cracked and I was on my feet and between the living room and the kitchen before I knew it.

"I'm tired of being in the middle. I am dealing with so much on my own and I can't focus on it because I'm so tired from mediating all the time and I didn't even realize it. If I'm not making sure Marlee and Madison aren't going it kill each other, I'm making sure that you and Mom aren't going to collide, or I'm making sure that you and Mom don't make Marlee and Madison upset. Madison is so stuck on her wedding that is a whole year away, but she's already freaking out about having you both there," I yelled, staring down at my shocked parents.

"I didn't realize you felt that way," Mom said, shutting her laptop and sliding it behind her.

"That's because neither of you notice anything!" I knew if I didn't get mad, I would cry instead, and I didn't want comfort. I didn't want any of them to feel bad for me. I wanted them to feel bad about themselves. "You two just throw your money at your problems! You gave us whatever we wanted growing up. You only ever noticed what you wanted to about us so you could go and show us off to all your rich friends."

"You wanted to play soccer. That's why we put you in all those expensive camps and payed for the best coaches. If you didn't want to play, you should've told us, Super Star," Dad said. He took a step toward me and stopped when I raised my hands in front of me. They were shaking. I could barely get a hold of my thoughts anymore. I was so mad and sad for the version of myself that never did anything except stick to the plan and do what I was told with the promise of being a professional soccer player because I was so good at that. It was so good that I was so good at that. Why wouldn't I want that? I loved soccer. I loved being on the field, but the only thing I cared about now was how everyone had expectations for the way I should be feeling.

"I've had a lot of time to think because that's about all that I can do and what I learned is that I've had to be everyone else's support system for so long that I have no idea what I want or why," I said. Mom sat up a little straighter now, putting on that tight look I'd seen so many times when she was enduring someone she'd rather tell off.

"Your dad and I have always been supportive of you girls," she said.

"Sure, when it benefitted you."

"Margot, that's not fair," Dad snapped.

I walked back to the couch to collect my phone, ignoring the shocked expression on Marlee's face to turn and point at our parents. "What's not fair is the number of dinners I had to make so you two could go take work calls or check emails or hop on a video call. What's not fair is that Marlee and Madison always come to me first with their problems and ninety percent of the time, we sort it out together. You have no idea how many heart-breaks I sat through with Madison during high school or the number of times I drove Marlee to the bookstore because she was obviously overwhelmed by your fighting and just wanted to go do homework in peace."

"Why did you never tell us this? You all could've come to us," Mom blurted, face red with frustration as tears ran down her cheeks.

"Because when you're told as a kid just to wait until mom gets off the phone, you stop asking."

The room was silent, and I was sure they were both recovering from the low blow because my stomach ached like I'd been dealt one too. Mom let out a deep sigh and looked toward the kitchen, her eyes glassy. Dad placed his hands on his hips for a moment, taking that stance he usually did before delivering a final warning to behave. Only, his eyes were set on the floor and his lips were pressed so tightly together that it made my eyes burn.

"Super Star"

"Stop. Just, stop," I told him, my keys clanging together as I waved my hand. "For once I wish you would just see me, see us, as who we are and not what you think our potential is."

I don't know how I got the words out without a waver in my tone, because a sob burst from my lips as the cool air hit me on the porch moments later. I let myself fall apart for just a moment when I sank into the driver's seat of my Jeep, long enough to let out a single wail that made me so pathetic that I forced my hand to push the ignition button and put the Jeep in reverse before I had even calmed my breathing. The Jeep slid a little in the road, just enough to send me back to that moment before I was airborne and colliding with the tree in the ditch a year ago. I knew I couldn't stay here. I couldn't stay here and reminding myself of that over and over was how I found myself cruising up the road toward the country club and away from my messed-up family and that ditch that changed everything.

I stopped next to the curb outside that two-story cabin and began to wipe the moisture from my face. I was afraid of what I looked like, so I avoided the mirror. I could already feel that my eyes were swollen and as I rubbed them with the sleeves of my sweatshirt, I realized I'd left wearing an old pair of sweatpants from high school and the oversized sweatshirt with Will Ferrell dressed as Buddy the Elf across the chest. I groaned and let my forehead rest against the steering wheel. I stayed like that as the thoughts swirled through my mind. There were all the frustrating moments after the injury, the toughest soccer practices, and the good and bad days on the field before I graduated high school and left home. There were other moments too, like the times I convinced my sisters to go for coffee one Saturday that our parents were fighting, which started our tradition of café chats after life got chaotic.

The groan I let out developed into a kind of deranged yell that made me feel a little better and also made me feel incredibly stupid. The moment got worse when the passenger side door opened, and Dax Krune climbed in wearing a pair of jeans and a half-zip red sweater. He pulled the door shut and we sat in silence for a moment.

He never dressed up. Did he really have to show up all dressed up now, when I was wearing old sweatpants and a stupid sweatshirt that didn't even fit?

"I am not self-destructing," I finally said. What the hell? I'd already made my parents mad. I spilled an entire childhood of sisterhood secrets, so Madison and Marlee would be upset. Why not let him know that I was mad at him too for taking pity on me when the last thing I wanted was pity. I pivoted in my seat so I could look at him straight on before launching into my argument.

"You said that my family is so rich and I'm so privileged because I get whatever I want and you're right. I know that. What you don't know is that my parents fought all the time when I was growing up and that they were always somewhere else, even when they were physically present. There was always a phone or a computer or something right in front of them instead of engaging with us and I ended up holding everything together. I'm like the glue between my parents and my sisters and it was all working just fine until that stupid accident when I needed help getting upstairs at home and when everyone kept looking at me like I'd fall apart if anyone mentioned soccer. Maybe things weren't fine. I don't know, maybe they never were and all I was doing was trying to save a sinking ship. I don't really care, but I do care that people keep treating me based on how they think I should be acting because the truth is that I don't even know if I know who I really am. I'm not going to just take it anymore when someone tries to tell me what I should be feeling or how I should act or ..." I groaned and turned in my seat, so I was staring at the road again as I felt tears building in my eyes.

"I knew that I couldn't play soccer forever. Even the pros retire and do something else for a long time afterward. I'm not stupid. I know I need another plan. I just don't ... I'm not crazy smart like Marlee or extroverted enough to network my way to the top like Madison. I couldn't imagine myself doing anything my parents saw as important enough for me other than soccer and now that I'm facing being finished with that career before I can even start, I just don't know. I think a part of me didn't plan on needing to deal with all of this until I was a lot older, had a whole life of my own outside my family, and was at an age where my athletic ability declining is acceptable and not something out of my control. Why is it that everything has always been outside of my control?"

The Jeep was quiet for a long time. I only now noticed that it had started to snow as the flakes landed on the windshield and melted within seconds.

"If there's anything else you want to say, I'm all ears," Dax said. "Might as well get it all out. It might help you process how you feel about it."

I let out a deep breath, the first one I felt fill my lungs entirely since I'd left the cabin.

"I'm good. That's it."

"All right," Dax said and reached across the gearshift to turn off the ignition. He pulled the key fob from the cup holder before I could think to reach for it. "Come on."

The snow crunched under his feet as he climbed out of the Jeep and shut the door. I didn't have any choice but to go with him and despite the twist of anxiety in my gut about walking into his family's evening on Christmas Eve, it was still better than going home to face my parents and Marlee.

Chapter 15

The Krune's house looked a little like a Christmas version of Superbowl Sunday. Dax led me straight to the stairs which made my view limited, but there were paper banners of snowflakes taped along the mantle of the fireplace, plastic bowls with chips and pretzels and other snacks lined up on the kitchen counter, and the TV played a mix of trap versions of Christmas songs as photos of past Krune Christmas's flashed across the screen.

A loud cheer drew my attention for a moment as we reached the top of the stairs. There were more voices than just Daren and their parents. It made me a little nervous about joining a whole group, but also less nervous about crashing a family-only party.

"Come on," Dax said as I hesitated, pulling me out of my concern so I could follow him into his room. He shut the door behind us. He'd cleaned the entire space since I'd been here just a day ago. There weren't clothes on the floor, and it looked like he'd even wiped down the wooden floors. Dax pulled open the doors of his closet and stood looking over the clothes hanging there for a moment.

"Well, I have more ass than you do, but these should work," he said and pulled a pair of black joggers from a shelf. He slipped a sweatshirt off a hanger that had a Berkely logo across the chest before tossing both items to me.

"There's no way you have more ass than I do when my sport is all sprints. We run hills at least once a week," I said as I caught the clothes.

Dax turned from the closet with a smile on his face that made my face warm.

"That bikini you wore to our first swimming workout kind of gave away all your assets, no pun intended," he said with a laugh and pulled my keys from his pocket. He sat them on the bedside table. "I got more ass than you, Sinclair."

"I got in a fight with my family on Christmas Eve and found out I have no butt. This has been a great holiday," I grumbled as I folded the clothes over my arm.

"I didn't mean ..." Dax let out a sigh before continuing. "I only meant that my pants are bigger, and they might not fit you super well. Your ass is fine. You're a college athlete. Of course, you have a nice ass. It's just not big enough to fit in the pants of a guy that's probably a hundred pounds heavier than you are."

I was suddenly very aware of how small I was next to him. I wished I could pretend that I'd never worn that stupid bikini to the pool. My entire ass was basically out. I almost fell down that embarrassing rabbit hole all over again until he started talking.

"You can have the room. I'll be downstairs with the others. Don't feel like you have to join, if you don't want to. I won't tell them you're here. It's just my parents, Daren, and two of Daren's friends who are here for the holiday. They're winter warlocks. The bathroom is just down the hall. Make yourself comfortable. I have my phone on me, so text if you need anything. I can bring food up, if you ..."

"Oh. Um, no. I'm fine. Thank you," I answered, hugging the clothes tighter to my stomach as he nodded slowly, looking over the room as though assessing if there was anything else he might have forgotten to mention.

"I'll be downstairs," he said and left, shutting the door behind him.

Dax was right. He did have more ass than I did, but the joggers didn't look half-bad on me. I changed into his clothes and spent a lot of time in the bathroom splashing cool water over my face until the puffiness had mostly subsided around my eyes. Part of me wanted to avoid people at all costs. Knowing what to expect and that Dax hadn't told anyone I was here made it a lot easier to leave the room and go downstairs toward the sounds of laughter. I stopped in the living room to listen to the voices, putting together a mental picture of the six of them gathered in the dining room when the photos flashing across the TV screen caught my attention.

They were randomized. A photo of Dax and Daren standing next to a snowman in the yard when they were grade school age was replaced with a more recent photo of the family sitting on the second-floor deck together. The next photo was of Daren sitting on the floor in front of a Christmas tree as he held up a sweatshirt with a University of Colorado logo across the chest, wrapping paper strewn around him on the floor. The screen flashed and the next photo faded in. It was Dax standing on the tallest podium in a pair of swimming jammers with his goggles perched on top of his head. He had a medal around his neck that was in the shape of a Christmas tree. He was probably twelve or thirteen years old.

"Have you had dinner?"

I turned from the TV to face Danielle Krune. She didn't seem surprised at all to see me and was carrying a plate filled with a little bit of everything. There was a pot roast, a small serving of potatoes, a handful of pretzels and chips, and even a brownie with some red and green sprinkles on top.

"Sorry. I didn't mean to crash the party or anything," I said, feeling my cheeks heat.

She waved a hand and held the plate to me. I was hungry enough that I took it and didn't wait before popping a chip in my mouth.

"Dax didn't sneak you in as quietly as he thought," she explained.

My eyes burned and I quickly blinked away the tears. This was not going well. Maybe there was a reason everyone seemed to pity me.

Danielle gasped. "This is one I love, but I didn't at the time. It was a horrible day."

It took me a moment to realize she was talking about the photos. She nodded toward the TV screen where a photo of the entire Krune family was on display, the four of them standing in front of the cabin with strange smiles on their faces. It was like they were all posed, Daren's scowl giving away the true emotions behind all the forced smiles. Danielle and Lucas didn't look a ton different than they did now, but I'd known Dax long enough that I could tell that he was probably a freshman at the time.

"We came to Crescent Peak later that year because Daren went to a basketball camp at the start of Christmas Break. He didn't end up getting to go for very long though because the boys got into a car accident and Daren broke his leg. It took him out for most of the basketball season and Dax had to take time off from his private lessons to heal. They were both off that day. Traveling in general can be stressful and it only made things worse. They kept arguing. Daren ended up punching Dax in the backseat of the car. I don't know if he would appreciate me saying this, but I will anyway. Dax is my more sensitive child. He feels things deeper, and he doesn't usually react that much when his brother isn't the nicest, but that day after Daren punched him in the arm, Dax turned around and punched him in the face. Lucas and I lost it."

"I can't imagine Dax getting mad like that," I said, studying the photo of them in front of the cabin before it changed to one of Danielle and Lucas kissing and holding a set of keys between them, the cabin in the background.

"He doesn't normally, which was why his dad and I were so reactive to it. We were nearly here, so the remainder of the drive was a screaming match between the four of us, blood in the car from Daren's nose, and Lucas and I grounded them both and sent them to their rooms as soon as we got here. Dax was always our easy child, so it was strange to us how he'd reacted. Not only that, but he said some pretty terrible things the next day that got him in more trouble."

"I never saw him as the kind to push limits," I said as the TV changed again to another family photo in front of the Christmas tree, this one from just a year ago.

"He's not. Dax is a people pleaser. I think it's part of what has made him so successful in swimming. He's easy to coach," Danielle said, turning from the screen to look at me. "His dad and I were so surprised by his behavior that we came down pretty hard on him, too hard. In hindsight, we punished him more for being mouthy than we did Daren for worse behaviors. We just didn't expect it of Dax and it wasn't until I caught him in the gym one morning that I realized he was just stressed. We do a lot of out-of-character things when we are stressed like punching brothers or losing our patience with a sweet boy."

"That was all right before the state swim meet. Dax said he shouldn't have competed and did anyway to win the state title. Training through an injury is stressful," I said, watching as the photo switched again to one of Dax and Daren in the middle of a snowball fight in the yard.

"He wasn't supposed to compete. You're right. He insisted and so the coaches let him. He didn't train through the injury though. He didn't swim much at all until that day," Danielle said as the TV switched to a new photo again. "I felt bad about being so tough on him, so I made him help me with breakfast in the morning so we could talk. He ended up enjoying it. He likes to cook and he's good at it, but baking is what he really enjoys doing. We all really liked swimming season because it meant there were extra cookies and fancy breads around the house."

"Baking?" I asked, turning away from the photo of Daren and Dax next to gingerbread houses. Danielle smiled and nodded, taking the empty plate from my hands and setting it on the coffee table.

"When he needs a break, he finds something to bake. Mostly he experiments with making baked goods a little healthier. You should ask him about his protein waffle recipe," she said and moved toward the front door. "Want to join us in the dining room? There's a contest going to see who can make the best gingerbread house."

"Um, yes. Thank you," I said, confused when she opened the front door and stepped onto the porch. The doorbell rang through the house, enticing a black cat I didn't know they had to crawl out from under the couch.

"I'll get it!" Danielle called toward the dining room. I was a little surprised when the cat easily leaped onto the couch and then the armrest to brush against my arm. "Do you have pets?"

"No. Madison is allergic," I said and scratched the cat behind the ears. "I'm not a huge pet person, so I've never really thought about it. Marlee always wanted a cat though."

Thinking about my sisters reminded me why I was here in the first place. If Christmas Eve had just been the three of us, that stupid fight would never have happened.

"Ready?" Danielle asked, already inching toward the dining room. I nodded and followed her.

❄

I WASN'T SURPRISED that my gingerbread house place last. I did not have an eye for design the way Madison did at all. Not only that, but my construction was subpar, and the entire thing collapsed before judging. I did enjoy eating the pieces though. I left my phone in Dax's room, so it wasn't until nearly ten that I overcame my dread to check it.

"I can't believe no one has called," I said. There were a few text messages, one from Dad telling me to be safe and another from Marlee detailing what happened after I left. I clicked out of that one without reading it.

"I let them know you're here," Dax said.

When I turned to look at him, he was shirtless. Why was he always shirtless? He tossed his sweater toward a corner of the room. Jeans just fit so differently on his hips than the tight swimwear I was used to. They sagged along his hipbones, only making his abs look more pronounced somehow. Maybe I just hadn't noticed before. I knew he was muscular, your typical swimmer physique with round shoulders and a narrow waist. He'd indulged in lots of sweets and even had a beer when Daren and his friends opened a pack. Still, his stomach was flat.

"I'm going to the bathroom," I said and left before he could reply. The bathroom smelled like boy, that deep scent of men's cologne with a tinge of sweat from a pile of clothes next to the shower that looked to be Daren's. My eyes were less puffy than before, but still puffy enough that everyone surely knew I'd had a rough night. I could only imagine how horrible they looked when Dax had found me.

I did my best to freshen up, waiting long enough to give Dax time to change. A knock came at the door that startled me, causing me to knock over the soap despenser.

"I'm in here," I called out.

"It's me," Dax said through the door. "You okay?"

I took a deep breath and opened the door. He wore a pair of flannel pajama pants and a gray T-shirt. He looked over me before turning to the counter and taking a toothbrush from a black toiletries bag setting on the counter. He put some toothpaste on the bristles and popped it in his mouth before pulling open one of the drawers and removing a new toothbrush, still sealed in the packaging from a stack.

"You can stay here tonight, if you want. Daren's friends are staying downstairs, so you can crash in my room," he said as he handed me the toothbrush.

I don't know what I'd expected. I didn't want to go home. I hadn't really planned to, but I also hadn't thought about sleeping here. I turned the toothbrush over in my hands for a moment as he began brushing his teeth.

"Thanks, Dax," I said and pulled the plastic away from the brush. I brushed my teeth next to him, learning that Dax tracked how long he'd been brushing using his smart watch. I cringed a little when it came time to spit, wiping my mouth with the back of my hand as I straightened up. I tugged the elastic from my hair and let the bun unwravl so my hair hung around my shoulders.

"You should wear your hair down more," Dax told me as he held a brush out. I took it and began brushing the tangles out. "It's pretty."

"You should dress up more often," I said as I finished, accepting that I'd have bedhead in the morning.

Dax let out a laugh. "What you saw is the only pair of jeans that I own."

"You only have one pair in your whole wardrobe?" I asked as he moved into the hallway.

"How many do you own, Sinclair? You're like the queen of athleisure. I bet you own more leggings than anything," he said, opening his bedroom door and waiting for me to walk in ahead of him. I didn't reply and not just because he was right. I hadn't thought too much about how many pairs of jeans I had until now and I was pretty sure I only had two. I knew that I only had two nice bras that I rarely wore and maybe nine sports bras that were regularly rotated through my weekly wardrobe.

Dax pulled the sheets back on his bed and flipped the light switch, so the only light came from the sliding door. I heard him settle into the mattress with a sigh. I almost asked where he expected me to sleep, but it was so obvious that the words never materialized. I sat on the edge of the bed and slowly laid down. The bed was large enough that we didn't touch.

"Hey, Margot?"

"Yeah?"

He let out a deep breath. "It's okay if you don't know what you want, but there has to be something you'd like to do, maybe something you've never allowed yourself to do in the past."

"Like what? Are you asking me if I have a bucket list or something?"

"I mean, if you want to call it that."

"What kind of thing am I supposed to want? Sky diving? Skinny dipping?"

"Skinny dipping!" Dax laughed and I could feel him move in the bed. "That's something I've never done. That could be kind of fun."

Madison had gone skinny dipping once. It was a dare at a sleepover when she was in high school and gained her a lot of attention from boys when the word had gotten around.

"Maybe someday," I said, surprised I was even considering it. It was so unlike me to do something risky. Maybe that was the point. "You know, yeah. Maybe that would be fun."

"I've been in a lot of pools, but never naked."

"Dax," I chided, unable to keep from giggling. "I guess, I'll add it to my list."

"Definitely add it to your list. We'll keep adding to it in the morning," he said and adjusted again beside me. Maybe it wasn't a bad idea, skinny dipping, and the whole list thing. Maybe what I needed was to be a little freer like Madison. I'd always admired the way Marlee didn't seem to care at all about what people thought. Maybe what I needed was to forget about my injury and soccer and just come back to it when I was more relaxed. It's what Dax did. Dax was on his way to the Olympic trials. The more I thought about it, the more I was sure he was right.

❄

THE ROOM WAS HOT. Winter witches didn't get hot like this. Witches had powers guided by nature that meant we could regulate our temperature. Winter witch or summer witch, I shouldn't feel this hot. I knew it was a dream when the sound of a car door shutting drew my attention to the left and Dax was sitting there in his Berkeley sweats, hair still damp from showering. He smiled at me, and I reached for him.

I pulled his lips to mine by the back of his head. His hands found their way to my jacket, tugging the zipper down as we kissed until he could push it off my shoulders. I pulled at the hem of his sweatshirt, eager to feel the contour of those swimmer's abs.

"Backseat," he said against my lips. "Come on. Backseat."

We pulled apart my heart picked up pace as I stepped out of the truck and climbed into the backseat the same time he did. As soon as he sat down, I climbed on top. I straddled him, feeling the hardness press against me. He stifled my moan with a kiss, fumbling with the hem of my shirt enough that I broke our kiss so I could pull it off. He traced his fingers up my abs, over the band of my sports bra, and drew a light circle around my breast before giving it a tight squeeze and moving to the other. As I reached for his waistband, he lifted me off of him and sat me in the seat beside him. Then he pulled me back into his lap so that I was facing away from him now. He held me tight, one hand cupping my breast and the other easily sliding between the fabric of my sweatpants and underwear. I bowed against his chest, the back of my head resting on his shoulder.

I could feel his breath on my ear when he asked, "You up for the challenge, Sinclair?"

Then something landed hard against my stomach, and I was startled. I was staring at the ceiling of Dax's bedroom now. He was still asleep, but he had shifted and now had an arm draped across my midsection. I was lying in his bed, still very aroused from the dream, and the fact that I was wearing his clothes that smelled just like him nearly threw me over the precipice.

I managed to slip out of the bed without waking him. I gathered my things from the side table and made my way down the hall, down the stairs, and out the door. I didn't realize that it was just two in the morning until I was pulling into the driveway next to Mom's SUV.

Chapter 16

I MADE it to my bedroom without anyone noticing. Dax and I didn't have plans to work out in the morning because of the holiday and thank God for that because not only did I not go back to sleep, but I wasn't sure I could face him in that little of clothing just hours after the dream I'd had. I sat in my bedroom scrolling my phone, switching between apps as I ran into soccer content until I decided to do something productive instead. I went to my desk and opened a Google Doc and started making a list of things I'd like to do before ... I hadn't thought too much about what kind of a list this was. Things to do before you die didn't really fit the bill.

To Do Before Soccer

I LISTED SKINNY DIPPING FIRST, still feeling a little stupid for agreeing that it would be fun to do sometime. I knew the point was to loosen up, but who was I kidding? I could pretend all I wanted, but I'm not Madison or Marlee and that was fine. I was Margot Sinclair. Just thinking about what that meant made my chest ache.

My phone buzzed on the desk and I glanced down at the screen, heart skipping when I saw it was a text from Dax.

. . .

> You snuck out before I could give you your Christmas present.
>
> Can I come by later?

PRESENT? Why did there have to be a present? What kind of present did a guy give to a friend who was a girl anway?

> No. Family stuff.

I CRINGED as I hit send. It was too harsh. I wasn't mad at him. It's not like anything happened for me to be mad or sad or anything. I just felt awkward as hell and I just wanted to be friends and not weird.

> I'll let you know. We have things to do other than morning workouts. I started a list.

> An actual list? Can I help?

HE SENT HIS EMAIL, and I shared the Google Doc. A moment later and his profile appeared at the top of the page and I watched as his curser made its way down to the page until he began to add to the list.

. . .

To Do Before Soccer:

1. *Skinny dipping?*
2. *Raid the liquor cabinet at Lawson Rathbone's cabin*
3. *Go to the Winter Solstice Gala with a date*
4. *Watch a terrible movie and eat a pint of ice cream*

WHEN HE CALLED, I didn't hesitate. I wanted to talk to him. I put the phone on speaker and stared at the blinking curser.

"I hope I didn't wake you. It's only like five," I said. I heard a clang in the background, making me wonder if he'd left his house.

"I was up. No worries. I'm doing my lift early today. No swimming because of the holiday, but I wanted to do those band exercises for my shoulder again. I'll do some light lifting and probably clock a mile on the treadmill," Dax said. I heard the sound of him moving his phone around and then the line went quiet. "Did I do or say something last night?"

Here we go.

"No. You were fine. It was nice and all of you to invite me to stay and your parents were super nice about it."

"Okay. Well, I just wondered because—"

"Because I should've said something before I left. It was rude."

"No. Not that. You didn't want to go home last night, and I just assumed you wouldn't want to wake up before the sun to go back to everything there. I thought you'd be around in the morning for a while."

That was the plan. I knew I'd come back home, but I wasn't excited to get back even though it was Christmas morning. I felt more at home by the idea of watching the Krune's open presents around their Christmas tree than I did sitting with my family around ours right now.

"Yeah. Well, I don't know. It just felt ... I couldn't sleep and I can't stay away forever and I ... I didn't know what to. I just felt ..."

I leaned back in the desk chair and held my breath, fighting the emotions rising in my throat and the tears stinging my eyes. I took a deep breath and as I let it out, Dax spoke.

"You had another panic attack, didn't you?"

Another? It took me a moment to remember how he'd found me at the McAdam's mercantile. I was so embarrassed and angry with him that I didn't think about what it really was, a panic attack that he'd caught me in the middle of. God, he'd sat in the snow and was just with me through it, not even saying anything to try making it better like everyone else felt compelled to do. He just sat there, and I hated that it was exactly what I wished everyone else would do, just let me have a moment and then move on with our lives. I hated that it was exactly what I wanted and that my stupid brain had ruined it last night with that dream.

"Maybe," I said with a sigh. "I'm just not used to this. I'm usually so good under stress. I'm the player you want to take the game-winning goal because I didn't crack under pressure."

I heard the phone shift on his line again and it sounded like he took a seat.

"Sometimes, when we are so used to everything being important and everything being high stakes, we don't know how to deal with the little things like doing something just for the fun of it. I felt a little that way when I started baking. My instincts were to make it a competition and see how good I could get. You know, push the limits. Sometimes, you need to learn how to have fun. It sounds a little crazy, but I think competitive people have a hard time."

I watched the cursor blink. I could hear him breathing on the line and found myself matching his breaths, easing my anxious heart. The sound of doors in the hallway pulled me from my meditation.

"I gotta go, Dax. I'll talk to you later," I said and waited for his response as I heard another door open.

"Yeah. Okay. Merry Christmas, Margot."

"Merry Christmas, Dax."

I didn't hang up right away and neither did he. We sat in the silence for a few seconds before he hung up and then I sat a little longer, thinking about the sound of his breathing on the phone and how it had felt against my ear in my dream.

❆

CHRISTMAS DAY WASN'T AS AWKWARD as I thought it would be. We made lunch a buffet and ate it as we opened presents, so the entire event lasted just a few hours and then Dad went back to his new rental cabin and Madison and Jared left for the McAdam's house. Christmas had gotten pretty copy-paste over the years. Madison always gave everyone clothes of her own design. Marlee has given gift cards ever since the year Madison told her not to buy her any more books. Mom and Dad bought us clothes and jewelry. Jared was welcomed to the family with the promise of Denver Broncho season tickets and a spot with Dad's tailgate buddies.

Nothing was open in Crescent Peak and Mom was busy turning Dad's office into her own, so Marlee and I joined the McAdam's for an afternoon. We sat on the back porch of the mercantile, the heaters and fire pit going and hot chocolate sitting on the coffee table. Jared's mom and uncle were prepping for dinner. The smell from the smoker had me hoping we could stick around for dinner too.

"Since you two are here, can I do a final check on your dresses?" Madison asked, already setting her mug aside and standing up before either of us could replay.

Marlee groaned. "You already checked mine this week."

"Okay. Fine, but I haven't checked Margot's since she stormed out of here and I had to just run with the measurements I had. I'd like to check."

"I don't have the right kind of stuff on," I said. I wasn't sure that was true, but I doubt I was wearing light-colored underwear.

"Then strip down. It's fine. Margot, this is a reflection of my work as a designer," Madison said, slipping into that girly whine that she used when she was trying to convince boys to do something for her. She let out a squeal when I stood up. I didn't say a word as I followed her into the mercantile, but I did catch the apologetic look Marlee shot me and Jared's shrug.

"I adjusted the fit on the skirt a little so it wouldn't hug your hips as tight," Madison said as she walked to a door behind the register. She disappeared inside while I awaited my fate. The dress was just as beautiful and frightening as I remembered. The amount of skin showing made my heart skip, but my brain immediately reminded me of that bikini I wore to the pool. I had definitely worn less, and the dress really was beautiful.

"Go try it on and let me know when you're ready. I can help you zip it up." Madison shoved the dress into my hands and went back to the register where she pulled out her sewing kit.

I decided to take her advice and just strip down after I discovered that I was wearing a bright red thong. The dress revealed enough that it made it impossible to wear a bra underneath, so I slipped into it completely naked and did my best to fasten the back before pushing the curtain aside and walking into the middle of the store. Madison had moved a full-body mirror there so I could get a look at myself. I understood what she meant about the hips now. I hadn't realized how tight the skirt was before, but feeling the comfortable stretch of it at my thighs as I joined her made the entire thing feel more wearable and less ... Well, over the top.

I stepped in front of the mirror and felt the smile pull at my lips before I could process all the emotions. I didn't see how little fabric it was. Instead, I saw how it highlighted all the squats I did during team lifts. I saw the way the structured fabric gave me more of an hourglass shape and supported my boobs more than I'd ever imagined a backless dress could. I'd never felt so feminine and even better, it was comfortable despite how it looked.

"Who's out shopping on Christmas?" Madison asked.

I looked away from the mirror as she started toward the

entrance. Through the front window, I saw the bed of a truck pull into a parking spot.

"That's Dax," I said and hurried toward the dressing room.

"Isn't he your friend?'

I had to stretch to reach the zipper and even then, I couldn't get the right angle to pull it down. "Yes, but I don't want to see him like this."

The bell above the door rang just as I was ready to ask Madison to help me get out of the dress.

"Hey, Madison! Congrats on the engagement," Dax said.

"Thank you! I have most of the wedding planned already if you can believe that."

Anyone who knew Madison wouldn't be surprised by that fact. I tried again to pull the zipper down and felt my arm cramping instead.

"Is Margot around? I wanted to give her something," Dax said. I heard Madison stammering, trying to work out what lie to give him. I closed my eyes. I'd have to see him today anyway. He seemed sure of that. I also really wanted out of this dress.

"Madison, I need help with the zipper," I said.

"Margot, Dax is here! He wants to give you something. Just come out," she called back to me.

"Just come help me out of it."

"It's not that kind of white dress, Margot," Madison said with a laugh. I was relieved to hear her voice getting closer. I backed up in the dressing room to make space for her. "It's just Dax," she whispered once she'd slipped through the curtain. She gasped loud enough that I thought my heart would leap out of my throat and run away. I nearly clapped a hand over her mouth. "Dax?"

I shushed her and spun around so I didn't have to face her. God. Between my two sisters, Madison was not the one I wanted to admit my dreams to. I wasn't even sure what it all meant. I liked Dax. We were good friends. He made me feel better about everything. He made me feel like I wasn't alone in it all and I didn't have to say a word to him. He just knew. The sexy dream and the way I couldn't stop thinking about how he looked in those stupid dreams just messed it all up.

"Does he know?" Madison whispered. I heard the zipper slide down and I gladly shoved the whole dress to my knees and climbed out.

"No. Don't say anything. Don't do anything. We are just friends," I hissed and began pulling on my clothes. Madison was pink in the face when I turned around, and I could tell that she was ready to burst with excitement. "We are friends. There's nothing there. Something weird happened and it was just really embarrassing, and I want to forget about the whole thing. Please, go away. Just, go away."

"Fine. Okay," she said, her smile dimming. She slipped out of the dressing room while I was still getting dressed. I heard her say something to Dax before the sound of her heeled booties echoed off the mercantile floor.

"I guess you didn't get my text," Dax said, sounding just a few feet outside the dressing room. I fell into the wall as I tried pulling my leggings on.

"I sat it down when I got here. I haven't looked at it all afternoon," I told him as I righted myself and tugged the stretchy fabric over my butt. I pulled my sweatshirt on next and used the mirror to redo my ponytail and make sure I hadn't missed any stray hairs.

"I wanted to give this to you before the gala," Dax said as I walked out of the dressing room. He pulled a piece of paper from his back pocket and handed it to me. "Merry Christmas."

It was folded in half long-ways. I unfolded it and thought I was looking at a paper receipt before I saw the words *United States Olympic Swimming Trials* in bold at the top. Beneath it was a date, time, and barcode. After a long moment, I finally looked up at his wide smile.

"You did not just give me a ticket to the Olympic trials," I said, looking down to check the date again.

Dax laughed. "My parents bought a bunch so they could fill a section with all our friends and family. Why wouldn't I give one to you?"

"Okay. I guess I just didn't know that I was ..." I wasn't sure what to say. We were friends. He had a bunch of tickets reserved for friends. It wasn't weird. Maybe for other people it was weird to give such an expensive and once-in-a-lifetime gift, but not where we came from.

Dax's smile dimmed and he shifted from one foot to the other. He took a slow step closer, glancing toward the back door which was still shut and muffled the sound of laughter on the back porch.

"I don't mean to get all mushy and stuff or anything. Okay, so, I'm just going to say it because you've been pretty vulnerable and real with me and ..." Dax sucked in a deep breath, his cheeks turning pink as he thought for a moment. It made my heart speed up. I was sure I could see a glimmer of hope in his eyes when he looked up at me. It was almost an unspoken message that yes, we were on the same page and even though I didn't want to admit it aloud he already knew.

Dax let out a sigh and held his hands out in resignation.

"I feel close to you. I've never had a lot of friends, and I don't care to have a lot of friends, but it's hard to find someone who really gets it. I have teammates I'm close with, but they're all competitive and it's not like an outside-the-pool friendship where we can just hang out and have other things in common to do. The people I hang out with outside the team are good friends and all, but they also don't understand what it's like to be this kind of an athlete. You get it and I feel like we've both been through some of the same struggles. You know where I've come from, how I grew up. It's just so easy talking to you and it's like you've been with me through it all the entire time, even though we didn't really talk through school and we don't ever see each other at college. So, thank you. Take the ticket. It would mean a lot to me if you would come. I bet my family would let you fly out with them. They all think you're great, by the way."

"Well, thank you," I said and folded the ticket again between my hands. The pause was deafening. "Dax," I said and looked up from my hands. He looked like he already knew what I was going to say and it made my stomach do somersaults. "You're a really good friend. I think I needed you, well, needed someone to ground me and remind me the world is bigger than just what's in front of me."

He smiled a little, but it looked almost sad. Why did I always do that? I had to make this amazing gift about myself and stupid soccer. Even when I was thanking him for showing me more, I was thinking about my shortcomings on the field. The irony was not lost on me and I hated myself for it.

"I think we'll be friends for a long time," he said with a laugh. "You can be grounded for life."

I laughed, thankful for the humor. It felt a lot less awkward, and it was almost like being back at the rec center together, just us. He pulled me into a tight hug and the smell of clean linen and sandalwood made my chest tighten just before he released me and took a step back.

"I added to your list," he said.

"Yeah. I know. I saw. We are not raiding your friend's liquor cabinet."

"We definitely are," Dax said with a scoff as we walked to the entrance of the mercantile. "He makes plenty of money and he told us to make ourselves at home. He won't mind."

I ignored him and opened the door, a gust of wind carrying snowflakes through the door. Dax paused to brush them from my sweatshirt. His gaze flicked from my shoulder to my face, and he smiled.

"I guess the next time I see you will be at the gala," he said and started to back toward the parking lot. I watched him go, giving a final wave as he climbed into his truck before I shut the door.

Chapter 17

Marlee and I didn't want to spend any more time than we had to at the cabin, so we spent the entire day of the Winter Solstice Gala at the McAdam's to get ready. Marlee didn't complain about the tedious process once. She let Madison put more make-up on her than normal and let her curl her hair. She waited silently when it was my turn in the chair, but she didn't leave the room once and there wasn't a single fight the entire day. It was a Christmas miracle.

"Marlee, what do you think about getting a cat?" I asked once Madison had finished curling my hair. They both looked at me like I'd lost my head.

"I'd rather have a cat than a dog. That was a little out of left field," Marlee grumbled.

"If I wasn't allergic, I'd love to have a dog. Cats don't act like they even like humans," Madison scoffed and approached me with a small brush and an eyeshadow palate.

"That's why I'd have a cat. We have that in common," Marlee said with a smile. She was standing at the far side of the bathroom vanity looking at herself in the mirror. She'd been there long enough that I couldn't tell from her nondescript expression if she was admiring herself or looking for her usual sullen, dark-clothed self in the reflection.

"Why are you asking anyway?" Madison asked, setting the

eyeshadow on the counter and turning with an eyeliner pencil in her hand.

"Can I skip the eyeliner and just wear mascara? I don't want it to smudge," I told her. I could see she wanted to argue, but she tossed the eyeliner back into her cosmetics bag and fished out a tube of mascara instead.

"Like I was saying, that question really was out of nowhere." She lifted the wand to my eye, and I stayed perfectly still as she worked, trying to focus on Marlee who'd stopped staring at herself in the mirror and was now bucking her heels around her ankles.

"I was just wondering. The Krune's have a cat."

"Am I still dropping you off there on the way to the club?" Marlee asked. It was the plan. Madison has gotten so giddy about whatever was between Dax and I that it made me cringe when I talked about him around her. I made sure not to look her way when I answered.

"Yes. I'm going to hitch a ride with him," I said.

"Hitch a ride?" Madison exclaimed and whirled around to face me. "Dax is not your Uber. He's your date tonight."

The way she said the last part made my face heat.

"We're going together so the elders won't bug us about not being in relationships."

I caught Madison rolling her eyes as she put on her lipstick in the mirror. The door opened and Joanne McAdams peeked her head in. She smiled and moved all the way into the room, closing the door behind her.

"You all look beautiful!"

"Thank you," Madison said and surged forward to hug her future mother-in-law.

"Thank you for letting us come over so early," I told her, motioning between myself and Marlee who sat up straighter on the lid of the toilet.

"Yeah. Thank you. That casserole at lunch was great, by the way." Marlee stood up and gathered her keys from the counter as Madison shoved the last of her things into her clutch. I stood up from the chair and checked my phone. Part of me expected Dax to send a message, but he hadn't texted all day. I sent him a message that Marlee and I would be leaving soon as I followed the group into the hallway.

"Is that the wedding dress?" Mark yelled from the living room down the hall. I heard him groan and launch into a defense as soon as Joanne and Madison started into their reprimands.

"I know you aren't supposed to see the dress before the wedding, but brides these days aren't all that traditional. I thought I'd ask," Mark said. When I joined them in the living room, I could see from the smirk on his face that he knew exactly the kind of reaction he'd get from the comment. It was easy to see why Jared was as onery as he was.

"Okay. We're ready, Jared!" Madison called out. She hugged Joanne again and then Mark, though she swatted his arm when she pulled away and they both laughed at whatever it was he'd told her. "Can you get a few of us?"

"Yeah. Of course," Joanne said and took the phone from Madison.

Madison pulled Marlee and me by our wrists to the Christmas tree. I stood on her left and Marlee stood on her right, the three of us pressed together and smiling at the camera as Mrs. McAdams snapped photo after photo. Madison didn't allow us to break our positions until we heard a pair of men's dress shoes on the hardwood floor.

Jared was the kind of outdoorsy man who looked just a little out of place in a suit, even as handsome as he looked in one. He'd left most of the stubble on his chin, which Madison ran her fingers over when she rose on her toes to kiss him. He smiled when she tugged him into our places by the Christmas tree to pose for more photos. Marlee and I took a few with them before I made up the excuse of being late to the Krune's and we left them to finish their photoshoot in the living room.

"They are cotton candy," Marlee said as we buckled ourselves into our seats in her Jeep.

"What do you mean?" I asked, noticing how high the slit in

my skirt was now that I was seated and the fabric fanned around my thigh. I'd have to make sure to put a napkin in my lap at the dinner table or maybe just not sit at all.

"Madison and Jared as so sweet and fluffy and pink like cotton candy. I love them, but it hurts my stomach a little," she said and put the Jeep in reverse.

I wasn't sure what to say because I wasn't sure what she meant. Madison and Jared were adorable together and it was reassuring to me when I saw the way he looked at her, especially when she didn't notice him staring. He adored her and that part made my gut clench because the twinkle in his eye when he met eyes with Madison across the table at lunch on Christmas Day was the same Dax would give me when we practiced in the mornings. It was the knowing look he gave me after I'd messed up during my lesson and he was seconds away from making some joke about it.

"You don't get all tense when we get to the turn anymore," Marlee said.

It took me a moment to realize we were heading up the mountain now. I looked in the rearview mirror at the metal barrier I'd smashed through a year ago. She was right. I didn't avoid driving past it anymore and though I still felt a little on edge when I drove by, I barely noticed when Dax and I took that turn on the way to North Ridge.

"Yeah. It feels less overwhelming," I told her. Neither of us spoke as we passed our family cabin. The windows were dark. Mom must already be at the club, pretending to be with Dad or whatever it was they were planning on telling everyone tonight. Part of me wanted to bail on the whole gala just because of that situation.

"Let me know if you need a ride later," Marlee said as we pulled into the Krune's driveway. "I'll probably be in my pajamas at the cabin though."

"You are going to at least make an appearance at the gala, right?" I asked. I didn't have to tell her that Madison would kill her if she didn't at least stay long enough to show off her dress.

Marlee grumbled something I couldn't hear as I climbed out of the Jeep.

"I'm going to the gala, but I'm not spending the entire night there. I have stuff to do," she said, truly meaning the words.

I shut the door and was just halfway up the sidewalk to the front door when she backed into the street. It was such a short walk that I didn't bother putting my coat on. I didn't need it anyway, being able to regulate my temperature with my powers and all. It wasn't long after I rang the doorbell that the door opened, and Lucas Krune invited me inside.

His tie hung loose around his shoulders, but he was otherwise dressed to go.

"You look great, kid," he said and gave me a one-armed hug. "Margot's here!"

Danielle was halfway down the stairs when her husband turned and yelled. She winced at the sound but smiled lovingly at him and pecked him on the side of the head when she joined us.

"Margot, you're beautiful!" she said and hugged me. She wasn't much taller than me normally, but her stilettos added another two inches. She took a step back and opened her white clutch to take out her phone. "I should've done this the last time you were here, but I guess now is better than never. Can I get your phone number?"

"Oh, um, sure," I said and unlocked my phone as well, not realizing she was waiting for me to tell her my number. I gave up on creating a contact and told her my phone number instead, watching as she typed it in. My phone vibrated in my hand a minute later. I knew the text message was from her, but the message surprised me.

> The door code is 523523. You're welcome anytime.

A WHISTLE DREW my attention back to the stairs. Daren and his friends were hurrying down the steps. I wasn't sure which one of them had whistled at me, but I didn't care to say anything. It was clear they had other things on their minds than picking fun at me considering the way they skirted around Mr. and Mrs. Krune.

"Who's driving tonight?" Lucas asked as the three boys gathered their keys from the kitchen counter. The boy who asked me out at McAdam's Mercantile raised his hand.

"I am, Lucas!"

"Sounds like a plan, boys," Lucas said. "Call if you get in a spot. Don't do anything too wild tonight. The roads are slick at night outside the mountain."

"No worries. Quentin and I will make sure Daren's a good boy tonight," he teased, reaching over to touch Daren's hair. Daren ducked out of the way and slapped his hands aside with a smile and showed him both his middle fingers before his parents could see.

Lucas leaned toward me and whispered, "Text us if you need anything. You can stay here tonight if you'd like."

Something about their kindness or maybe it was how at home I felt here, melted away my nerves for just a second before the room filled with cheers and whistles. Daren, Noah, and Quentin were all cheering and attempting to yell over one another. Lucas grumbled next to me as he walked by to retrieve his keys and wallet from the coffee table.

"He even styled his hair!" Quentin said.

I followed his gaze up the stairs where Dax was. He wore the typical black-tie attire of a warlock man at the Winter Solstice Gala. The suit was tailored to fit his broad shoulders and tight mid-section. He was fastening the button on his suit jacket as he walked down the stairs, looking up as he reached the final steps and catching my gaze. He smiled and then his eyes moved from my face to my dress and a different look crossed his face. It was almost shock, like he hadn't expected me to look the way I did. I thought I would feel vulnerable in the open-back dress with the high slit, but I felt so feminine and sexy instead.

"What you looking at, little bro?" Daren asked, sending both of his friends into fits of laughter.

"Daren, if I hear that you pulled anything like that with a girl tonight—"

"She know I'm joking," Daren told his mom and then looking to me for confirmation. I turned toward Dax instead who's cheeks were pink with embarrassment.

"We're going to go ahead and go. We'll see you guys there," Dax said. His hand met my exposed skin for just a moment before he lowered it to the small of my back, putting a layer of fabric between us.

"Oh! I wanted to get a picture of you two," Danielle said.

"We'll take some when we get there. I promise," I assured her, inching out the door the same way Dax was until we were too far over the threshold for anyone to stop us. The air cleared as soon as we were safely outside. I caught the frustration on Dax's face before he saw me looking and smiled instead.

"You were so red," I told him as we walked to his truck. He reached out and playfully pushed my shoulder before realizing I was in a pair of heels and nearly toppled over.

"Shit!" he cried out and quickly pulled me to his side. We both burst into laughter once I caught my footing. He walked me to the passenger side of the truck and opened the door. I climbed in and when I reached to pull the door shut he was still standing there between the door and the truck. He hesitated for a moment, hand resting on the doorframe next to my ear.

"I didn't mean to stare. I'm just not used to seeing you ..."

"I look like I'm playing dress up."

"I was going to say that you look hot," he said and smiled. "I mean it. You look great, Sinclair. How the hell are you going to dance in that dress though?"

"Be glad that I don't dance. I'll skewer your feet with these heels, if I do," I said and looked down at my nude heels. Dax laughed and shut the door, leaving me just the time it took him to round the front of the car for the driver's seat to calm the butterflies in my stomach.

Chapter 18

Dax parked his truck a few rows back from the entrance to the lodge. We made sure to stop outside the main entrance to take photos with the giant grizzly bear ice sculptures that manned each side of the stairs to the doors. Dax stopped another couple on their way in and the husband and wife each took our phones and began snapping photos of us between the statues.

"Thanks," I said when the woman handed me my phone.

"Have a nice night. Happy solstice," Dax told them and pocketed his phone when the man handed it back. I moved to the side as another group of people passed for the doors. I was struck by how different I look in the photos. I looked curvy, like one of those social media influencers. Dax looked handsome as always, though I still preferred him in his sweats or those jeans that fit just right on his hips.

"Ready?" Dax asked. He extended his arm to me when I looked up. I moved to shove my phone in my pocket before remembering that I didn't have any. "I got it."

"Thanks," I said and let Dax take my phone and tuck it away with his. I looped my arm in his and we ascended the stairs. It was chilly inside in the best way. It was invigorating and heightened all my senses, made my power feel effortless in my veins. The more winter witches you had in one place together, the more powerful they became and it was palpable. Dax must have felt it too because he looked more relaxed next to me and the way he smiled as he surveyed the room was so boyish that it eased my nerves about the night. Maybe the gala would actually be fun.

"How about a dance?" Dax asked and started for the dance floor just ahead.

"I'm not good at dancing. I don't really know how," I said and slowly followed after him. He turned to face me, laughing.

"You can't be that bad," he said and extended a hand.

"I'm not good. I promise," I said with an awkward laugh. He pulled me into the crowd anyway as the loud pop song carried through the room. Before I could do more than sway, the song ended and a soft ballad replaced it. The people around us began to split into couples or leave the dance floor.

"Here," Dax said and pulled me closer. He took my left hand and draped it over his right shoulder before taking my right hand and holding it up. A hand rested against my back, his skin warm compared to the cool air. "The man usually takes the lead, so let me lead. No one can accuse you of being a bad dancer that way."

I snorted but relaxed and mirrored his movements. After a quiet moment, it became an easy dance, choreographed even. I focused on his chest, inhaling the smell of his spiced cologne when I noticed the engraving on his silver tie clip. I let go of his hand to run my fingers over the letters.

"What does the I stand for?"

He let out a sigh, which made me look up at his smirk.

"My middle name is Ian," he said a little hesitantly.

"Dax Ian Krune," I said.

He chuckled and took my hand again, pulling us back into position as we swayed.

"Yes. My initials are DIK, or Dick if you asked my brother."

I gasped. How had I not noticed it the first time?

"Ouch," I said. Thankfully, the tension eased, and he laughed. The song ended and another ballad began.

"What's your middle name, Sinclair?" Dax asked, taking a step away from me and holding our entwined hands high. I spun around, feeling a little stupid but loving it nonetheless. He stepped closer and replaced his hand at my back, this time putting us just a few inches apart.

"Rose," I said.

"MRS."

I scoffed and said, "Sometimes it feels like my parents tried to set up my whole life before I was born. Growing up everything was designer, carefully curated. I hated it."

"You used to wear those long basketball shorts when we were kids," Dax said. The words threw me so far into my memories that I knew exactly the navy pair of shorts he was talking about. I didn't like the shorter shorts all the girls wore because they were too girly and I didn't want to be put in that box with Madison. I was capable and in control and I wanted everyone to know it. I wanted to be the girl who didn't just go along with the crowd and I wanted to wear nice clothes that were also comfortable.

"Those shorts were comfortable."

"Yeah. They were also too big. You always wore baggy clothes. You still keep pretty covered up. Well, normally," Dax said and eyed my dress with a smirk. "That's why I was … Again, I didn't mean to stare earlier, but you don't usually wear stuff that shows off your body."

"Madison made it," I said. "You had a mouthful of metal for most of high school."

Dax laughed as the song changed again, a much more upbeat rhythm breaking us apart.

"True and somehow I still got dates," he said as he followed me off the dance floor, still swaying and nodding his head to the beat. "Did you date anyone? I don't remember you having a boyfriend in high school."

That was because I didn't have one. I was too focused on soccer to date anyone. Sure, there were boys I liked, and I'd even kissed a couple at school dances and that time I did show a brief interest in finding a boyfriend freshman year. I'd never been on a real date though and I turned down the couple that had asked because I didn't want to get distracted. Madison's grades dropped whenever she had a boyfriend, and she struggled to find time to study and do homework when she went on dates and I just didn't think it was worth it. I had my entire life to date. I just assumed that a boy would fit into that and if he didn't, then the timing wasn't right, and it would happen later. That was sort of the problem though. I put everything off until later. It was always another item on my list of things to do once I'd gone pro.

"I've never dated anyone," I said as we made our way to the buffet table. The line was short, as most people were already seated with food or already finished with the meal. In about another thirty minutes or so the dance floor would empty in preparation for the solstice dance.

"Oh! Wait!" Dax exclaimed as we filled out plates, startling a little old lady who joined us to refill her champagne glass. "What about Brody? You two had a thing."

I handed Dax a cloth napkin rolled around silverware before taking my own and starting toward the round tables on the other side of the room.

"I never dated Brody Price," I said, searching for an empty table so we could be alone.

"What? You two definitely had a thing. I remember that," Dax said and nudged me. I followed him past the rows of tables and toward the door in the back.

"No. There was never anything with Brody. We were chemistry partners senior year, so we had to do our semester projects together. There wasn't a thing," I said as we moved into the next room. It was a large space with a small kitchenette to the right and large windows on the left that overlooked the mountains. There was a foosball table and a pool table in the middle with squishy leather couches and armchairs next to the windows. That's where Dax led me.

"Okay, well, I know Brody had a thing," he said as he sat his plate on the coffee table in front of the couch and began to unroll his silverware.

I sat down next to him with my plate in my lap.

"What?"

"Yeah. Brody was on the swim team, and he told a few of us

once that he was hanging out with you and that he was going to ask you to prom."

"Okay. Well, I told him we could go as friends if he didn't find a date first."

"Oh my God, Sinclair! You are so naïve!"

"I'm not naïve!"

"You so are. You're just as innocent as you look most days," Dax said and sliced into his chicken. "Have you ever kissed anyone?"

"I've kissed three people, thank you," I corrected, pointing my fork at him before spearing a potato. He laughed and lowered his hunk of chicken back to his plate.

"Okay. Fine. I'll give you that, but what kind of kissing are we talking about?"

"Don't be gross," I said and took a bite.

He laughed and shook his head. "It's not gross to kiss someone you're into or ..."

The implication was there in his tone, and it made my stomach twist. I sat my fork down entirely, not sure I would be able to pick it back up anytime soon.

"Maybe there was a little tongue."

"A little tongue and what, you just sat with your hands in your lap?"

I threw my roll at him, and he caught it in his right hand. "*One* of those guys was a little handsy. He grabbed my butt, and it was weird. That's it."

"It's not weird when you're into it. You just had the wrong guy."

"And you would know?" I challenged, giving him the same eyebrow-raised look he'd given me.

"Not about the boy part, but I've grabbed a couple of butts in my day."

I would've thrown another roll at him if I had one.

"So, there were three boys, some butt grabbing, end of list," I said with a laugh, watching as he passed the roll back and forth between his hands like a baseball. "What about your list, Casanova?"

He chuckled and tossed the roll at me. I caught it and immediately sat it down with the rest of my discarded meal. Dax adjusted on the couch, turning so he had one leg resting on the cushion between us and an arm resting along the back.

"My first kiss was in the back of a bus on the way to swimming practice, no tongue in case you were wondering. Then, there were a couple of dates freshman and sophomore years. I grabbed a few butts and such. Then came Hannah senior year. We were together most of senior year. One thing led to another," Dax said with a shrug.

"One thing led to another?" I asked in disbelief.

"One thing led to another, Sinclair," he laughed, his cheeks turning pink.

"Why are we even talking about this?" I asked. The silence fell and I suddenly wish I hadn't asked. His smile dimmed a little and he lowered his leg to the floor so he could stand.

"Because we are friends," he declared and unbuttoned his suit jacket. "How about we play a game of pool?"

I unbuckled my heels and stepped out of them before standing up. "Sure. Fair warning, I'm pretty good."

Dax smiled as he racked the balls at one end. I felt a lot more relaxed now that my feet weren't crammed in those stupid heels. I held both pool cues while he moved the triangle of balls further onto the table. When he straightened up, he slipped his jacket off and laid it over the back of the leather armchair behind him. He joined me in front of the white ball, taking the pool cue from me.

"All right, hustler," he said and stepped back. "Ladies first."

Butterflies filled my stomach again as I leaned over the end of the table and took aim.

"It's not hustling if I tell you I'm good at pool," I told him and took the shot. Breaking was not something I was great at comparatively, but the balls spread out in a way that favored me. "Solids."

Dax nodded his head as I stood up, moving into place next to me. "If I win, you have to learn how to do flip turn in the pool."

I laughed. "Everything is always a competition with you."

"And you can't resist." The smile he shot me was so challenging that I felt my cheeks heat.

"If I win, you have to do soccer drills with me," I said and motioned for him to take his turn. He smirked and shook his head.

"Game on," he said and leaned over, his back muscles flexing as he pulled the pool cue back and took the shot.

We both played with such focus that were rarely spoke and the game took long enough that we'd missed the traditional solstice dance without realizing it. I kept a step ahead of him the entire way and when he had a brief moment of an upset, he botched his turn and sunk the white ball. He let out a sigh and straightened up as I took the game-ending turn and whirled around from the table to point an excited finger at his chest.

"My turn to play teacher!" I poked his chest and he held his hands up in resignation.

"Okay. Fine. Monday morning you can do your worst, Coach Sinclair. I swear I can take it."

"We'll see about that," I told him and went to the armchair to check my phone. I pulled both of ours out and was surprised that I had several texts from my sisters.

> Daren and his friends are so annoying.

> It's ten o'clock and Daren is wasted.

> Margot, you and Dax need to get to the deck now!

> There's a fight on the deck!

"Dax," I started. When I looked up, his ear was pressed to his phone and was struggling to pull on his jacket.

"What happened?" he asked, leading the way across the room. He let out a groan and picked up speed, leaving me to jog after him after I snagged my heels from the floor. No one in the main hall gave me a second look as I pattered barefoot after Dax who only moved quicker until he threw the glass door to the large deck open. I slipped through and stopped next to one of the high-top tables to slip my heels on as Dax faced my sisters, Quinton, and Darin. Darin sat on the cooler he always brought to the gala. It used to be hidden under the deck and he'd sneak beers when we were all underaged, but now it just felt like a trashy frat boy's way of ruining a sacred witchy event. There was a smear of red on his white button up and the cracked blood just beneath his nose told the whole story.

"What did you do?" Dax asked, looking from his brother to Quinton who was the first to answer.

"I tried to stop them. It was a stupid fight and Daren is drunk enough that he got pissed off over nothing."

"It wasn't nothing. I'm not going to let Noah tell me that I'm immature!" Daren didn't have to speak at all for anyone to tell how drunk he was. You could smell the beer on him.

"Yeah, sneaking cheap beers to a black-tie event and picking a fight is real mature," Dax grumbled, ignoring him when his brother tried to stand up and was pushed back down on the cooler by Quintin.

"I got some water," Jared said, the glass door shutting behind him. He handed two bottles of water to Dax. Dax tossed one at his brother who fumbled it and dropped it between his feet. Dax hesitated before he handed a bottle to Quintin.

"How much have you had?" he asked.

Quintin shifted from one foot to the other, crossing his arms and then uncrossing them. "I'm good, man. I've only like six in."

"Noah was sober. He got in his truck and took off," Jared said.

I looked at my sisters next. Madison looked annoyed like she really wished Jared would just go back inside with her to dance. Marlee looked exhausted, more than just her usual irritation. Her eyes looked different than when she dropped me off at the Krune's and I realized it was because she didn't have mascara and liner under her eyes anymore.

Ugh.

I moved to her side while Dax and Quintin tried talking Daren down who was going on about the whole fight again. Marlee let out a sigh when she noticed me.

"I'm fine."

"It's okay that you're not."

"It's not a big deal. I'm just going to go home and sit by myself like always. I have stuff to work on anyway."

"Marlee, I know that you say that so you have an excuse to get away when you're uncomfortable."

Marlee took a step away from me and held her hands up. Everyone but Madison was too busy trying to reason with Daren to notice her.

"Does it matter what I do? It's not what anyone wants from me anyway!"

"Marlee," I started, taking a step forward only for her to take another step back. She looked toward the door, then Madison, and then her eyes landed on the stairs that led down to the parking lot.

"I'm going to go home. I'm fine. No one bug me," she said and started down the stairs. Madison and I watched as she walked through the sea of parked cars until she reached my blue Jeep.

"This has been great," I said under my breath.

"I just want to go dance," Madison whined. "I was having a great time until Jared decided to break up the fight. He's such a nice guy and I love that about him, but I really wish we could just forget this happened."

"Go dance with your fiancé, Madison," I said with a sigh and moved forward to help Dax. I patted Jared's shoulder and nodded toward my sister. "I got it. You go."

"You sure? I don't mind," he said.

"I know, but I got this. Dax and I were on our way out anyway," I said. I noticed the way Dax hesitated before he grabbed onto his brother's right arm. He and Quintin lifted him to his feet, each draping an arm over their shoulders. Dax gave me an apologetic look.

"Let's take these idiots home," I said.

"Hey! I wasn't acting like an idiot," Quintin defended.

"Just shut up and go, Quintin," Dax said as they started toward the stairs. I followed behind. The cooler could stay behind on the deck, hopefully for good. I was glad it was a short drive, because Daren complained the entire time. Dax groaned when he pulled into the driveway next to Noah's truck. I held the door so Quintin and Dax could guide Daren inside. Noah was sitting on the couch watching the TV.

"You suck," Daren told him. Noah stayed relaxed on the couch.

"Yeah, I know. I shouldn't have said that, man. I'm sorry."

"Good," Daren said and surged away from Quintin and Dax to sink into the couch next to Noah. He leaned forward with his head between his hands. "I think I might hurl."

"I got it!" Dax called out and rounded the couch for a chip bowl next to Noah. He emptied the last of the tortilla chips into Noah's lap before setting the bowl in his brother's lap just before he made a horrible retching sound that made me turn away.

"Hey!" Noah yelled.

"Hang on, Sinclair. Don't go anywhere," Dax told me as his brother vomited into the bowl. I would love to go anywhere else right now. Dax ran into the kitchen and came back a moment later with a bottle of champagne and a couple of plastic cups with his dad's medical clinic logo printed on the side. "I'm not letting our night end on a bad note. Come on."

I gladly followed him back to the truck.

Chapter 19

"Who are you texting?" Dax asked as the sign for North Ridge came into view ahead.

"Marlee," I said with a sigh. "She just hasn't been right. I mean, she's never outwardly happy the way most people act, but she's been extra on edge since our parents announced they are divorcing, and it's been concerning and ..."

The truck was silent aside from the soft indie music from the radio.

"I don't usually step in for my brother like that. Any other time and I would've called him an Uber and made his stupid friends figure it out when they got home," Dax said and turned into the parking lot of the rec center. "We're not kids anymore. He's an adult and he knows how to deal with his own problems. He just chooses not to. I choose not to clean up his mess for him."

"You shouldn't have to," I told him as he kept going past our usual spot near the front of the entrance.

"Neither should you," he said. It sounded so simple, and my first thought was to defend my sisters. They didn't get into trouble like Daren did, but the result was still the same. They always told me first. I didn't always do anything, but I did drop everything to help them figure it out or to make them feel better. Just like how I was texting Marlee about how it wasn't healthy for her to shut herself away every time she was upset. My therapist would be proud of me because I totally saw now that I ran away from my own problems and made myself feel better by doing more for others than they often did for themselves.

"I treat myself like such an asshole," I groaned.

Dax parked in the spot just in front of the outdoor pool and turned off the engine.

"Not tonight, you don't," he said. "Grab that bottle and the cups."

He got out of the truck and started for the gate. He looked at it for a moment before turning to face me.

"I bet we could use our powers and pick the lock with icicles," I told him.

He waved a hand at the idea. "Nah. That lady at the desk won't even look up at me if I just walk past. Watch this."

He left me at the gate and jogged down the sidewalk toward the main entrance. I didn't stop him. He was probably right, but I also thought I could just as easily pick the lock. I set the champagne bottle and the cups on the concrete and used my powers to conjure two icy rods. They'd be strong enough to withstand being shoved into the small opening, which was what I did next. I listened carefully and paid attention to the feel of the rods moving the pins. About a minute later, the door swung inward, and I tossed the icicles into the bushes.

I grabbed the bottle and cups and went inside, pulling the gate shut behind me. I went to the edge of the pool. The patio lights that were strung around the whole pool cast warm light over the water. I was dying to dip my feet into it, feel the buzz in the veins as the winter chill worked to recharge my powers. I wondered if this was how summer witches felt at the beach.

The door to the building opened and Dax paused for a moment in surprise. I raised the champagne and cups for him to see with a laugh.

"I told you," I said.

"Well, this way the door to the indoor pool is open. We'll probably want the locker room at some point," he said and joined me. He took the champagne bottle, and I immediately pulled my heels off and tossed them to the ground behind us. My heart skipped at the loud pop of the cork, and I laughed as I held both plastic cups so he could fill them halfway.

"Cheers!" I said as he sat the bottle on the concrete and took a cup from me.

"To living without expectations," he said, that challenging look twinkling in his eyes again that made me think back to the list.

"Living without expectations," I said and pressed my cup to his. We both drank. I sat down at the edge of the pool, letting out a sigh of relief when I let my legs sink into the pool. Anyone else would think this was crazy, but for a winter witch a polar plunge was like soaking in a hot bath after a long day.

"Hold this," Dax said and handed his cup to me. He shrugged out of his jacket and made a dramatic display of tossing it toward the nearest pool chair. He missed and it fell to the concrete, but he didn't bother to move it. He undid his tie from around his neck and tossed it away too, the dark fabric falling through the air like a ribbon. He undid the top two buttons of his white dress shirt as he sat down next to me. I could see down the collar as he leaned forward to pull off his shoes and socks next, dipping his feet to the ankles in the water next to me.

"This is the best I've felt in so long," I said and took another drink. A few weeks ago, having more than a small glass of champagne would've been pushing my diet too far. Here I was now more relaxed than ever with maybe three glasses worth in a plastic cup.

"You know, you didn't protest this once?" Dax said with a chuckle. "A week ago you would've told me just to take you home so you could get up early for a workout. You definitely wouldn't be drinking with me."

"You're right. I probably wouldn't have left the gala at all."

Dax started to laugh harder now, pulling my attention away from the ripples in the pool.

"What?" I asked and elbowed him.

"You broke the law, Sinclair."

"What law?" I asked and downed the last of my cup because

why not? Before I could reach for the bottle, he'd raised it to my cup for a refill.

"You broke into that gate back there. You and I should definitely not be here right now."

"I guess that is breaking and entering, isn't it?" I said with a giggle and took another sip. "It doesn't feel like it. This place just kind of feels ..."

"It feels like ours," Dax said, holding my gaze.

"Yeah. It does."

Silence passed between us for a moment before he sat his cup aside.

"You know what would make it better?" he said and stood up. I realized what he meant as soon as he turned toward the pool and my stomach started doing somersaults in response. I thought my heart might beat out of my chest.

"No. No way are we skinny dipping right now," I said.

"Who said anything about skinny dipping?" he said and looked down at me and winked.

"No way. You wouldn't," I said as he turned back to the pool and bent his knees. He dove into the water, emerging a few feet ahead of me with a wide smile on his face and blonde hair falling across his forehead.

"Come on, Sinclair," he teased.

"I have my hair and makeup done."

He swam closer and I reflexively pulled my knees to my chest.

"The point is to live a little," Dax laughed, close enough now that I could see the curves of his muscles as his shirt clung to him.

"Madison would kill me if I ruined this dress."

"Forget about your sisters and do something for yourself," Dax said, reaching out for me.

I let him take my hands and closed my eyes. I let out a squeal and leaped into the water, a release so glorious rushing through my veins that I couldn't help but laugh when my head broke the surface. It was almost overwhelming how happy I felt, how free it was. I opened my eyes and looked back at Dax's blue eyes.

"Atta girl!" he cheered as I struggled to tread water. The dress was light, but the tulle had gathered awkwardly around my legs, making it hard to get a good kick to keep myself afloat.

"I'm sinking. The dress is a little stuck," I laughed as I tried to tug the skirt away from my legs. Dax moved closer, wrapping his arms around me and keeping me up. I stopped swimming and let him hold me while I tugged the fabric until it was more comfortable. When I looked up, my nose brushed his and my heart jolted. Something in his eyes was different, softer. I reached out and brushed his hair back so it wasn't hanging over his brows.

"Atta girl," he said again, this time in a breathy whisper. Forget butterflies. Everything inside seemed to melt, and I was glad he was holding me or else I might've sunk to the bottom of the pool.

I bit down on my bottom lip, unsure what to do. I should move. I freed my skirt. I could swim on my own now. Still, I stayed in his arms as the thoughts ran through my mind, only brought back to the moment when his hand cupped my cheek. He pulled my bottom lip free with a brush of his thumb and then his lips met mine. They were gentle at first before my senses caught up. I kissed him back, deeper, his hands holding his face to mine and his breathing picking up pace. I wrapped my legs around his hips and when he pulled me tight against his chest with muscles I could feel against my bare back, I felt the tightness of him press between my legs and I remembered how close were and not just physically.

I pulled away with a gasp, feeling the tears sting my eyes.

"I've wanted to do that for so long," Dax said between breaths before his expression changed to concern. "Margot?"

"I don't want to mess this up. I don't want to mess us up," I said, swimming backward before finally sprinting the final yard to the stairs of the pool. The dress wrapped around me again as I stepped out of the pool, the fabric heavy enough with water that it slipped from my chest, and I raised my arms to cover myself.

By the time I made it to the locker room it was obvious that the dress was wet enough that it wouldn't stay on, so I let it slip to my hips once I'd reached the locker room. I pulled a towel from the stack on the shelf beneath the counter and stepped out of the dress. I wrapped the towel around myself as a knock came at the door.

"Margot?"

I closed my eyes as a tear slipped down my face.

"I just want to make sure you're okay. I'm sorry. I didn't mean to ..."

The room was silent and after a few seconds, I went to the door and cracked it open. Dax was still wearing his slacks and button-up, dripping water all over the floor. I opened the door the rest of the way and he moved into the locker room. I noticed his eyes linger on the white dress in the middle of the floor before he looked up at me again. He launched into an apology, but I didn't hear a word of it. Whatever sliver of resolve I had left crumbled now that he was in the room and he was still him, still gentle and so damn considerate of my feelings while challenging them at the same time, still so sexy and wearing far more clothes than he usually did when he was in the locker room with me.

He stopped speaking when I dropped the towel, leaving just my nude thong to cover myself. His mouth parted and his eyes stared hungrily at my chest.

"God," he breathed.

"I don't want to be friends," I told him as another tear spilled onto my cheek.

"Good, because I don't want to be friendly with you right now," Dax said and surged forward. He lifted me and I wrapped my legs around his hips, gasping as he gripped my ass and walked to the vanity. He sat me down and stepped into the space between my legs, one hand palming my breast while the other cupped my cheek. I kissed him hard as my fingers worked at the buttons of his shirt, getting just two done before he pulled away long enough to undo the rest and slip out of the shirt.

"You look so hot like this," I told him as he stepped forward again.

"I've been dreaming about what these looked like since you wore that damn bikini," Dax said and cupped both my breasts before placing soft kisses there. My fingers found the buckle of his belt, which I managed to undo before he took over. He pulled himself free and didn't wait for his slacks to fall before he tugged my thong out of the way and sunk into me with a moan.

"Good?" he asked, eyes finding mine and thumb stroking my cheek reassuringly.

"Good," I confirmed and tightened my legs around his hips, watching the smile spread on his face as I took him deeper.

I let my hands wander as he started to move, hips rolling deliciously. I wanted to feel every contour of his muscles, the way they tensed with each thrust. I kept exploring until his breathing quickened and he moved a hand between us, his fingers finding a sensitive spot that left my hands tight on his shoulders until we were both sent over the edge and left panting as though we'd just finished a day's workout.

"I've been dreaming of that for so long," he said between breaths.

"Me too," I said and pulled him closer.

Chapter 20

My dress was soaked and wouldn't stay on, so I wore Dax's suit jacket like a dress and my heels as we went back to the truck. His wet shirt and slacks clung to him so tight that it made me squirm in my seat as we made our way through downtown North Ridge and up the mountain to Lawson Rathbone's cabin. I waited patiently while he typed in the gate code and then again as he unlocked the front door. When we made it to the stairs, I was in his arms again and his shirt was off.

We fell asleep in the master bedroom upstairs and were still entwined when I woke up the next morning. I raised my head off Dax's bare chest and held him tighter when I saw his smile.

"Morning, Sinclair," he said and kissed my forehead. "Sex with you is amazing. You have stamina for days."

I laughed and rolled onto my back next to him. "Time to refuel."

"I'll see what Lawson keeps in the kitchen," Dax said and sat up. I watched him as he pulled on his underwear and then went to Lawson's closet. I remembered what his mom had told me about Dax's hobby and favorite way to relax.

"How about your famous protein pancakes?" I asked.

He emerged from the closet a moment later dressed in a pair of black sweatpants and a white shirt.

"I bet I can make that happen," he said and paused for a moment.

"What?" I asked and sat up in bed.

He smiled and shrugged. "Just looking."

"I need food. I didn't eat dinner last night. I'm hungry," I said.

"Yeah. Me too." He sent much a look that made my heart skip. I pulled the sheets up to my chin and stuck my tongue out at him.

Dax groaned. "Later then."

"Later. I promise," I said, my brain already filling with thoughts of all the ways I wanted him. He left the room and after getting my fill of snuggling in the sheets, I reached for my phone. I was a little surprised when I saw that it was closer to lunch than breakfast. It was eleven-twenty and there were messages in the group text with Marlee and Madison. Marlee had texted at nine and then again thirty minutes ago.

> Did you come home last night?
>
> Where are you?

THE NEXT MESSAGE came through as I held the phone, this one from Madison.

> You hooked up with him, didn't you?

I DECIDED to keep the theme of last night going and didn't bother responding. They didn't need me. I wouldn't make myself available until I wanted to be, so I set my phone on the side table. I went to the closet and found a stack of women's athletic clothes.

I pulled on a pair of slinky leggings and a long-sleeved crop top and went downstairs to find Dax.

He was already busy mixing batter in a bowl while a skillet heated up at the stove. I went to the sink and started washing the dishes. As I finished with the final bowl, Dax's hands slunk around my waist and his lips found my neck.

"Breakfast is ready," he said.

"Do you realize it's almost noon," I turned and he stepped aside, motioning to the plate on the counter. The pancake was a perfect golden brown with a couple of banana slices on top. I picked up the fork and cut off a hunk. It was dense, but full of cinnamon and nutmeg and just a pinch of something that still made it sweet like a normal pancake. I finished chewing and turned to Dax next to me.

"So?" he asked, waiting patiently as I swallowed.

"Delicious," I said and swatted him on the butt. "Good job, Krune."

He chuckled and pulled another fork from a drawer next to him before taking a bite of the pancake. It didn't take long to start feeling full and with my mind off my growling stomach, it switched to other subjects like everything that had happened last night. Eventually, I would have to face my sisters and answer some questions before I saw him again for morning workout. Anxiety started to creep into my chest, but I knew I needed to ask.

"So, um, after everything last night and with us ..." I wasn't sure how to approach the topic without just saying it outright. Maybe that was what I should've done though because now I couldn't find any words at all and my chest hurt and I swore my face was bright red.

"I'm all yours, Sinclair," Dax said and moved the plate aside so he could lean his right arm on the countertop. "Call me what you want."

I chewed on my lip for a moment.

"Boyfriend?"

"That's what I was hoping you'd say." He smiled and leaned in to press a kiss to my temple. "What do you want to do today?"

I didn't want to do anything but this. I knew I didn't want to leave Lawson's cabin, not yet.

"Let's work on the list," I said. "How about a movie with a pint of ice cream?"

Dax laughed and followed me as I made my way toward the giant living room. There were two large sectionals in this room and another sitting area near the windows. The TV was as large as they came and hung above a big fireplace that Dax decided to get going.

"Why did you add that one to the list? It seems so normal," he said as the flames whooshed to life. I looked away from the Netflix screen I'd been scrolling through.

"Well, I rarely eat ice cream, athlete diet and all. I think it's been years since I had more than a small cup on a holiday or something. Eating a big sundae while watching a sappy romance just seems like something a girl should do at least once," I said. It was something Madison would do.

Dax straightened up from the fireplace, the flames already sending a wave of warmth through the room and adding to the romantic feel of the moment.

"I'll grab the ice cream," he said and started back to the kitchen. I searched for a throw blanket, finally finding a fluffy brown one that blended in with the back of the armchair, and curled up beneath it as I continued my Netflix search for a sappy movie. Dax returned a moment later with a whole carton of ice cream in one hand and two spoons in the other.

"I hope chocolate is okay," he said and plopped down next to me. "It's all he had."

"Chocolate is great," I said and held out the blanket so he could slide next to me. I continued my search until I found a new release that looked promisingly terrible. As the opening credits rolled to the upbeat pop song, I sat the remote aside and accepted a spoonful of ice cream from Dax.

We were mostly quiet through the movie, snuggled together on the couch eating ice cream until we'd finished what was left of the entire pint. I was sure my stomach would hurt later, but it made me feel rebellious to indulge this way. The entire day was an escape from literally running away from Crescent Peak to be in this luxurious cabin to the way I hadn't thought at all about the fact that we'd missed a workout.

"Well, that's one thing checked off your list," Dax said and moved his arm from around my shoulders as the credit rolled on the TV. He took the empty ice cream carton and our spoons from the coffee table and went to the kitchen while I exited the movie and looked over the suggested titles.

"You know, that was so cheesy, but I also kind of enjoyed it," I admitted when he returned. "That movie was not good, but it was kind of fun."

"It's like those reality TV shows," Dax said, his cheeks flushing at the look I gave him. "I don't watch them, but my mom hosts a weekly wine night with her friends when a new season of that one airs. You know, the one where the guy or girl or whatever gives out roses?"

I laughed and returned to scrolling Netflix. It had been so long since I'd watched anything, now that I'd thought about it. School kept me busy and soccer kept me busier.

"What would you say is your comfort show?" I asked.

Dax sunk into the couch next to me and said with his hands held up as in praise, "Doctor shows."

"Like Grey's Anatomy?" I asked, surprised by his answer.

"Yeah. That. Others," he said with a shrug. "Both of my parents are in medicine, so I grew up hearing all kinds of things about the body and it's interesting, but it's super interesting to see how different shows portray it. They get it wrong a lot and I just think it's kind of funny. It's a bit of a guilty pleasure. What about you?"

I felt my cheeks heat. "Grey's Anatomy."

He laughed in disbelief. He took the remote from me and began working his way through the right apps until he found Grey's Anatomy. We started with the first episode and quickly turned into taking turns giving commentary. He told me all the medical facts about the episodes that he'd learned from his parents and where the inaccuracies were. I told him what I knew about the cast and the production. We got through most of the season, leaving it on while we made an early dinner in the kitchen. We even left it on in the background while I sat on the countertop and we kissed as we waited for the oven timer.

We snuggled on the couch after dinner until we'd both gushed so much about medical facts and Grey's Anatomy trivia that we'd gotten our fill for the day. Dax stood up from the couch and stretched his arms high over his head.

"What do you say we check off another item on your list?" he asked.

I didn't have to ask to know what he meant. He started down the hall toward one of the front rooms, whichever it was that stored all of Lawson's alcohol. I stood up and pulled the elastic from my right wrist and began to gather my hair at the crown of my head, walking toward the giant windows on the other side of the room. The water fountain to the pool was off and it looked like ice had started to crust over the grooves. The pool water was still, the snow melting when it met the water. The patio just outside was fully furnished. I lowered my hands from the bun on top of my head and opened the door.

The patio had a large sectional and two lounge chairs large enough to seat two people comfortably. There was an outdoor kitchen so nice that I almost wish I'd known about it sooner. Dax was a good cook and I bet that translated to the grill perfectly. On the other side of the patio, the stone met the edge of the hot tub. I walked toward it, mostly to admire how fancy it looked surrounded by all that polished stone with one side overlooking the rest of the yard and the mountains beyond. Inspiration struck and I couldn't resist the chance to check two items off my list at once.

I pulled off the athletic top and peeled the tight leggings from my legs. A kind of electric feeling shot through me as soon once I was completely naked. I almost laughed from the thrill of it as I stepped into the hot tub. It took a bit to figure out how to turn it on, but once I did the jet filled the tub with enough bubbles to hide beneath. Just as I'd gotten comfortable in the hot tub, the sliding door opened and Dax stepped out, slowing his pace as he approached the hot tub with a growing smile on his face.

I adjusted under the water, rising just enough that the warm water still covered the intimate bits.

"You're a little overdressed for this party, Krune," I said before I lost my nerve. "Unless you don't want to strip in the snow. I hear men shrink in the cold."

"Winter warlocks don't shrink in the cold." A red flush rose to his cheeks, and he smiled. "Don't be so smug. I can see those peaks from here, Sinclair."

I sank deeper into the water at that, pressing my thighs together and backing to the seat of the hot tub as he approached the edge of the tub. He smiled and leaned down, setting a pair of champagne flutes and a bottle down that I hadn't even noticed until now. He straightened up, his hands going to the hem of his shirt. He pulled it over his head and tossed it onto the same lounge chair I'd folded my clothes on.

He was drawing out the process as a tease, that much was obvious from the onery grin on his face. I didn't mind. I studied the ridges of his abs and the curves of those swimmer's shoulders, trying to decide what part of him I wanted to inspect closer once he was in the water. He laughed at my impatient groan as he decided to pause to open the champagne bottle. He poured two glasses and sat the bottle down beside them, raising his eyes to mine with a look in his eyes that nearly cry out for him to hurry up.

His hands went to the waistband of his black sweatpants, and he slipped them off. His boxers were next, and he threw them on in a heap on top of my clothes, turning enough to give me a view of his tight ass. I thought my heart would explode with nerves as he turned his gaze back to me, fully naked and definitely not shrinking like I'd joked before.

He lowered himself into the water and reached back for the champagne flutes, handing me one when he turned to face me.

"To skinny dipping," Dax said and raised his glass to me.

"To raiding Lawson's liquor cabinet," I said and clinked my glass to his.

I was all so perfect. The chill of the air was invigorating and made my powers tingle, the champagne easing my nerves, and then there was Dax looking at me in such a way that I sat my glass aside and moved through the water to press myself against him.

Chapter 21

Skin to skin. My mouth was on his, tasting the sweet champagne on his lips and gladly sucking it off his bottom lip. His hands slunk around my waist, gripping my ass and pulling me against his hard body. I ran my hands down the front of his body, over every curve and ridge, feeling his racing heart against my palm as he cupped my breasts.

The back of my knees met the seat of the hot tub as he squeezed tight, his lips leaving gentle kisses down my neck and onto my chest. Before I could sink into the seat, he gripped my hips and lifted me onto the cool tile. The temperature would've been a shock to most, for a winter witch it sent a zap of electricity through my body and I nearly lost myself in it. I let out a moan as he lightly bit my right breast, his hand tracing a line from the dip of my neck down, down, down.

My eyes flew open when he reached that sensitive spot to see that he was watching me, grinning at my reaction. Oh, the way that look almost sent me over the edge ... I bit my lower lip and tipped my head back, feeling his hand on my chin immediately, pulling my attention back to him.

"Eyes on me, Sinclair," he said with that onery smile.

I was lost, completely broken beneath him, a mess of pleasure so thorough that I was left feeling drunk and completely spent. So, I thought. Just when I thought I'd hit bottom, another wave began to build at his coaxing fingers, quicker this time. Before the wave could wash over me, Dax lowered me to the tile, cradling my head with one hand and using the other to prop himself up above me.

His hips met mine and as he began a steady rhythm, that wave crashed over me again so intensely that I was glad this cabin's nearest neighbors were a mile away. Dax let out a moan and tightened his hand in my hair, allowing himself to rest his chest against mine as his breathing slowed to its natural pace.

I could've laid beneath him forever.

❄

I'D NEVER BEEN hungover before, but I'd heard enough about the feeling to know that that's exactly what I was the next morning. The night before was a blur of happiness that I remembered ended with Dax holding my hair back while I vomited into the toilet in the master bathroom.

Dax reached across the center console of the truck to squeeze my thigh. "You take that Tylenol I left by the bed?"

"Yes. I also ate the toast," I said. I'd wanted to skip the toast, but he promised I would feel better after I ate some carbs even though I was worried they'd reappear moments later. He was right and I did not throw up again. My stomach was more settled actually and my headache had mostly vanished by the time we climbed into the truck and started back to Crescent Peak.

"Good," he said and returned his hand to the steering wheel. "Want to come over? We could sit on the deck or something."

As wonderful as that sounded, my phone had reminded me an hour ago that I had plans.

"I can't. I have a call with Hadiza."

"Who?"

"Dr. Hadiza Morgan. She's my therapist," I told him, not cringing at the word *therapist* for once. Dax didn't seem fazed as he nodded.

"Oh. Yeah, I should get you home for that," he said as we

passed the sign for Crescent Peak. "Up for a workout tomorrow morning?"

I thought about my last lesson in flip turns. I didn't inhale water by the end of it, but I was still far from proficient. Maybe I'd wear that bikini again just to add a little something to our workout ...

"Yeah. I'll see you bright and early," I told him as he pulled into the driveway. My stomach did a flip as I thought about all the questions I'd be asked the minute I walked inside.

"I'll pick you up in the morning. Don't forget your dress," Dax said and pulled the white gown from the back of the truck. "I might want to take it off you again sometime."

My cheeks burned at the memories as I pressed my lips to his. I held the dress close to my chest and practically ran inside, hopeful to make it to my bedroom before anyone could catch me. Mom was in the kitchen and Marlee was reading on the couch when I closed the front door behind me.

"I got therapy!" I called out and rushed to the stairs, heart racing until I was safely behind my bedroom door. I tossed the dress on my bed, wondering what Madison would have to say about the state of it as I got set up for the video call. I switched to my to-do list in another tab as I waited for Hadiza, crossing off the items Dax and I had accomplished at the cabin and letting myself bask in the memories.

To Do Before Soccer:

1. ~~Skinny dipping?~~
2. ~~Raid the liquor cabinet at Lawson Rathbone's cabin~~
3. ~~Go to the Winter Solstice Gala with a date~~
4. ~~Watch a terrible movie and eat a pint of ice cream~~

I THOUGHT about adding *master flip turns* to the list when I heard Hadiza on the other tab. I exited out of the tab with the list to see her sitting in her office like usual, this time wearing a long-sleeve sweater dress in a bright pink color.

"I take it the week has been really good," she said with a smile.

My cheeks ached like I'd just eaten something a little too sweet, telling me there was no way I could hide the details. This was therapy. It was supposed to be all about me. I was allowed to be personal, so I told her about everything from the horrible family Christmas to leaving the gala with Dax and our weekend in Lawson's cabin. By the end of it, I was sure I'd filled most of our time and I wasn't sure what kind of therapy work we'd do, but I didn't care. It felt good to say it all.

"So, Dax is now your boyfriend?" Hadiza asked, clearly fishing for confirmation.

"Yeah. I've never had a boyfriend before."

"I find that a little surprising," she said with a laugh.

"Maybe it is. I don't know," I shrugged, thinking back to the conversation Dax and I had had by the pool table about relationships. "I told Dax that I just never let myself think about it. I liked boys. I had crushes and stuff, but I told myself I didn't have time."

"You told yourself that then. Has that voice spoken to you this time around?"

"No. It feels like that was so long ago. It's like that was someone else saying that," I said, surprised at just how separated I felt from that version of myself.

Hadiza nodded, a look of interest on her face. "That's called reframing, being able to see something that used to cause you anxiety from a new perspective."

"The idea of having a boyfriend never made me anxious," I said.

She gave me a knowing look, the one that always made me stop and rethink.

"No. I just didn't see the point in pursuing any of those boys," I said, immediately understanding what she meant. *I just didn't see the point.* "Oh."

She smiled. "You haven't ever seen the point in a relationship before because you thought it was a distraction. You came to therapy because you were having a lot of anxiety about your injury and how it has threatened your goal of being a professional soccer player. Would you say that's all pretty accurate?"

"Yeah," I said, a little worried about where this was going.

"You're here because you have a lot of anxiety about soccer."

"Well, not really about soccer."

"Okay," Hadiza said, weighing my words for a moment. "You feel a lot of anxiety about not having soccer."

I opened my mouth to agree but something about the words just rattled around my brain. Something about it felt strange, uncomfortable.

"Yes," I said slowly, still digesting what she said.

"What are you feeling?" she asked after a moment.

"I don't know," I said.

She shook her head. "Describe it."

I checked the time. Twenty more minutes. I paused a little longer, wondering if I'd regret being honest.

"I feel ... My stomach kind of hurts to be honest."

"So, kind of a sick feeling?"

"Yeah. It makes my brain hurt to even think about that."

"You don't typically think about what makes you anxious, do you?"

"I don't let myself think about that."

There it was again. It was like a punch to the gut. *I don't let myself think about that.*

"Let's talk about the things you like for a moment," Hadiza said, her tone a little lighter. "You have this great thing going on with Dax. It's new and you're embracing it, which is something you've never let yourself feel before. You have that list and you're taking steps with him to do it and you feel ..."

"I feel good. I never thought I'd feel good about breaking my diet, but he's right. Cake on your birthday isn't going to ruin the whole year of progress, you know?"

"You're right," she said. "You're challenging some past beliefs and learning that maybe reality is a little different than you thought. What I think is really commendable is that you basically came up with your own therapy tool. That list is a bunch of little goals that kind of contribute to the bigger goal."

"I see that, but I don't really see how they all connect," I said, thinking about the list and all the items I'd just checked off. "So, I know that they all work together, but I don't really understand yet how it all contributes to the whole soccer thing yet. I started it because it was really just a bunch of things to do before I went back to the program."

"By program, you mean you want to go back to the athlete diet and soccer training and whatever the specialist will have you do to address the nerve issues?" she asked.

"Yeah. I guess," I shrugged, pulling my right leg up so I could rest my chin on my knee. "That was the plan from the beginning. I'm just giving myself a break to reset like Dax did."

"He did the same thing?"

"Yeah. He had an incident in high school before a big race on his competitive team. He didn't feel great and so he took the time off from swimming entirely and then came back to it when he felt like he couldn't wait any longer."

"I see," Hadiza said. "Is that what you see this list as, another program to follow and then you'll have accomplished a goal?"

"What do you mean?"

She picked up her pen and jotted down something before looking up to answer me.

"I mean that you'll feel ready to face the specialist and training for the season again after you check everything off your list."

That was the entire point of the list. It was literally called *To Do Before Soccer*. I didn't answer her right away. I had that sick feeling again.

"Let's do some goal setting. Why not? You set the small goals for now. Let's look a little further out now," Hadiza said and lifted her notepad. She'd written the word *soccer* at the top and the word *injury* at the bottom. There was an arrow leading up from *injury* to the word *List*. Above that was another arrow going upward. "When you think about soccer. What comes to mind?"

"Going pro."

"Okay. That's a futuristic thought, right? That's something how many years ahead, you'd say?" She motioned to the empty space on her notepad.

"I don't know, maybe another four."

She drew four circles leading to the word *soccer* at the top. Four years. Four big goals.

"When you think about soccer now, what do you feel?"

I was so uncomfortable now. It had been building the entire session, but now my stomach churned so much that it hurt. My eyes stung and I tried to blink away the tears. I was not going to cry. I wasn't going to give her the satisfaction. Was that what I was avoiding? Trying to admit that she was right from the beginning about why I was in therapy?

"Let's take a second," Hadiza said. "Let's imagine the good things. It's work, but you come back. You work your way onto the starting team again. You have the same level of success and then you keep working hard like I know you plan to. People have already noticed you and now you've proven you're the real deal. You go pro. You leave college and make a professional team. How does that feel?"

"Good."

"What does that look like? What does life as a professional soccer player look like for you?"

Why did my eyes burn? Why could I not see it past the images of the professional soccer players I scrolled past on social media? I could see my family in the stands, sporting my number and my favorite team's colors. But Dax wasn't there.

"Margot," Hadiza said, her tone sending an angry tear rolling down my face. "Forget about what you think it's supposed to look like. Forget about what you think you have to do in order to be successful. Forget about what success as a soccer player looks like for now."

"There are things I have to do to make a professional team

and there are things that come along with being a pro. That doesn't change just because I'm a different person than Alex Morgan."

"True. But, when you do the things that feel right for you, you reach a kind of success that checks all your boxes. In other words, we all set our own paths. There are probably a million ways to score in soccer, right? Right foot kick. Left foot. Header."

"I see what you mean," I told her, feeling myself relax a little. She wasn't saying that soccer was a negative kind of anxiety after all. She wasn't suggesting that I didn't want soccer to be my life.

"There's a lot more that I'd like to discuss, but that's our time for this week," Hadiza said and raised the notepad again. She motioned to the three empty bubbles with her pen. "Try to come up with three big goals you would like to accomplish that would lead to a professional soccer career."

"I can do that."

"And," she said, raising her voice to refocus my attention on her. "And, come up with three goals you want to accomplish outside of soccer that are for yourself. Remember that these are the big goals. Three years to professional soccer. Three ways to accomplish that. Three personal things you want to be a part of that success."

"You want me to put my dating life in one of those personal bubbles, don't you?" I asked. I didn't need to say it aloud and she knew it from the way she smiled.

"I think *you* want to put a relationship in one of those bubbles."

I didn't deny it. We confirmed the date of our next appointment and then signed off the call. A few minutes later, my email pinged with a scanned copy of her notepad. I opened up another Google Doc and created two new lists, one for the big goals for professional soccer and another for personal goals.

Boyfriend or just friend, but hopefully boyfriend, I wanted him with me through the journey. So, I immediately added Dax to the list.

Chapter 22

I WAS EXCITED to get back to the rec center. Dax picked me up before the sun rose and we drove to North Ridge blaring a playlist of upbeat songs to get ready for our workout. He held my hand as we walked into the rec center, the same sullen-looking girl sitting at the front desk like always. I felt lighter on my feet than normal about the workout.

"Shit," Dax said as we passed through the glass doors to the indoor field. "I forgot my gym bag in the truck. Be right back."

I let go of his hand and turned from the door and my heart leaped in my chest. There was a soccer ball a yard ahead, just sitting on the field next to the soccer goal. I hadn't set foot on the field in over a week, not since I made that bet with Dax. Now that I thought about it, the bet was over and I hadn't realized it until now. I could technically skip my plans to master flip turns in the pool and spend the morning on the field.

The turn felt strange under my feet despite how short a time had passed since I'd been here. I dropped my bag to the ground and went to the ball, passing it from right foot to left and slowly walking further into the field. It was a strange feeling. It was familiar, but still foreign like running into and old friend and learning that they liked a different music and had a job you'd never thought they would.

I dribbled the ball to the other side of the field, picking up pace until I was jogging. It was easy, surprisingly easy. I didn't think about it. I just got started. I weaved side to side, passing the ball from one foot to the other, doing the warmup drill by memory until I'd completed the entire time for the first time since my injury. I was stunned. My heart hammered in my chest. My brain was a swirl of emotions.

"Ready?" Dax asked.

I lifted my eyes from the ball at my feet, catching a flash of something on his face. Was that disappointment? What was that?

"Um, yeah. Let's go," I said and left the ball.

I didn't really want to practice flip turns anymore and Dax didn't press. He warmed up in the lane next to me while I swam laps. Once he was ready, I got out of the pool and timed his sprints, telling him what I saw whenever he asked until he bobbed in the pool staring at me.

"What?" I asked. He didn't ask the usual questions after this sprint. He just looked at me in such a way that I worried a little about what he was thinking.

"You're thinking about soccer, aren't you?" he asked and glanced toward the clock on the wall.

There was no point denying it. I wasn't sure why I felt like I should.

"Yeah. I am," I told him as he pulled himself up on the edge of the pool to sit next to me. "I ran a drill while you were getting your bag from the truck. It was the first time I've been able to complete that drill."

"That's great," he said. "Doctor was right. Low impact workout to help gain some strength without risking further injury."

"Did you know that our bet is technically over? You said one week of no soccer and I did that," I said, playfully jabbing his bicep.

Dax stood up and lifted a towel from the bench behind us. He dried his hair before wrapping it around his hips. It almost distracted me from the subject. Almost.

"Okay, Sinclair. Point made," he said and extended a hand. He helped me to my feet.

"We don't have anywhere to be," I told him.

"Okay. You're not wrong. You can do fifteen minutes on the field while I wrap up here," he said with a wink. I didn't wait. I hurried to the locker room for my shoes, already dried off from the time I'd spent on the sidelines.

I was back on the field with the ball at my feet in minutes, running that same drill over and over. I knew I should incorporate a goal kick at the end, but I wanted to make sure I really had gotten stronger and that my first attempt hadn't been a fluke. I ran rep after rep until I started to feel my heartrate climb and it felt like being back at practice with the team. I could practically hear my teammates cheering me on, telling me how excited they were to have their best forward back in time for the season opener.

"Margot!"

I finished the drill before I turned to face him. Dax was motioned to his wrist. I begrudgingly ran back toward his side of the field and kicked the ball into the goal where I hoped it would stay safe until I could come back tomorrow. Dax pulled me to his side and planted a kiss at my temple.

"You're a little sweaty," he said with a laugh.

"Weirdly, I'm glad to hear that," I said and kissed him on the cheek.

We fell into a routine, starting with a pool workout together and then splitting so I could practice on the soccer field. Each day, I felt the soreness only soccer could bring creeping back and reminding me just how much I had to go toward being ready to start with the team again. I incorporated more and more with each session and found myself aching for more each time Dax would call me off the field.

"I know you would probably stay all day if I let you," he said as we walked toward the truck together.

"Absolutely," I told him, hiding my frustration behind the playful tone.

"You'll get there. Keep it light to gain a little strength like your doctor said and then go full time when they figure out how to treat the nerve stuff," he said.

"Yes," I said as we got into the truck.

My brain was still at the rec center as we drove back. Dax dropped me off in the driveway and I kissed him goodbye through the driver's window, the butterflies in the my stomach fading fast as I walked toward the front door of the cabin.

Marlee was sitting on the couch with her computer on her lap and she looked up with a groan when a loud bang came from the den to the left. She noticed me in the doorway and shook her head.

"What's wrong?" I asked.

She let out a long sigh and pointed toward the den. I heard Mom and Dad arguing now, something about some books on a shelf.

"They're already dividing up their assets. It's like they decided to split over a year ago. You know what, maybe they did. It's not like they ever acted like they enjoyed being with each other," Marlee said and tried focusing on her laptop again before looking up at me and setting it aside. "Madison was here. She wanted to ask Mom about some designs for the mother-of-the-bride dress and it ended in a big fight. Madison threatened not to invite them to the wedding at all because she's dramatic and over the top about everything. Dad got pissed and-"

"Lower your voice. If they hear then it'll just be a fight all over again over nothing," I told her.

"Nothing?" Marlee scoffed. "I don't really care about all that girly stuff like Madison, but the wedding is a big deal to her and Mom and Dad are both being shitty about it. I have to sit here and listen to them argue and try avoiding Mom because she says things that make me feel like she's trying to pit me against Dad."

"Just go somewhere else," I told her as I heard Mom in the background telling Dad to take a box with him when he goes today. Dad launched into an explanation of why he couldn't take any more things from the cabin yet.

"I'm working and I would like to be in my own space to do it," Marlee said and motioned to her laptop.

"Marlee, what are you always working on? You're always off in your own world, avoid everyone, and then you have the nerve to complain at everyone for not including you or not valuing your opinion when you don't ever care to involve yourself in anyone else. You think Madison is spoiled and self-centered, but you are no different!" I yelled. I hadn't yelled like that since Christmas. I was surprised how quickly it took for me to get there and I never thought I'd say those things to Marlee. Part of me felt bad, but then she rolled her eyes and sent me a smug look.

"I'm not at all like that brat," she said as though it was an obvious fact. She was already typing at her laptop again when I sent the next insult.

"Same story, different cover," I told her and started for the stairs. "Maybe it'll make sense to you now that I made a bookish metaphor of it."

Her mouth parted in shock and her face turned bright red. I hurried upstairs, convincing myself that I couldn't stay. I needed to do something. I needed to get somewhere, be productive. I turned around with my gym back still slung over my shoulder and went back downstairs, not answering Marlee when she asked where I was going. I climbed into my Jeep and drove back to North Ridge, back to the comfort of the turf field.

※

I MADE the most of my time so I could spend the least amount of time at home. Dax and I spent the morning together at the rec center. We spent most of our time in the pool, I even stopped the soccer drills so I could spend more time flirting in the pool. The few times we ended our workout in the shower together was enough of a reward for skipping soccer.

The mornings left me elated until he dropped me off at the cabin and the heaviness immediately fell on my shoulders. I knew I could do anything else. I knew I probably should, but I hadn't been spending my time at the field in the morning, so it wasn't like I was overdoing it by driving back to the rec center to practice. I started going the same time Dax did his afternoon lift in their garage gym so that I wouldn't miss any time with him. I'd spend a few hours running through soccer drills at the rec center, go home to shower and get ready, and then I'd go to the Krune's cabin for dinner and tea on the balcony with his family.

Everything felt balanced, but I was still focused on doing better. There was so much ground to make up if I was going to be ready to rejoin the team again by the next season and I pushed myself further each time, reveling in the soreness of my muscles each morning when I joined Dax in the pool.

I nearly slipped out of one of the rocking chairs on the Krune's balcony at the pop of a cork. I turned to watch Lucas Krune hold the champagne bottle away from his body, foam spilling from the top onto the deck.

"This is our last evening together, so I thought we should celebrate it," Lucas said.

I turned to Danielle for an explanation, and he gave it without me asking.

"Daren and his friends head back tomorrow morning. Lucas leaves tomorrow afternoon so he can get ready for appointments for the next week."

"Oh. Well, I'll miss all of you," I said and looked at Dax. I hadn't thought about how little time we had left together before he'd fly back to California for school. I'd be here. I'd be in Heritage City, doing my semester online. It was hitting me now that I was heading home where it would be just me to mediate between my parents as their divorce progressed. I slipped my feet out of my boots and pulled my knees to my chest, draping the fuzzy blanket over the armrest and letting the winter air chill my nerves.

"Toasts!" Lucas cheered as he filled the last of the champgne flutes. He handed one to each of us and we took turns toasting accomplishments. Daren was excited for a frat party coming up. Quintin toasted to the Krune's for letting him stay at the cabin, a sentiment that Noah echoed a moment after. Lucas raised his glass to good company and sent me a wink. Danielle said she was thankful for a full house at Christmas and hopeful for safe travels home. Dax gave a toast for friendship, and I thought I would melt into a puddle in my chair.

"To strength of mind and body," I said and raised my glass, the only on in the group that was still full. Daren had emptied his a few toasts ago and emptied the last of the bottle into his glass. Dax drank the last mouthful of his and set the glass on the table next to his parents'. He pressed a kiss to the top of my head and lowered his lips to my ear as the conversation turned from toasts to the next semester at college.

"You feel okay?" he whispered.

I pulled away to look at him, confused by the concern in his expression.

"Yeah. Why?"

"Just wondered. I know you like your champagne dry. That's why I told Dad to buy a brut for tonight," he said with a shrug.

"Oh. Well, I hope he didn't do that just for me," I said and hugged my knees. "I'm just full from dinner. I might drink it later."

"Dax, what do your classes look like?" Quintin asked. Dax straightened up and moved back to the rail in front of me, leaning against it as he took in the group.

"I have a lighter load than normal this year so I can get prepped for the Olympic trials in the summer," he said. Quintin turned his attention to me now and nodded in my direction.

"What about you?"

"I'll be in Heritage City for the semester. I'm doing the semester online so I can work with a specialist and then I'll fly back to California for the Fall semester," I said.

"You living with your parents?" Daren asked, wrinkling in nose. If it wasn't for all the people around, I probably would've too.

"Yep," I said. "I'm thinking about getting a job at one of the gyms in town or something."

"I bet you could do an internship with Danielle," Lucas interjecting, leaning forward in his rocking chair to look at me around his wife. "You could come to my practice too, but Danielle thinks you'd be great at what she does."

"Margot, honey, how about we go inside, and I take a look at your ankle," Danielle said, her voice low.

"I'm fine," I said and slipped my feet back into my boots.

"Mom, she sees a specialist in two weeks," Dax said and folded his arms over his chest with a smile. "She doesn't need two doctors."

"I know that, but I thought it looked swollen now. I just want to get a better look," she defended.

My stomach dropped as Dax's smile faded to a frown. I looked away when his eyes flicked to mine and I stood up, glad it was Danielle who followed after me first. I went inside and she directed me downstairs in case she needed any supplies. I reassured her that it was fine and that it must've been the lighting from the sunset that made it look weird, but she didn't act like she'd heard as I sat on the living room couch.

Danielle Krune sat a pillow on the coffee table and sat next to it, motioning for me to raise my right ankle as Dax joined us.

"Your doctors said they suspect you have some nerve damage?" she asked as I slowly raised my leg to the pillow.

I nodded when she looked up at me. "It's fine. It's actually gotten stronger from swimming."

She pushed the leg of my sweatpants up my calve to reveal my ankle. It was swollen. It wasn't bad, but it was easy to see. I noticed what she saw immediately, a purple spot on the outside of my ankle that I hadn't seen until now. My stomach twisted in anticipation, the guilt setting in when I heard Dax let out a long sigh.

"It doesn't hurt," I told them. "It looks worse than it is."

"It probably doesn't hurt that much with the nerve damage," Danielle said as she frowned at my leg. Dax put his hands on the top of his head.

"She's been doing about twenty minutes of swimming with me and fifteen minutes of soccer drills," he said, his eyes going from his mom to me. I could see the question there. His mom skipped right on by it and called me in the lie.

"That light of a workout wouldn't result in this," she said.

"Margot," Dax said with a sigh.

"My doctor cleared me to work out."

"Not like this, Margot. He said low impact. You're doing more than light workouts."

"I'm not overdoing it. I'm barely breaking a sweat!"

"You're working out twice a day, aren't you?" he asked.

I lowered my leg from the table.

"Margot, the way it's swollen, you shouldn't exercise at all until you see your doctor," Danielle told me, disregarding her son.

I wanted to cry. I was so frustrated.

"I want to go home," I said. The room was quiet for a long time. Danielle gave me a sympathetic smile and patted my knee before I could shrug away. It was the worst-case scenario. It was the last thing I wanted.

"I'll take you home," Dax said softly and went to grab his keys. I waited in the entryway impatiently, so on edge that I felt itchy. He walked too slow to meet me at the front door and once he'd opened it, I darted ahead and waiting for too long next to the passenger side door. He unlocked the truck and climbed in, sitting in silence as I waited for him to press the ignition.

"I don't need anyone feeling sorry for me," I finally said. I could still feel the ghost of Danielle's touch.

"I don't feel sorry for you," Dax said after a moment. It was a punch to the gut. I looked at him as he studied his hands on the steering wheel. With a deep breath, he turned to look at me, locking serious eyes with me. "You told me that you weren't self-destructing, but that is exactly what this is. If you don't want to play soccer anymore, Margot, you don't need an excuse. You don't need to destroy your body just so you can say that you tried to go pro."

"What? I can't believe you would suggest that! Of course, I want to go pro! It's been the dream my entire life!"

"You are a division one athlete, Margot! You know that you

have to rest. You know that you can't just will yourself better or be a better athlete by killing yourself in practices! This is not you wanting to be a professional athlete. This is you not coping with your anxiety. You may not be self-harming in the usual way, but you are overdoing it and you know that you are. You're a college athlete. You don't get to tell me that you don't know what's good for you and what's not," he said.

"I do know what's good for me! Where do you get off telling me how to be a college athlete and how to take care of my body when you swam in the state finals with an injury in high school and you work out twice a day?"

"It's different," he said and sat back in his seat in a huff.

"It's different because you're a future Olympian. Is that why?"

"No," he said and looked at me again. He didn't look angry now. He looked exhausted. He let out a deep breath. "You didn't have panic attacks when we started swimming. You didn't seem tense or fidgety when we were swimming. You never felt bad for skipping a workout or eating a damn pint of ice cream, Margot."

"I want to be a professional soccer player," I told him.

"I believe you. I believe you, Margot, and I think you can do it." He was sincere and something about his voice, the way his blue eyes pierced me now shattered something in my chest.

"Take me home, please," I said and wiped a tear from my face. I sat back in my seat and kept my eyes on the dash. After a long pause, the engine purred to life, and he backed out of the driveway.

The drive was short and silent. Dax moved at a crawl as we approached the cabin, so slow that it hard to tell when the car actually stopped. Amazingly, no one was parked in the driveway. I never got the cabin to myself like this.

"Margot," Dax said and let out a deep breath. "You can't be in control all the time. Life happens."

"I got in an accident that ruined soccer for me, my sister can't enjoy her engagement because my parents are getting divorced, and Marlee is weirder than normal. I think I know that life happens," I blurted.

"Yes, but you can't just fix everything. Some things can't be fixed and what's more, not everything needs to be fixed, Margot."

I kept my eyes on the dash. I wasn't even sure why I was still sitting here. We'd been in the driveway for a while and yet I felt like curling up in the seat. It was like moving bricks, but once I opened the door and got myself out the seat, I was hurrying toward the front door. I closed the door behind me and clapped a hand over my mouth as a sob burst from my chest. I went upstairs and locked myself in my room, noticing the truck still parked at the end of the driveway. It stayed there for nearly twenty minutes before Dax backed out and started back up the mountain.

He called a few hours later after I'd gotten ready for bed and told Marlee through my closed bedroom door that I wasn't feeling well. I almost let the call go to voicemail, but I rolled over beneath the sheets and took the phone from my bedside table instead.

"Hey," I said.

"Hey," he said. The line was silent for a moment. "I don't want to hurt you, Margot, but I think you needed to hear that. You have so much potential, too much going for you to think that you're limited by your abilities on some soccer field or by what you can do for other people. You aren't stuck. You won't be frozen in this moment forever and I just wanted you to know that, to know that I care about you and not what you can or can't do. Just you, Margot."

I squeezed my eyes shut against the tears. I tried to shut out all the emotions tugging at my heart, sending it into a frenzy.

"So, I only have a couple of days left before my flight back to California."

"Okay. Yeah," I said and took a deep breath before I said what I needed to. "I just need a little time to myself first."

It was quiet for a moment.

"Okay. I understand. How about Friday we take a final swim at Lawson's? I leave Saturday for the airport," Dax said.

"Okay."

"I'll pick you up Friday," he said. The line went quiet again before I agreed and hung up. I was suddenly much more awake than before. I got out of bed and went to my desk. I opened my email, deleting out the spam before I found the nerve to open Coach's email.

This time, I sent a reply.

❄

IT WASN'T until Dax drove out of Crescent Peak that I felt the awkwardness melt away in the truck and we slowly slipped back into our old ways. He told me about the classes he was taking this semester and told me about his roommates. I told him about my classes and how different they would feel being online instead of in-person.

I noticed the grin on Dax's face as we stripped down to get into the pool in Lawson's backyard, taking off my sweats to reveal that bikini I'd worn the first day at the pool. The cold water was heavenly as I let it wash around me, not caring about my long hair. Dax floated on his back next to me and we watched the clouds overhead until snow began to rain down on us. I kissed him as the snow melted against our bodies, kissed him deeply because I knew I wouldn't see him for too long afterward.

My hair was still damp as we drove home. Dax's had dried long before the trip back he looked handsome as ever as he parked his truck in the driveway of my family's cabin and turned in the seat to face me with a smile. That smile nearly crushed me and the way it melted from his face a moment later sent me to tears. He reached out and brushed the moisture from my cheeks.

"I know," he said in a whisper. "But don't. Please. Don't shut me out, Margot."

I took his hand from my face and held it between both of mine, staring at the lines of his palm for a moment as I struggled to piece together all my thoughts.

"I just need us to be friends right now. I need to figure some things out. I need the space. I need ..." I still didn't know what I needed. I didn't know what I wanted. My heart hurt for so many reasons, so many that I couldn't discern with him beside me right now. He filled an emptiness I never thought I'd fill, but I didn't need to fill a hole. I needed to repair it.

After a stretch of silence, he gave my hand a squeeze and then raised it to my chin, lifting my face to look at him. His lips twitched into a sad smile.

"You'll always have me, whatever you want that to look like," he said and brushed another tear from my face with the pad of his thumb. He lowered his hand and sat back in his seat. The distance between us felt wrong, too far, strange. I resisted the urge to apologize and to touch him again. It wouldn't make it easier. It wouldn't matter if I hugged him or if I sat motionless. It would still hurt like hell.

"I can't imagine not having you in my life," I told him.

Dax smiled and nodded; his eyes shimmering.

I got out of the truck and ran inside before I could fall apart.

Chapter 23

Online classes weren't so bad. It was kind of annoying to sit behind a computer in my bedroom for hours with old photos and cringy décor from high school around me. I needed to do something, but before I could accept a position at a local gym, Danielle Krune sent me a text with some information about an internship program at the hospital that I could take part in. It was unpaid, but it promised to keep me busy and that was worth more to me now than minimum wage.

I helped where I could around the hospital and quickly found myself spending most of my time alongside a couple physical therapists in the clinic. I shadowed their appointment with willing clients and it felt normal. It was like soccer, but without the practices and field work. It was strictly healing and exercises geared toward the client's goals. Most of the patients were elderly and were looking for increased mobility, but there were a few high school athletes that we put together plans for to make sure they'd be healed and strong for the sports they would return for. It was actually kind of fun to discuss that planning.

My own journey was much slower than I'd hoped considering that the specialist told me during my first appointment that the best plan considering my goal of going professional was to have surgery. I was admitted the next day for the minor procedure. The twelve weeks in the cast was the worst part. I made the best grades I'd had since starting college and I had a lot of time to shadow at the hospital. The therapists gave me a lot of pointers about my recovery and when the cast finally came off, I had more strength and mobility than the doctor had anticipated. It was the best-case scenario.

Even better, I was cleared not long after to return to school. I could practice. I could join team lifts. I was told to be conservative at first and check in with the team physical therapist, but I was cleared all the same. I emailed my coach and by the end of that day, we'd set up a day for me to rejoin the team for practice and I'd booked my flight.

I was way more nervous than I thought I would be. The flight back to California felt strange and that anxiety only increased until I felt like a live wire the day I walked campus to the soccer complex. It was weird to walk into the building and realize how much it smelled like grass and Clorox.

Movement from my left caught my attention and I opened my mouth to greet the two players before I got a good look at their faces. They both smiled at me and continued their conversation as they continued down the hallway ahead of me. I didn't recognize them. They were probably transfers from another school.

I followed them into the team locker room. It was exactly the way I remembered it. All the emotions from winning matches and team bonding sessions after a hard practice flooded my brain. The taller of the girls who'd passed me in the hall approached what used to be my locker, her jersey hanging at the back. I wondered if she took it down if there would still be a scuff mark on the wall from when I'd thrown my cleats in my locker after my last horrible practice.

"You ready to suit up, Sinclair?" a voice called to my right.

I turned to face her. I felt a surge of energy as I looked at my coach's smiling face.

"Yes. Hell, yes," I told her as she tucked a clipboard under her arm.

"Hit the field! Warm-ups!" Coach yelled, her voice echoing around the room. The giggling and chatter stopped immediately as the girls hurried through the door at the back that led down to the field. "Suit up and work in. Do what you can. We'll talk after," Coach said before following the last of the pack.

I dropped my duffle bag next to the bench in the middle of the room, fumbling to slide my gear on in my excitement. Music played over the sound system as the team split into groups to do their warmups, the drills I could do in my sleep. I'd been able to complete them flawlessly for weeks, my ball handling so like the way I looked when I watched past games. It was easy, so easy that it shocked me and I pushed myself even further as we moved into new drills.

I caught Coach watching me a few times. She'd whisper to the assistants on the sidelines, make notes on her clipboard, and even gave me a thumbs-up a few times. I was so excited by my progress that I wasn't quite ready when practice ended and the entire team returned to the locker room. I followed Coach when she called me over, leading me into the large office just off the locker room.

"How do you feel?" she asked.

"Great," I said as she sat her clipboard on the desk.

"Your movement looks good, reaction time just about where you left off," she said with a laugh of disbelief. "

"Thank you."

"Have you seen the physical therapist?"

"Not yet, but I emailed over the notes from my doctor last week and he said that everything looked great. I'm meeting today after practice to get evaluated," I said. I felt like I could cry, I was so happy. I'd done it. I came back after injury and was in good shape.

"Good. Do that," Coach said and pulled her phone from her pocket. "As long as the therapist is good with it, keep coming to practices and lifts. It's good to have you back, Margot. I mean that." She patted me on the shoulder and gave me a warm smile as she pressed her phone to her ear.

I took that as my cue to leave. I went back into the locker room and a few of the girls welcomed me back as I made my way to the bench to take off my gear. I was still buzzing with energy as

I sat and listened to them talk. I sat there until the room slowly emptied, still feeling like I could run laps. The three remaining players finished their conversation, standing up.

Ashley and I spent a lot of time together on the field, dribbling back and forth and weaving through opponents. She hesitated as she waited for the others to gather their things.

"It was good having you back, Margot," she said.

"I'll see you at practice tomorrow," I told her. She looked a little surprised by the comment but smiled and nodded.

I left after them, hoping my racing brain would calm down as I sat with the physical therapist. The appointment went just as all my doctor's appointments before had gone. The therapist was happy with the look of my leg and was glad to see that it wasn't even swollen after the long practice. It was reassuring to hear, but I still felt on edge. I hoped that it would go away during the walk back to my hotel. By the time I got there, I didn't feel any calmer. It was like I'd chugged a large cup of coffee or something. I felt like I was waiting for something, like I had a whole day planned out and just couldn't remember all the things I had to do. It was uncomfortable and it lingered even as I went to bed that night.

I was only in town for a week, but I'd fallen back into the routine halfway into the week. It took me a little bit to realize what that routine was. I forgot that I didn't really know most of my teammates that well. I knew them, like where they were from and a little bit about what they liked and their majors and such, but I realized when a few of them left practice to get ready for a sorority event that there was a lot I didn't know and it struck me now that I'd never asked.

"What sorority are you all in?" I asked as I slipped into my sandals.

Ashley looked up from her phone. "Kappa. You?"

"Oh, I'm not in a sorority," I told them.

"Oh. For some reason I thought you were," Ashley said. "Well, you can come with us, if you want. There's a beach party in a few weeks after the semester ends and a few of us are going to shop for new swimsuits."

"Are you all Kappas?" I asked. The other two girls, the two I hadn't recognized on the first day, nodded. The taller girl finished tying her thick blonde hair into a large bun at the top of her head.

"I transferred from Texas. I walked on in the fall. I'm Lola," she said and then nodded to the dark-haired girl next to her. "This is Jaylee."

Jaylee gave me a small smile. "I kind of worked my way off the bench after you got injured."

Oh. I should've remembered her then. Had I really not met them before?

"So?" Ashley started slowly. "Bikinis?"

Ashley had a car. she drove all of us to a little boutique not far from campus that had a wall full of bikinis. Jaylee was immediately drawn to a black bikini top with a string of pearls that tied at the nap of the neck. Lola found her way to a collection of pink swimsuits and motioned us over.

"Jack likes pink," she said and turned from us to face the wall again. There were several shades of pink, some with other bright colors mixed into the pattern, and a few with ruffles.

"How do you know he likes pink?" Ashley asked as Lola reached for one of the ruffled tops. It wasn't really my style, but the top on the rack behind it caught my attention. It was in a coral blue color and the straps were a lighter shade, that blue outlining the triangle top. There was a little silver ring between the two cups. I pulled the top from the rack and scanned the bottom section of the wall for a matching bottom.

"I was wearing that pink dress when we met at that frat party," Lola said and snagged a pink pair of bottoms that had a a similar ruffle detail as the top.

I found a pair of swimsuit bottoms that matched the top, the same light blue and darker blude color combination with silver rings holding the front half to the back half, which covered even less of my ass than maybe the swimsuit I owned did. I thought about Dax's reaction when I'd worn it that first day at the pool in North Ridge and I felt my insides heat.

"That's really cute," Ashley told me. Lola kept gathering pink swimsuits from the wall, whispering to herself as she inspecting them.

"I like that it has details, but it isn't going to be risky to wear," Jaylee said as she joined us with the black bikini in her hands.

Ashley gasped. "Not risky? Did you see how small the bottom is?"

"I don't know if you can call it risky if the idea is to have your ass out," I said with a laugh. Jaylee motioned to me as though I'd made the point for her.

"That's what I'm saying," she said as Lola joined us with several suits hanging from her arm. "How many are you going to get?"

Lola shrugged and looked down at the suits in her arms nervously. "I'm not good at making decisions."

"Sounds like you need to try them on and we need to rank them," Ashley said with a wry smile.

It was strange how comfortable I felt with them as we catcalled and debated which suits were better, Lola making a point to dramatically burst from the changing stall at the back of the room and strut around the little couch we'd crowed onto. It reminded me a little of being with my sisters. I almost forgot that I had a call with Hadiza until my alarm went off on my phone. Lola, still not able to decide, left the store with three swimsuits and swore that she'd take two back. Ashley gave me a look that told me there was no way she was doing that.

Jaylee told us about her family's upcoming vacation to Mexico. They would leave the week after the sorority beach party, which I got all the information for. They told me about what boys would be there and who they were hoping to be noticed by, all but Jaylee who was in a serious relationship. Lola and Ashley gushed about their crushes while Jaylee scrolled her phone and smiled at their girly comments as we drove back to campus.

I was glad that they didn't get a chance to ask about my dating life before Ashley pulled up to my hotel. I don't know why it made me so nervous. Dax and I weren't together, but it gave me the worst stomach ache to think about how things had been between us. I thought about him often, found my mind thinking about the feel of his arms when I laid in bed unable to sleep. That was the thing. I was elated to be back on the field. I cried the day I was cleared to practice again, I was so happy. Still, part of me left practice feeling a little let down. In the past, I would just go practice on my own some more or relax to whatever soccer game I could stream on TV. I found myself craving time with people more than being alone in my room. I also didn't want to practice outside of my scheduled workouts and my brain tried to chase away the acknowledgement each time it would creep into my brain.

Ashley, Jaylee, and Lola waved at me as I headed toward the hotel entrance. I hurried up to the third floor in time to hop on the video call with Hadiza, who sat in the same office she always had. Her smile was infectious.

"I take it everything on campus is going well," she said with a laugh.

I let out a deep breath and something about it felt like a relief, so much so that I felt a well of emotions settle in my chest. It took a moment to settle my nerves and keep it all from spilling over, even though the tears came anyway.

"What are you feeling?" she asked.

I took another deep breath as I tried to piece it all together. Today had been the most fun I'd had at college and it hadn't hit me until I realized I'd never been out with friends like that. I hadn't gotten to know my own teammates past the basics. My time at school was always so carefully planned between classes, practice, and keeping my mind on my goals on being the best soccer player that I could be.

"I think I messed up," I said through the sob.

"What happened?" Hadiza asked.

"Not now. Nothing happened," I told her and cleared my throat. "I've missed out on so much. I've been so focused on soccer. I don't spend time with friends. I didn't realize until today that even though I put so much into my performance on the soccer field, I haven't put nearly as much into the team. I barely know my own teammates and I told myself today that going out for just an hour wouldn't mess anything up. One hour today isn't going to take away from my progress toward going pro. So, I went out with three of my teammates."

I had to stop to slow my breathing again. I needed to refocus my thoughts, needed to be honest about how it felt today and how it felt knowing I didn't even know the name of the player that got off the bench because I left the team.

"How did it go?" Hadiza asked, resting her chin on her hand.

"It was the most fun I'd had in a long time," I told her.

"And that's the part that has you upset right now?" she asked, doing that squinty thing with her eyes she always did when she wanted me to confirm or deny her assumptions.

I nodded. "I'm sad, no, frustrated. I'm mad at myself because this is what I've done forever. I chase away anything that I think might be a distraction. I push away whatever might get in the way of soccer."

"I don't think it's really about soccer at all," Hadiza said and sat back in her chair. "Until your accident, soccer was dependable. What else in your life has been dependable, predictable for you?"

I hadn't expected her to suggest that soccer was dependable, but I knew exactly what she meant. I'd never denied it. Soccer was what I was good at. I never struggled to be the starter on any team I was on. I'd never faced a drill or a skill I couldn't master, even if it took some time. I knew what hard work on the field looked like. I knew what it took to be better and I pushed and pushed and got better and better just like I knew I would. There was an easy path to follow and I'd never been steered wrong.

When my parents argued, there was still soccer to be exactly what I expected it to be. When Dad worried that his company might go under when I was in middle school, it didn't matter because I would be okay with my college soccer scholarship and then my professional career. Soccer didn't need anything from me the way my sisters did or my mom did when she complained about my dad when she picked me up from school or like my dad did when he vented about Mom on the drive to soccer practices.

Marlee couldn't be there for me about dating because her dating life had been a wreck growing up. Marlee couldn't be there for me about school because she didn't know what it was like to need to study to make a measly B. Mom and Dad were completely emotionally unavailable. I needed soccer because I didn't have anyone else.

I don't really think it's about soccer at all.

I looked up from the keyboard at Hadiza, her small smile telling me that she had already seen the truth on my face.

"I gave you homework a while back, which you never did," she chided, chuckling as she opened the file next to her and turned until she found the right page. She lifted the list we'd started together months ago. "You were supposed to list out the steps you need to complete to become a professional soccer player *and* the things you would like to accomplish in the next four years that are just for yourself. Have you added to that list at all?"

More lists. Why did it seem that the answers were all on the lists?

"No," I told her as I stared at the blank circles on the page. "I haven't added to them."

I hadn't, but I wasn't stumped the way I'd felt before. It was easy to come up with the steps to being a professional soccer player, so easy that I barely thought about them. Instead, I thought about the way Lola snorted when she laughed, which was hilarious to me, considering how gorgeous and conscious of her appearance she was. I felt guilty about not knowing them until now, and I wanted to do better. I wanted to know more about the girls on the team. I wanted to have more of a relationship with whoever my roommate would be when I moved back to campus. I wanted to fill my days with more than just soccer. Dax liked to cook. I wanted to do something just because it was fun. I wanted to see more to my future than just soccer because even if I did go pro, I couldn't be the best forever. The chances of being the best at all were slim. The truth was that soccer couldn't be forever, not even for the best soccer player. There was more to life than soccer. Christmas Break with Dax and today with my friends proved that there was so much joy in life to be had and I was missing it all, avoiding it because I thought soccer would promise me more. Happiness is found in the moment, not something the future could promise.

"I think I want to declare a major," I said.

After settling on sports medicine as a new major, one that didn't require too many more classes than I'd already taken thankfully, I opened my Google Drive to find the list Hadiza had talked about. I opened a different one instead.

The list Dax and I made was in my *recent* tab even though I knew I hadn't touched that document since I left Crescent City. It had been edited a few weeks ago by Dax according to the timestamp when I opened it up. It looked almost exactly the same except for one addition that made my chest tighten.

To Do Before Soccer:
~~1. Skinny dipping?~~
~~2. Raid the liquor cabinet at Lawson Rathbone's cabin~~
~~3. Go to the Winter Solstice Gala with a date~~
~~4. Watch a terrible movie and eat a pint of ice cream~~
5. Watch Dax Krune at the Olympic Trials (click here for ticket)

Chapter 24

"You didn't tell him, right?" I asked from the passenger seat of Daren's Charger.

"No, but I still don't understand why you haven't told him yet," he said as he took the turn into the parking lot a little too fast. I held onto the door handle to keep from sliding into the center console.

"I haven't ... Things just haven't lined up," I said, not really sure how to answer him. The truth was, I was being a bit of a coward about telling Dax all the things that had happened since Christmas. I'd taken the ticket in the Google Doc as a good sign and just ran with it. The next month of waiting was hard and I nearly called him, but I felt like I needed to get settled into my version of reality, the one I was choosing entirely for myself, before I brought him into it. The anxiety tried sending me down a million rabbit holes about how he might not fit into my life now, but deep inside I knew he would. He said he wanted me in his life, even if we were just friends. I couldn't imagine not having him.

"My family is already in the stands. They've been watching the entire trials in-person. Mom has been cheering so much that she sounds like Dad now," Daren chuckled.

"Thanks for picking me up. I'm sorry you had to wait an extra three hours. If I knew the flight would be so delayed, I would've told you," I said as I got out of the car. Daren was at the front of the Charger waiting on me as I flattened the Berkeley T-shirt I'd bought especially for today and adjusted the hem of my shorts.

"Margot, it's fine," Daren said as he led the way to the entrance. "If I hadn't waited, it would've been another hour to get to the airport."

He was right. If he hadn't been there ready to pick me up, thank God he'd tracked my flight information, then I wouldn't make Dax's heat at all. As we approached the ticket kiosk with our phones out, a horn blared and cheering erupted.

"Heat started," Daren said next to me as a woman scanned the barcode on his phone.

My heart hammered in my chest as I waited for the man to scan my ticket and allow me through. Once he had, I sprinted ahead until I realized I had no idea where I was going. I slowed and let Daren point the way since it was too loud to hear a word he said. Most of the crowd was on their feet, so it was impossible to get a good look at the pool as we hurried down the walkway. Daren started up another set of steps as the cheering grew somehow louder than before. I saw them before they saw me.

Lucas Krune let out a roar and turned to his wife, pulling her to his chest and letting her go so roughly in celebration that she stumbled into the blonde girl next to her. They held each other for a moment as they cheered before they looked back toward the pool, Danielle and the blonde girl holding a banner with *Krune* painted across it in blue. I ran after Daren who was immediately pulled into his Dad's tight hug.

"What happened?" I asked, my yell lost in the cheering.

"Margot!"

Lucas Krune reached past Daren and pulled through the row, placing me next to himself and Danielle. They both went to hug me at once, resulting in an awkward half-hug with both of them as I was jostled around. The announcer's call was garbled, which worsened as the entire Krune clan began shouting.

"What happened?" I yelled again as the crowd simmered from the event.

"Oh my God! You're Margot!"

The blonde girl was dressed in a similar Berkeley T-shirt as mine, complete with a custom *Krune* tattoo on her right cheek. She reached across Danielle to grab my hand, pulling me closer. There was no room to get a hug, so she just held onto my hand as she began talking over the announcer calling the time for the next event.

"Dax says you're like his best friend. He's told me all about you," she said.

It felt like being punched in the stomach.

"This is Taylor. She's on the women's swim team," Danielle said, hugging me to her side.

"Our teams cross paths pretty often. We ended up getting to know each other pretty well this year thanks to Olympic stuff and all," Taylor said with a shrug, glancing up at the scoreboard overhead as it flashed the event schedule for the day. I'd missed most of it, but it seemed that I'd missed a whole lot more than swimming.

"Did you two train together?" I asked, pulling her attention from the screen.

She shook her head and then shrugged. "Not really, but we did meet to help each other keep times and such. So, kind of?"

"There it is!" Lucas yelled, patting me on the back. He pointed at the screen. "Two-hundred-meter butterfly."

We had twenty minutes before the heat.

"Twenty minutes is a short turn-around to be ready to swim again," I said. Lucas did a double take, glancing from the screen to catch my gaze before he turned with a smile.

"That wasn't Dax's heat. It was his teammate's," he said and clapped me on the back. "Hunter just secured his spot on the team."

"Oh. So, Dax hasn't competed yet?"

"Not today. You should've seen him in the prelims. He was the front runner pretty early. It wasn't a surprise that he made the finals and he's the favorite to win the two-hundred-meter butterfly."

Butterflies of a different kind filled my stomach. No one sat down as we waited for his event. This was Dax's best event. I remembered all that time we'd spent timing sprints in the pool over Christmas Break and I wondered how much faster he was now. He was already swimming a qualifying time then, so surely that made earning a spot on the team likely.

I felt a little sick when the athletes filed out toward the pool, not a single one paying any attention to the cheering crowd. The camera panned over the group as they got ready in front of their starting blocks and my stomach did flips when I saw Dax on the big screen. He took his place on the block, arm muscles flexed, and then he launched himself into the water at the buzzer and the sick feeling in my stomach turned to pure adrenaline.

I cheered so loud between Danielle and Lucas that my throat started to hurt. Dax kept just head of the swimming in the lane next to him, so close that if he slipped back into his old form, he'd lose his place. I hoped that he kept his focus as he turned at the wall and cut through the water beneath like a shark. He came up for a brief second, both arms launching from the pool and pulling him ahead.

He did another flip-turn at the starting point, resurfacing with the same amount of intensity that he'd started with. The man in the next lane was just on his heels as he swam for the end of the pool, the two of them far enough ahead that it was unlikely anyone would overtake them. Dax reached the end of the pool seconds ahead, completing his flip-turn and starting into the final sprint ahead still in first place. My ears hurt from the cheering around me as Dax swam faster and faster, creeping further ahead of the swimmer next to him.

He bobbed beneath the starting block, his eyes going to the big screen above the pool where his time and place were displayed. The last of the swimmers reached the finish now and Dax held a fist up into the air. He was on the big screen, smile wide and hair sticking up as he pulled off the swim cap. The announcer's words were lost in our cheers as I hugged Danielle. I took the end of the banner when Taylor shoved it into my hands and we turned to hold it at our chests, jumping up and down so much that it was hard to read the name painted across it even as our little group was projected onto the big screen above the pool.

"I hope everyone's passports are current!" Lucas yelled, giving Daren a high-five and turning to slap my hand with enough force that it stung.

Dax leaned on the lane divider, talking with the second-place swimmer. They both hugged before exiting the pool as the announcer's voice boomed through the area.

"Dax Krune will join the US Olympic Team, finishing first with a six-second lead on the second-place swimmer, Zach Chambers. Chambers will join the Olympic team for the second year in the two-hundred-meter butterfly and the one-hundred-meter butterfly alongside Krune."

We stayed just long enough to confirm on the big screen after the event that Dax really had made the Olympic team. It took a long time for us to come down from the excitement and I was still buzzing as I rode with Daren to the hotel where we were all staying. The hotel was huge, in the swanky part of the city and had a fancy restaurant just off the lobby that the Krunes had already made reservations for.

I waited while they all checked in, my eyes landing on Taylor who quickly typed away at her phone. She looked up and smiled when she caught me staring.

"Hey," Daren said, elbowing me and startling me out of my thoughts. "We're going to all change into clothes for dinner and head to the restaurant a little early for drinks. Dax and Hunter are on their way here. They'll clean up and meet us."

"Okay. That's cool. Great," I said, reaching for my suitcase.

Daren smirked. "Relax. He'll be excited to see you."

"Yeah. Sure," I said, trying not to think too far into it as he went to grab his suitcase by the front desk. It didn't work. My brain filled with too many thoughts. He'd saved that ticket for me, yes, and I booked a flight to watch him swim. I hadn't even booked a hotel room because I thought ... I was so stupid. This entire thing was stupid of me.

"Want to head up?" Taylor asked, stopping next to me. "You

didn't happen to bring a hairdryer, did you? I forgot mine and those hotel ones don't dry my hair fast enough."

"Yeah. I did. Um, could I get ready in your room? Mine isn't ready yet," I told her as the panic started to set in. I couldn't process what she'd said, just that she'd agreed, and I followed her into the elevator as I tried to control the panic clawing at my chest.

Great. I might have a panic attack in her hotel room.

Taylor opened the door, and I rolled my suitcase in after her. She didn't wait long before asking me about myself, launching into an excited tangent about how much Danielle had helped her once she found out that I was studying sports medicine. Of course, she was planning to be a surgeon and Danielle had connected her with surgeons she knew just like she'd gotten my the internship in Heritage City. I turned away from her as she stripped to her bra and underwear, a matching lacy bra and panty set laid out on the bed next to her.

"The Krunes are the nicest people," I told her as I unzipped my suitcase and pulled out my blue silk dress. Madison had made it for me when I told her about the trip, insisting on making yet another dress to show off my best features. The skirt was knee-length with tiers of flirty ruffles. The top plunged nearly to my navel. It fit me perfectly. I don't know how Madison did it, but she was able to make structured dresses that you didn't need to worry about being a possible wardrobe malfunction.

"They are the best and I am so thankful they've been so welcoming to me," Taylor said, walking past me for the full-length mirror on the back of the hotel room door. She wore a short black dress that showed off her sporty legs and cinched waist. She already looked date-night worthy but turned then to the makeup bag in her hand. She pulled out all the necessary tools and palates and then two palm-sized boxes.

"I wasn't kidding when I said that Dax talks a lot about you," Taylor said as she finished blending the foundation on her skin. "He said you two grew up together. We're excited that you came."

I stepped into my nude heels, wishing I'd packed more

makeup and at least a straightener. Taylor must've noticed my thoughts as she finished curling the ends of her blonde hair, because she asked if I wanted her to do mine next. I was so nervous that I needed to do anything else that wasn't standing in the middle of her room in my uncomfortable heels, so I moved to the mirror and let her work.

"I don't want to come off weird, but," she said as she finally finished with the last piece of hair. My brown locks hung in loose curls around my face. I don't know that I even looked this girly at the Winter Solstice Gala. Maybe it was just the fact that I was wearing a dress that would highlight my chest, which I know Dax had liked, and I had jumped on a plane to chase after a boy I'd called "just friends" not long ago. "I think you and I will be good friends."

"Really?" I asked, not sure what else I was supposed to tell her.

"Yeah. We have a lot in common. Dax says we do, anyway," Taylor said and reached for one of the little boxes. She opened it and pulled out the necklace and earrings. She leaned close to the mirror as she put them on and I remembered that I was supposed to buy jewelry to match this dress.

"He's going to be so excited that you're here," she said and opened the next box. My chest constricted when I saw the ring, a princess-cut diamond set in a silver ring. She took it from the box and placed it on her ring finger on her left hand.

It felt like the room had closed in. I went to the bathroom and closed the door. I nearly lost myself before I focused on the night ahead. Hadiza called it grounding yourself. I thought about the nice hotel I was in, how kind Taylor was, how Dax had just made the Olympic team, I was here to celebrate with him, and I was finally in a place all my own with skills that made the anxiety manageable for the first time. I had everything I wanted and it didn't matter that Taylor had an engagement ring. I still had Dax. He was still the best friend I could ask for and he would still be excited that I was here. I was excited to be here.

I could cry about it later after I'd figured out where I'd get a room this late.

"Hey! It looks like the boys beat us downstairs!" Taylor called through the door. I took a final breath and joined her with the sincerest smile I could muster. We rode the elevator down together as my heart picked up pace. When the doors opened, there was a group of people standing in the lobby. It took me a moment to realize all the nicely dressed people were the Krunes. Dax and Hunter stood on one side, both in slacks and button-up shirts with their medals still around their necks. They must've dressed at the arena and just arrived because they both had rolling luggage in tow and duffle bags on their shoulders.

I felt like my stomach dropped to my heels when Dax's eyes landed on me. He smiled before turning his attention to the squealing blonde that had rushed for him. He let go of his suitcase and let the duffle bag slip to the floor in time to hug Taylor. He lifted her off her feet for a moment before setting her back down with a laugh. He turned to Hunter and clapped him on the shoulder as he took two steps forward to wrap his arms around Taylor. She cupped his face and rose on her toes, kissing him full on the mouth, a kiss that quickly deepened enough that they'd surely be embarrassed by the display if they weren't so absorbed in the moment.

Dax turned his gaze on me again with that wry smile I loved so much and I felt all those fears and the last of the anxiety that kept me frozen in place melt away. I met him halfway across the floor and threw my arms around him, kissing him hard. He responded immediately, his hands pulling me tight to his chest as he deepened the kiss, hands gripping my hips for a second before he pulled away.

I hadn't heard the cheers and Daren's catcalls until now. Dax was red in the face and from the burning in my cheeks, I probably was too. He turned toward the group and hurried to gather his things on the floor.

"I'm going to drop this off in my room," he said and pulled

the duffle bag onto his shoulder again. He returned to me with his suitcase in tow. "Can you help me get it upstairs?"

I took the handle of the suitcase as Daren, Taylor, and Hunter laughed behind us.

"Help him upstairs, Margot," Daren said with a laugh that only made my cheeks heat more.

"Make it quick, Krune. We have reservations in twenty," Hunter teased.

Dax pulled me along by my hand. Thankfully, we didn't have to wait for the next elevator and were able to dart inside. His hands were on me again before the doors fully slid shut, not breaking the kiss until the elevator opened on his floor.

We practically ran down the hall, waiting far too long to unlock the door. Dax burst inside ahead of me, tossing his duffle bag aside and turning to face me. The hotel room door shut behind us and my stomach twisted in anticipation.

"I hope you can get your money back for the room, because you're not spending the night alone tonight, Sinclair," he said with a smile, lifting his hands to start undoing the buttons of his shirt.

I let go of the suitcase and reached for the zipper at the back of my dress as I walked toward him. "I didn't book one. I hoped—"

His lips were on mine again as his fingers pulled the zipper the rest of the way down my back. I undid the last of the buttons on his shirt as he slipped my underwear down the curve of my ass. I did a little wiggle so they would fall the rest of the way to the floor as I shoved the shirt from his shoulders. He pulled his arms free from the fabric and lifted me, never breaking the kiss as he carried me to the bed and laid me beneath him.

"We have fifteen minutes," I said as he pulled away to undo the buckle of his belt.

"I can do a lot in fifteen," he said with a laugh.

Our bodies melted together the way I remembered. It was like the first time all over again, sending that wave crashing down and tears flooding my face by the time he'd settled on the bed next to me and only the sound of our heavy breathing filled the room.

"You found the ticket," he said.

I rolled onto my side. "I had to complete my list."

He smiled and propped himself up with an elbow, brushing my curls behind my shoulder.

"Did you complete it?"

The smile that pulled at my lips was more than happiness that I was here, happiness that we were more than just friends. This was pride.

"I am studying sports medicine. I'm still on the soccer team."

"That's great! So, you still have a shot at going pro."

"I do, but only if I want it. Right now, I'm just happy to play. If I get the opportunity and I still want to play then, then I will. I have a few more years to decide," I told him, butterflies taking flight at the excitement that lit up his face.

"Sounds like you have a lot of time to fill in the meantime," he said and pulled me toward him by my hip.

I giggled as he pulled me on top of him. "We better start making a list."

Fifteen minutes quickly became twenty and then who knew how long it had been. We'd definitely missed dinner, but I didn't care. For the first time in my life, I felt entirely content.

ACKNOWLEDGMENTS

This book was difficult for me to write. I stopped writing it after several chapters because I needed to take a break emotionally. Like Margot, anxiety is something I struggle with and when I was writing this book in January of 2024, there was a lot of change brewing in my life. That paired with Margot's struggles was too much to balance at once.

So, I took a break. I considered not coming back to this series. Then, I decided to rebrand the series entirely from just the Winter Witches trilogy to the Seasons of Witches series to better encompass all my ideas for witches across all four seasons.

I was so excited to come back to Margot's story because I think anxiety, especially mental health concerns within the sports community, is not often discussed in a way that shows how strong these characters are. A lot of people struggling with anxiety and depression present to the outside world like Margot, like they have it all together and can be a rock for other people. I wanted to show that through Margot, but I had to get myself in the right headspace first to do it.

When I came back to this book in the fall of 2024, the story unfolded quickly and developed into a romance unlike any I've written before. Dax and Margot are adorable and I have my husband to thank for a lot of that. Like Dax, he knows exactly how to call me out when I'm not being fair to myself or when I need a break. He can always tell before I can and I adore him for that. He is the best and without him, my writing career would look very different. So, thank you to Alex. I love you.

This book wouldn't be the best version it could be without

my editor, Lucia Ferrara. I've worked with Lucia on almost all of my books and I value our relationship so much. She works so hard and gives me the deep feedback I need to create well-rounded characters. I promise I'll get "farther" and "further" sorted out with the next book along with all those embarrassing typos.

When I first started publishing my stories, my son was an itty-bitty baby propped in a corner of the couch or sitting in his high chair playing cars while I typed away on my computer. Now, he's big enough that he can tell everyone that his mom likes coffee and books. My writing schedule looks a lot different than it did when he was little, but seeing the excitement on his face when we open a copy of my paperback book for the first time makes me so proud that I dared to publish my first book for a whole new reason.

Finn, you're the best and I love you. I hope that no matter how you feel about my writing career or cringe when people tell you about what I write, you will approach your own life with a bit of bravery to do the things that make you feel fulfilled. The world is a lot better off when we all chase after what brings us more joy.

And lastly, thank you to everyone who has read my books! I wouldn't have the career I do without my amazing readers and the people who have supported me along the way. Thank you so much.